Praise for the works o

Devil's Slide

...*Devil's Slide* though, is phenomenally written! Emotional, exquisitely paced, and tense for almost the entirety of the tale, readers are kept on the edges of their seats, never sure how things will turn out.

-Carolyn M., *NetGalley*

Amid Secrets

Amid Secrets, the third novel in the Falling Castles series, is definitely a tale filled with suspense, multiple dilemmas, and lots of twists and turns in the plot. Just about everyone we have met in the first two books of this series ends up in some sort of crisis or life-changing event. In other words, this is another exceptional mystery, intrigue, and romantic thriller by Stacy Lynn Miller.

-Betty H., *NetGalley*

Absolutely brilliant. The whole series has kept me engaged, and on my toes and hooked me in. Great storyline, fantastic characters throughout the book, gripping suspense storyline, cannot fault this author at all.

-Jo R., *NetGalley*

Blind Suspicion

With the first book ending on a cliffhanger, I was very much looking forward to reading this sequel and it was so satisfying. Lynn Miller knows how to keep things interesting, and I'm learning that the different volumes in her series never feel repetitive...In summary, drama, romance, and mystery—what's not to like? I hope to see more books in this series.

-Meike V., *NetGalley*

Honestly? Stacy Lynn Miller is probably one of the better authors I've come across in the last few years. If you want something fresh, gripping, entertaining and keeps you guessing to the end, this author is for you. *Blind Suspicion* is the sequel to *Despite Chaos*, another fantastic read, I recommend you read it first.

-Jo R., *NetGalley*

This novel is a very enticing and captivating story full of love, drama, loyalty, family dynamics (both good and bad ones), romance, mystery and so many other things...

-Laurie D., *NetGalley*

Despite Chaos

I honestly do not know what to say! Fantastic story. Everything I've read by Stacy Lynn Miller has been entertaining, engaging, and gripping. *Despite Chaos* is yet another amazing story, it's a must book to own in 2022. It's a 5/5. And with a cliffhanger like that...Can't wait for that sequel.

-Emma S, *NetGalley*

Stacy Lynn Miller has a great ability to write messy, complicated people that are easy to like. With this first book in the "Falling Castles" series, she does it again with Alexandra Castle and Tyler Falling.

-Colleen C., *NetGalley*

This is a well-written, slow-burn romance. There's romance, competition, blackmail, embezzlement and jealousy. The story was fast-paced, and I enjoyed every minute of it. The love, support, and understanding of Tyler's husband was astounding. Hands down a great read and I recommend getting a copy.

-Bonnie K., NetGalley

Beyond the Smoke

This was really good! This is the third book in Miller's Manhattan Sloane Thriller series and is the best written book of the series. I was caught up in the mystery, it kept me turning the pages, but so did the romance.

-Lex Kent's Reviews, goodreads

I loved the first two novels, but I think this one might be the best yet…I've enjoyed all the mystery, excitement, action, and intrigue in the plots of these books, but I've fallen in love with these characters, and want to know what's happening in their lives. This is the mark of an exceptionally talented author.

-Betty H., NetGalley

From the Ashes

I have been looking forward to reading *From the Ashes* by Stacy Lynn Miller since I read her first Manhattan Sloane novel back in April. I fell in love with Sloane, Finn, and all the other characters in this story while reading the first book, and I wanted more, especially since the story didn't completely end with the first novel. I'm happy to say I loved this book as much as the first one.

I highly recommend both novels, though, so get them both. You won't be disappointed.

-Betty H., NetGalley

From the Ashes is the sequel to *Out of the Flames* with SFPD Detective Manhattan Sloane and DEA [Agent] Finn Harper...Miller is a wonderful storyteller and this story had me sitting on the edge of my seat from start to finish. The first book in the series, *Out of the Flames*, was a 5-star read and *From the Ashes* is the same as it ducks and weaves and thrills and spills all the way to the end. The chemistry between Sloane and Harper is palpable...Miller certainly knows how to write angst into her characters. This book is a thrill a minute and I can't wait for the next one.

-Lissa G., NetGalley

Out of the Flames

This is the debut novel of Stacy Lynn Miller and it's very, very good. The book is a roller coaster of emotion as you ride the highs and lows with Sloane as she navigates her way through her life which is riddled with guilt, self blame, and eventually love. It's easy to connect with all the main characters and sub-characters, most of them are all successful, strong women so what's not to love? The story line is really solid.

-Lissa G., NetGalley

If you are looking for a book that is emotional, exciting, hopeful, and entertaining, you came to the right place. There are characters you will love, and characters you will love to hate. And the important thing is that Miller makes you care about them so, yes, you might need the tissues just like I did. I see a lot of potential in Miller and I can't wait to read book two.

-Lex Kent's 2020 Favorites List
Lex Kent's Reviews, *goodreads*

If you are looking for an adventure novel with mystery, intrigue, romance, and a lot of angst, then look no further.

...I'm really impressed with how well this tale is written. The story itself is excellent, and the characters are well-developed and easy to connect with.

-Betty H., *NetGalley*

WHISKEY WAR

STACY LYNN MILLER

About the Author

A late bloomer, Stacy Lynn Miller took up writing after retiring from the Air Force. Her twenty years of toting a gun and police badge, tinkering with computers, and sleuthing for clues as an investigator form the foundation of her Lexi Mills crime thriller series and Manhattan Sloane romantic thriller series. She is visually impaired, a proud stroke survivor, mother of two, tech nerd, chocolate lover, and terrible golfer with a hole-in-one. When you can't find her writing, she'll be golfing or drinking wine (sometimes both) with friends and family in Northern California.

For more information about Stacy, visit her website at stacylynnmiller.com. You can also connect with her on Instagram @stacylynnmiller, X @stacylynnmiller, or Facebook @stacylynnmillerauthor

WHISKEY WAR

STACY LYNN MILLER

BELLA
BOOKS
2023

Bella Books, Inc.
P.O. Box 10543
Tallahassee, FL 32302

Printed in the United States of America on acid-free paper.

First Edition - 2023

Editor: Medora MacDougall
Cover Designer: Heather Honeywell

ISBN: 978-1-64247-460-2

PUBLISHER'S NOTE

Acknowledgments

Thank you, Louise, Kristianne, Diane, Sue, and Barb. This incredible crew of beta readers pushes me to be a better writer.

Thank you, Linda and Jessica Hill, for believing in my work and making a dream come true.

Thank you, Medora MacDougall, my editor, who brings out the best in me.

Finally, to my family. Thank you for loving and encouraging me.

Dedication

To the Queens of the Speakeasies:
Texas Guinan, Helen Morgan, and Belle Livingstone

PROLOGUE

Half Moon Bay, California, November 1929

Livid didn't come close to describing Grace Parson's mood. Hours earlier, Rose Hamilton had been dangling precariously over the cliff at Devil's Slide. The only thing preventing her from falling into the ocean waves beating the jagged rocks below was Grace holding on to her right hand and Dax Xander's firm grip on her left. If not for Dax's strength after Grace's grip had given way, she would be crying over Rose's battered body at the morgue now, not hanging up her drenched coat and fixing her a stiff drink in her hotel room. And Grace rested blame for the entire nightmare squarely at Frankie Wilkes's feet.

Grace was aware of Frankie's drive to make Half Moon Bay the West Coast tourist destination for the rich and famous, but she hadn't known how far he would go to make it happen. Her eyes were now wide open. His ambition had turned into unimaginable greed, driving him to do the unforgivable—put the woman she loved in grave danger. She had no option but to correct her enormous lapse in judgment—after tending to Rose.

"Here, drink this." She handed Rose a tumbler she'd filled with a generous portion of whiskey. "It will calm your nerves."

"I'm fine, really." Rose accepted the glass, but her hands didn't shake as much as Grace expected they would following a near-death experience.

"Well, I'm not." Grace snatched the tumbler from her hand and downed its contents in three large gulps. The whiskey burn took the edge off enough to allow her to put herself in Rose's shoes. She would be unconscious from fright if she had been the one hanging by a hand over a two-hundred-foot drop. But Dax had calmed her with a single touch moments after pulling her to safety. Even the blind could see her effect was more potent than all the illegal whiskey in the state.

That immediate restoration of internal peace was nothing short of miraculous, and the sting it caused in Grace's heart had taken her by surprise. For four years she'd told herself that Rose was merely a physical salve for the emotional scars left from losing the love of her life needlessly. The authorities had declared the overdose accidental, but Grace knew better. None of her wealth or Hollywood fame could save her sweet Harriet. The isolation and heartache that came with living a lie, being forced to hide her love for Grace, had taken their toll. Too much for the owner of Grace's heart to bear. Grace knew now that the sting she'd felt when witnessing the deep, enduring love between Rose and Dax was the same pain she'd experienced the day she'd learned of Harriet's death.

Letting Rose go the night Dax first appeared at her table at the Seaside Club had come with a heavy heart. She'd finally realized why Rose had been attracted to her. When she wasn't in front of the movie camera, she presented a male appearance just like Dax with slicked-back hair and men's formal suits, down to the suspenders Rose adored. Saying goodbye was the greatest performance of her life, but she'd gotten through it because it was what Rose needed. However, tonight's harrowing events showed her that she hadn't put Rose in the past. Rose had become more than a therapeutic. Despite all her previous denials, she not only loved Rose but was madly can't-live-without-her in love with her. As much as it pained her, now was the time for another believable performance.

"You're shaking." Rose retrieved the empty glass and returned it to its place next to the crystal decanter atop the small dining table. "Let's sit." She gently guided Grace to the tufted settee. Her gaze shifted, inspecting Grace up and down. She gasped, briefly throwing a hand over her mouth. "Your tux is ruined. And your shoes. I don't think either is repairable."

"My clothes are the least of my concerns. How are you?" Grace scrutinized every inch of Rose, starting with her face. Not a scratch was on it, including her cute button nose. However, her long wavy brown hair was still rain-soaked and matted from the storm. Rose's long winter coat had protected her arms, but her wrist appeared swollen. "Your hand. Did I hurt you when I clutched it at the cliff?"

"It's nothing." Rose moved her wrist and shoulders in a circular motion, testing their mobility. "I can tell it will be sore for a few days, and so will my arms. It's been years since I've hung from the pull-up bar."

"Even longer for me, I'm afraid." Grace resumed her detailed inspection, gasping and falling to her knees on the plush carpet when her eyes settled on the fabric of Rose's dress at the bend of her legs. Sizeable tears and bloodstains signaled significant cuts, but the dress extended to her shins, making it impossible to assess accurately. "You're bleeding." Grace gestured with her chin at the lower hem of her dress. "May I?"

Rose nodded.

"You know, Rose, until a few weeks ago, I didn't have to ask before raising your dress." Grace told herself she was hoping to extract a smile from Rose to take her mind off her injuries, but part of her hoped for the return of the Rose she knew before Dax's reappearance. Her selfish side wanted to elicit a response that would present Rose with a choice between her and Dax, culminating in them making love until dawn. This was no time for selfishness, though, so she added a playful wink to telegraph the supposed innocent nature of her comment.

Grace hissed when she raised the hem and exposed a series of scrapes and splotches that looked like a painful, bloody version of Morse code's dashes and dots. "Holy hell, Rose. That must hurt like the dickens. I should clean you up."

Rose slowly lowered the trailing edge of her stage dress before raising Grace's chin with a hand. The look in her eyes left no doubt that Rose had understood the true intentions of her earlier comment. "I should go." She kissed Grace on the forehead. It was the type of goodbye kiss that made Rose's choice clear, leaving the back of Grace's throat thick with grief and regret.

She stood tall, padded to the door, and retrieved Rose's smudged and ripped coat. She helped Rose put it on, letting her hands linger on her shoulder blades a second longer than she should have. "Can I drop you at the Foster House?"

Rose turned on her heel slowly. "I should walk." The soft tone in her voice let go of Grace gently and with an air of certainty.

Grace pulled a folded sheet of paper from her breast pocket and handed it to Rose. She didn't release her grasp for several extra beats. "I've jotted down every way to reach me if you ever need my help or just want to catch up."

"That's very kind of you, Grace. I doubt I'll still have a job after tonight, but if I do, you'll always have a front-row seat at my show."

"If I have anything to say about it, you will." Grace would see to it tonight. As Rose twisted the knob to open the door, the finality of their goodbye wrung tighter in Grace's chest. When she stepped through the door and it closed, four words echoed the pain of not fighting for her. "Goodbye, Rose...for now."

Once Grace changed into a more presentable tux, one of the three she'd brought on this trip, she rang the hotel reception desk on her room phone and waited for the clerk's well-rehearsed greeting. "This is Grace Parsons. Please get a message to Mr. Wilkes that I need to speak with him immediately in my suite. Before you do that, my husband should be in the Seaside Club or Room 208. Please send him up as well."

"Of course, ma'am. Do you require anything else?" the young man asked.

"Another decanter of whiskey and a fresh set of glasses." The ache lingering in Grace's chest said she wasn't done drinking tonight. And if she handled her meeting with Frankie Wilkes the way she planned, he would also need a snort.

After returning the phone's earpiece to its cradle, she filled her glass to two fingers and sank into a chair at the round dining table, her face to the door. She ticked off in her head the questions Frankie needed to answer tonight. If the answers were as she predicted, she would have to establish her dominance, and their business arrangement would have to change on the spot.

Minutes later, the distinct sound of a key operating the lock pulled Grace's attention toward the door. Her confidant for the last eleven years, husband for the last ten, stepped inside, his expression morphing from expectant to concerned at his first glimpse of Grace. Clive approached and kissed her on the forehead. "You look haggard, my sweet. What happened tonight?"

She recounted the horrifying events of the evening, adding, "I've summoned Mr. Wilkes to get answers, and I'm sure the conversation won't be cordial."

"I'll be sure to keep the peace." Clive patted the revolver hidden in a shoulder holster beneath the left flap of his suit coat. He wasn't a towering man like Frankie Wilkes, but the military training he received during the Great War made him an excellent shot and bodyguard. He could put a bullet through a man's eye at a hundred yards while fending off a gang of a dozen ruffians.

"I know you will, my dear."

A rap on the door drew their attention. Clive pressed a hand on Grace's shoulder to stop her from getting up to let in the visitor. "I'll get it." He pulled out his pistol and readied it chest high when he eased the door open. Grace's muscles relaxed when Clive lowered his weapon and held it against the side of his thigh.

The door opened wider to Frankie Wilkes, clad in his traditional three-piece dark suit, high-collared white shirt, and red silk tie. "Is everything all right, Grace?"

"Have a seat." Grace gestured toward the dining chair next to her. Clive returned his gun to its holster and assumed a position behind him, ready to provide the element of surprise if needed.

"I don't have much time. My hands are full tonight."

"I'm sure they are, considering Riley King won't be returning from his whiskey run tonight. Your club manager was careless and nearly cost Rose Hamilton and me our lives." Grace pushed back the horrible image of Rose dangling over the cliff, holding on by a fingertip.

"What happened to them? They've been missing since leaving after Rose's first show tonight. I had to announce that her second show was canceled."

"I was taking Rose for a drive between performances to show off my new Roadster when Riley flew around the curve from the opposite direction, nearly hitting us. I'm afraid he and his truck landed at the bottom of Devil's Slide. The whole incident terrified the poor girl, so I took her home."

A lie was better until Grace gauged Frankie's response. This town had a human communication system more robust than Western Union, and he controlled it. If his spies had already relayed the actual events of the evening, he would call her on it and demand remuneration. But Frankie uncharacteristically flinched, cocking his head back a fraction. This man was clearly surprised.

"And the whiskey he was hauling? That went over too?" he asked. "Those barrels were supposed to supply the club for a week."

"A man lost his life tonight, your own nephew, and you're worried about whiskey?"

"That whiskey represents over ten thousand dollars in lost revenue. I would think you would care about that."

"My concern for profit does not exceed my concern for human life," Grace said. "Now, I want answers, Mr. Wilkes. I heard a disturbing rumor recently that Riley King had something to do with the death of Mr. Foster, the holdout who was keeping you from completing your quest to own the entire marina."

"You mean *our* quest. You have been behind this idea from the beginning."

Five years ago, when Frankie approached her about his vision to make Half Moon Bay the West Coast version of Atlantic City, Grace had had her own idea. The town's isolated location and proximity to San Francisco were an ideal combination. Convinced it would attract the wealthy and movie-making crowd with sexual appetites similar to hers, it took her only one day to agree to bankroll his operation. Her investment had paid off in spades and allowed her to insert her way so tightly into the underground fringe community that her name had become synonymous with the Seaside Hotel and Club and the discretion they provided.

"Providing money does not make me a conspirator."

"A court of law might not see it that way. Your money paid for everything on this street, including trying to convince that old man to sell."

"I gave you money to buy him out, not kill him." An uneasiness overtook Grace. She didn't sign up for violence.

"Killing wasn't the plan." Frankie nervously rubbed the back of his neck in apparent frustration. The feeling was mutual. "I brought in Riley and Jimmy to scare him, but he fought back."

"So their response was to push the poor man down the stairs? I can't have this blowing back on me."

"You have nothing to worry about. The only two people involved are dead, so there's no one to connect the dots."

Yesterday's local newspaper headlines suddenly made sense. Jimmy Gibbs's plunge over Devil's Slide a few days earlier had been no accident, bringing Grace to a horrifying realization— Frankie Wilkes had someone help him over the cliff. Now, he'd racked up two bodies—or more—in his quest for land and power.

"I see. And neither death bothers you?"

"The old man was an accident, but he deserved what he got. Jimmy was getting cold feet when that Foster bitch started asking questions, so Riley and I had no choice. If he talked, we'd all be implicated, even you. I did you a favor by taking care of him."

"Favor? A person's murder can never be colored a favor. You've gone too far." Grace waved her hands in front of her face in disgust. Her underlying fear of incrimination was something best kept to herself. Parting ways was her best option, even if it meant stepping away from Rose. "We agreed on twenty-five thousand, double my original investment, if either of us ever wanted out. I want out."

Frankie leaned back in his chair, smugly tugging on his suit vest and adjusting his tie. "I wouldn't give you the money if I had it."

"Then I will buy you out."

"That's out of the question. With the Foster and Gibbs killings, we're tied at the hip. Neither of us can walk away."

Clive reached beneath his suit flap to where he kept his revolver. Grace knew he would pull the trigger and send a bullet into Frankie's head if she gave him the signal, but the situation had yet to reach that point. More importantly, she wasn't sure if she could cross that line even to save her own skin. Rose's maybe, but not her own. Changing course to avoid the appearance of weakness, she waved him off. For now. But Frankie's next reply would determine if he would need further convincing.

"If that's the case, the terms of our agreement must change. Your unilateral decision to involve our enterprise in murder will cost you. Our fifty-fifty split on the monthly profits is no longer acceptable. Sixty-forty will compensate me for your lack of judgment."

Frankie's eyes narrowed like those of a raging bull a second before he sprang from his chair, palms on the table. Before he could straighten his knees, Clive pushed down on his shoulders, forcing him back into his seat. The pressure was less than what he'd once used on a crazed, starstruck fan who had tried to steal a kiss from Grace at a San Francisco movie premiere but was sufficient to let Frankie know more would be in store if he didn't cooperate.

"If you want to walk out of here in one piece," Clive said, "I suggest you give the woman what she wants."

"Fine. Sixty-forty." The muscles in Frankie's jaw rippled as the last bit of fight left him. Hopefully.

"And one more thing," Grace said. "Rose Hamilton stays on the payroll singing at the club for as long as she wants a job. If she asks for anything, and I mean anything, she gets it."

CHAPTER ONE

January 1930, two months later

The lunch crowd had picked up a smidge today, giving Dax hope that their business slump might turn around. Since the Seaside Club expanded its menu and dining room hours last month to include lunch seven days a week, lunch traffic at the Foster House had dropped by a third. Frankie's crusade to bankrupt the Foster House so he could take over the entire marina was escalating.

Their head waitress, Ruth, had put her best positive spin on the downturn trend earlier this morning. "Wait for the spring and tourist season. Parents won't want to bring their kids to a place that turns into a speakeasy at night, and the beachgoers won't want to stare at a basement wall when they eat. Our view of the marina will bring them in."

Spring was two months away, though, and tourist season was nearly five. Dax doubted the Foster House would last five more weeks if business didn't pick up. Each week she and her sister barely met payroll, settled the bills, and had less and less left over for themselves. And each week, the seven barrels of whiskey remaining from Riley King's final load were looking more and more like their most straightforward way out. But everyone who had a role in the events culminating in Riley's death, including her sister, had agreed to not bring up those barrels hidden in Charlie's auto repair shop until they had no other choice. That time hadn't come yet, but Dax feared it wasn't far off.

At the end of the day, she locked the main door of the Foster House and flipped the window sign to the closed side. After collecting the day's receipts from the cash register, she picked up the small stack of mail the postman had dropped off during his midmorning route. She gave the main dining room one final visual inspection but didn't find a single task undone. Why would she? Every day since the reopening, Ruth had ensured every table was cleared and wiped down, the floor swept, and the collection of shakers and condiment bottles was filled before her crew left. Dax expected nothing less from her and wasn't disappointed. Everything was complete.

Dax pushed through the swinging door into the kitchen, discovering May scraping the griddle clean. She studied her for a moment. Her sister's stamina had doubled since getting her new leg brace, allowing her to work longer without sitting on one of her kitchen stools. Some days her limp was barely noticeable, as if the horrible car accident that had left her lame had never happened. But that was a stinging memory Dax could never forget. If she'd been more attentive. If she'd been focusing more on the traffic and not the incredible first kiss she'd shared with Heather Portman hours earlier, she might have slammed on the brakes of the Model T a second before the pickup truck ran the stop signal and collided with them.

May wiped her sweaty brow with a forearm, pushing back several strands of long brown wavy hair that had strayed from the tie at the back of her head. She glanced over her shoulder toward Dax and let a tired smile form on her lips. "Another great day. There were four more customers than yesterday and not a single dish or glass broke."

"You'll never let me live down breaking an entire bucket of dishes when I saw Rose for the first time, will you?"

"Not on your life. It's a story to pass down when you and Rose take in a child or two." May's carefully selected words didn't escape Dax. She seemed to have accepted the harsh reality that she would never have a child of her own, giving up hope that her banker husband would find work in the city despite the stock market crash in October and come back for them or would join them in running the restaurant he'd inherited when his father had died. The last time she had mentioned Logan's name, in fact, was on Christmas while reminiscing about the last holiday she and Dax had spent together in San Francisco. It was a sore spot, one that Dax dared not pick at.

"Living under the same roof with Rose would be a necessary first step." Dax had taken Rose's rejection of her invitation to live and work in the Foster House hard but respected her choice. Well, mostly. She understood Rose not wanting to give up the money Frankie Wilkes was paying her and would have been happy if Rose kept her singing job and paid May rent if it meant they slept in the same bed every night. But the longer Rose waited for the right time to not upset her boss, the harder it was becoming for Dax to live with her decision.

"She'll come around."

"Will she? I'm beginning to doubt we'll ever live together."

May removed the dishrag from her left shoulder and tossed it in the nearby laundry hamper. She sat on her stool at the center chopping block and gestured toward one across the table. "Sit with me. Cleanup can wait."

Dax took her seat and placed the receipts and mail on the worn surface. Between them on the table sat the crumbly remains of an apple pie in a quarter-full tin.

May handed Dax a clean fork and picked up one herself. "Nothing takes the mind off disappointment better than pie."

"And your company." Dax slid her fork beneath an ample portion and brought it to her mouth. Sweet apples and bits of flaky crust complemented by a burst of heavenly cinnamon melted in her mouth, surfacing warm memories of her childhood. Living with strict parents who detested desires and attractions like hers had come with suffocating isolation, but May's baking always provided Dax comfort. Every dessert was sprinkled with love, and Dax could taste it in every bite.

May swallowed her first mouthful. "Your time will come. Rose has lived on her own for five years and has a job at the Seaside Club that fits her like a glove and pays well enough for her to support herself. And when the Seaside started its lunch service, they became our direct competitor. If Rose moved in with us right now, it might look appropriate to the town busybodies, but her boss might take it as an affront. With good paying jobs a scarcity, we can't expect her to put hers at risk."

"I get it. I do." But understanding Rose's choice to not accept Dax's invitation to move in with her didn't mean she was okay with it. Sure, Rose shared her bed two nights a week on her days off, but that wasn't nearly enough to keep the powerful pull of loneliness at bay. When her head hit the pillow of her empty bed on the other five nights, Dax ached to envelop Rose in her arms. And waking to cold sheets the next morning was a dispiriting way to start the day. Figuring out a way to spend more time with her had become imperative.

"But it's not enough," May said, agreeing. "It's been years since the accident that made it impossible to climb the stairs to our bedroom. But I remember how long it took to get used to sleeping alone downstairs and how lonely I was early on. The physical connection between lovers can be powerful, but I felt the most intimate with Logan when we fell asleep together. That closeness took on a dimension of vulnerability that didn't compare to lovemaking."

"I feel the same way. My body aches if I don't have Rose in my arms when I fall asleep."

"Be patient, Dax." May eyed the small stack of dollar bills on the table. "We're experiencing tough times, and many of us will have to sacrifice to make it through."

Dax did the math in her head, subtracting the regular charges with the grocer, butcher, and Edith's department store. They would be short for Sunday's payroll unless they had the same number of customers in the next two days.

She tapped an index finger on the stack of cash. "Do you think we're going to make it this week?"

May patted Dax on the hand. The topic clearly made her uneasy. "I'm confident we will, but I'm sure the ladies will understand if we're a few dollars short." She sifted through the stack of mail Dax had brought in from the dining room, harrumphing at one small envelope.

"Who is it from?"

"Logan."

May's unchanged expression when she opened the letter was perplexing. After nearly four months apart and not a word from her husband in two, she should have had some type of emotional reaction at hearing from him. Dax expected either elation at hearing from the man she once loved enough to marry or anger for abandoning her and Dax in a strange city to fend for themselves. But her sister's reaction was nonexistent, as if she'd received a receipt for the week's groceries. That meant one thing—she'd given up on her marriage. While she was sad for her, if Dax were honest with her, she would tell May that Logan didn't deserve her. He was selfish, arrogant, judgmental, and unforgiving—her sister's exact opposite.

"What does he say?" Dax asked.

"The same drivel as last time. No job. No buyers for the house. He blames you. And he's not coming." May balled up the letter and tossed it toward the trash bin along the nearby wall. She made it.

"We could use a distraction tonight," Dax said. "How about we catch Rose's first show tonight?"

"Don't they have a two-drink minimum? We can't afford that this week."

"The last time Rose stayed the night, she said the club manager would waive the drink requirement for us as her special guests. Besides, Jason is completely hooked on your biscuits. A few of those would have him buying the drinks for us."

"I'd love to see Rose sing again." May wrapped the four biscuits left over from today's lunch service into two paper napkins.

Two hours later, May had on her Sunday dress, and Dax had broken out her cleanest knickerbockers, a white button-down shirt, and a second pair of shoes—black oxfords. The goal of impressing Rose had also inspired Dax to slick back her short brown hair with a perfectly formed part on the side. Though the Seaside Club didn't have a strict dress code, patrons were expected to dress according to social graces, and tonight, she and May planned to put their troubles behind them by looking their best.

Once Dax locked the front door of the Foster House, she extended her left arm, bent at the elbow, to her sister. "Shall we?"

May hooked her arm around Dax's, adding a smile bright enough to light up the nighttime sky. Not since their trip to San Francisco to get May's new brace had they dressed up in their finest, but Dax intended to make tonight a special occasion. She planned to sweeten her invitation for Rose to move into the Foster House by telling her that Logan was no longer in the picture. If Rose still wanted to sing at the Seaside Club, she could move in and pay May a small amount every month for her room, like she did at the boarding house. Her idea had the benefit of being the truth. The town's busybodies would not think twice about May renting the spare room to a hometown friend to make ends meet.

May walked with a noticeable limp tonight, an expected byproduct of a ten-hour day at the helm of the Foster House kitchen. Dax firmed her grip until they safely passed the rickety sidewalk boards in front of their establishment and transitioned to the smooth concrete of Wilkes's properties. She remained on May's right, nearest the curb, to steady her if she wobbled. It had taken only one incident of her sister stumbling into the gutter for Dax to learn from which side to better protect her.

When they reached the Seaside Hotel, Dax held the door open for May, keeping her steady while she descended the twelve steps to the basement. A month ago, using her old worn-out leg brace, those stairs would have been impossible. But she easily reached the bottom landing with her newly fitted one, and her broad smile made the danger Dax, Charlie, and Rose went through to get that load of whiskey from Riley King to pay for the new brace worth it. Well, almost. Charlie still wasn't the same. She kept busy repairing cars at the garage, but Dax could tell she had yet to come to terms with her part in Riley's death.

An oversized guard stood sentinel at the nondescript entrance of the speakeasy. Fortunately, he no longer made Dax as nervous as a cat. Jason, the bartender who had taken over management of the club following Riley's death, had given the hulking giant a standing order: any friend of Rose, including Dax, was welcomed. Anytime. No passwords. No frisking her for weapons. And no eying her up and down as if she might become his next punching bag.

May offered the man a bunched-up napkin when he opened the door for her and Dax. "I thought you might like a few biscuits. I made them myself."

"Foster House biscuits?"

"They are." May narrowed her eyes and asked, "Why?"

The guard scanned the basement corridor up and down as if checking for spies. "They're the best in town." His eyes sparkled with approval as he extended his open hand, palm up. "Thank you, ma'am. These *are* a special treat."

The Seaside Club was dimly lit for Rose's first show of the evening. Jason stood at the end of the bar, waving his recognition. He whispered into the ear of a server, who escorted Dax and May to a front-row table covered in a crisp white cloth and then asked for their order. "Jason said the first round is on the house. What will it be?"

"Please thank Jason for us, but we're just here to see Rose tonight," May said. She never accepted gifts, yet she doled them out regularly. "Could you see that Jason gets this?" May handed the waitress the remaining two biscuits she'd carefully wrapped in a paper napkin. "And if you sneak one, he'll never know the difference." May added a wink.

"Of course, May." The waitress returned her wink and scurried away.

Dax scanned the half-full Friday night crowd with the locals augmenting the handful of off-season tourists, an average number of patrons for this time of year, according to Rose. The lights dimmed a smidge, and Lester emerged from the swinging door a few feet left of the corner stage. The elevated platform was large enough for his piano and Rose, but not much more. He sat on the dark wooden bench and tinkled the piano keys. A moment later, Rose appeared through the door and took the stage.

"Ladies and gentlemen," Lester said into his microphone. "The Seaside Club is proud to present Miss Rose Hamilton."

Those were the last words Dax heard clearly. The moment Rose opened her mouth to sing, Dax swam in the seductive, rigid waves Rose had added to her hair with a flat iron. Her calf-length blue sequined dress shimmered in the spotlight, making it impossible to focus on anything but the treasures hidden beneath the loose fabric. The curve of her waist, the swell of her breasts, and the slopes of her hips were all meant for her.

Tendrils of smoke created by patrons dragging hard on their Lucky Strikes drifted through the light stream between Dax and the stage. They added an alluring haze that made Rose sexier than she could remember. The vision even surpassed her years of fantasies when she'd thought she'd never see Rose again. She'd envisioned Rose in beautiful dresses, walking in the park or on the beach, but never in her wildest dreams had she conjured up a scene like this. The petite young Rose with whom she'd shared her first kiss had blossomed into a Hollywood-like sex symbol, and she was all hers.

May jabbed an elbow into Dax's side, drawing her attention from Rose while she took a polite bow behind the microphone stand. Dax shifted her stare, discovering May and every other patron in the club applauding wildly.

Dax returned her gaze to the stage, but Rose had already left. She searched her out and discovered Lester acting as a buffer between Rose and a zealous, alcohol-fueled guest who had grabbed her by the arm. His wrinkled suit and three-day beard suggested he was down and out, but bad luck didn't excuse overstepping like he had.

Rose's expression had turned from tired to troubled in an instant. Dax readied herself to lunge from her chair and coldcock the brute, but Lester snapped his fingers over his head. The sharp sound caught the bouncer's attention. He whistled before fast-stepping toward the stage. Jason did too. The brazen drunkard appeared ready to fight when each gripped him by an elbow.

"Hey, friend," Jason said, using a calm voice. "The lady has to rest her voice before the next show. So how about a cup of hot joe and a sandwich on the house? Then you can call it a night."

The man relaxed his stance when Jason patted him lightly on the chest and gestured with his head toward the back corner of the club. "Joe and grub would be nice. I haven't eaten all day."

"Then let's get you fed so you can go home and get a good night's sleep." Jason whispered something to the bouncer, prompting him to disappear behind the swinging door leading to the kitchen. Meanwhile, Jason led the man to an empty table in the back. The ease with which he defused the confrontation was an impressive example of how a calm head could prevail in the hairiest situations.

Rose appeared more relaxed and kissed Lester on the cheek before striding to Dax and May's table. She greeted May first with a friendly hug but let the one with Dax linger a second longer. Her smile lit up the room when she sat between them. "I'm so glad you two came. It's been, what? Nearly a month since you were here for my Christmas show?"

"And the club was so beautifully decorated," May said.

"I was surprised," Rose said. "Frankie never decorated for the holidays before."

"What brought about the change?" May asked.

"I think Grace may have had something to do with it. After the awful events at Devil's Slide, I told her that holiday decorations might help get me in the festive mood. The place was completely decked out when I returned to work the following Thursday."

Dax tightened at the mention of Grace Parsons, rolling her neck to relieve the tension. While Rose's ex-lover graciously had stepped aside, clearing the way for Dax and Rose to rekindle their love, the actress plainly cared for Rose more than she'd let on. Despite Grace's label for her affair with Rose, what she had termed a mere distraction, had clearly turned into love on her part. Thankfully, it was healthy enough for Grace to keep her distance, at least for now.

The waitress dropped off Rose's customary cup of hot tea with honey and two unexpected cold bottles of Coca-Cola. "Jason sends his compliments. He thought you two might be concerned about Rose but wanted to assure you he always puts her safety first."

"Tell Jason thank you." May raised her bottle in appreciation, tipping it in the server's direction. "And if he ever hankers for biscuits, they're on me at the Foster House."

Jason's overt kindness didn't escape Dax. She assumed he was vying for Rose's affections, but she didn't feel the least bit threatened by it. Unlike Riley King, who came on strong with Rose every chance he could when he wasn't screwing up the nightclub operations, Jason didn't give her a predatory vibe. He didn't come across as a man who considered Rose a prize to win over. On the contrary, he seemed to care for Rose genuinely but was gentleman enough to keep it to himself.

Dax raised her bottle. "Yes, please thank Jason. We all care for her."

While Rose sipped on her tea to soothe her vocal cords, the three women chatted about last week's thunderous winter storm, Charlie's upcoming birthday on Sunday, and the two families who recently moved from town in search of work. They shifted to the slowdown in business for the Foster House and Charlie's Auto Repairs and the hope that drier weather and the tourist season would bring a big enough boost to carry them throughout the year. The ease with which the conversation flowed felt like they were already family. The only thing that could have improved the moment for Dax was knowing Rose would come home to the Foster House after her last show and crawl into Dax's bed.

Dax scanned the other tables. Some were filled with single men and one with a single woman, but most were taken by couples. Everyone was drinking, and the couples laughed, flirted, touched, and kissed. It felt good to sit with Rose in public, but she wished she had the freedom of other couples. She wanted to flirt, caress, and kiss Rose when the feeling struck her, not when they were shielded from public view or alone in the Foster House after hours. That level of acceptance, though, was a long way off, if not impossible.

Frankie Wilkes approached the table, positioning himself between Rose and May, his back turned to May. The slight was obvious. The Foster House was his biggest competitor and the last stumbling block from establishing his monopoly on the marina businesses. May was its heart and soul.

"Great show tonight, Rose," he said. "I didn't recognize a few of the songs."

"Those were Lester's. They'd be a big hit if that Victor man didn't think his signed talent w-w-wouldn't w-w-work with a colored man."

"There are some things you can't fight, Rose."

"We'll see about that." Rose nuzzled her calf against Dax's beneath the table. Though camouflaged by the chair legs and the trailing edge of the tablecloth, the motion was still risky, and Dax understood Rose's daring and got the message. Prejudices were all around them, but Rose had her unique way of protesting with furtive caresses and singing Lester's masterpieces. Both were more reasons why Dax loved her. Rose never accepted intolerance for how people were born. Skin color, speech maladies, and who a person loved should never dictate how people treated one another.

"Is there anything you need, Rose?" Frankie asked.

Rose stroked Dax's leg again. "There is something. The stage is too small, and it's falling apart. I'd like something done a-a-about it before I fall off or through it."

Frankie rubbed the back of his neck. "The town doesn't have a carpenter since the Flynns moved away last month. I'd have to hire one from the city."

"There's no need, Mr. W-W-Wilkes." Rose gestured her hand toward Dax. "My friend here is an expert carpenter. She trained under her father for six years and w-w-worked for Bishop and Sons in San Francisco for nine."

Frankie shifted his stare to Dax and narrowed his eyes in certain skepticism. "The dishwasher at the Foster House is a carpenter?"

Dax squirmed at the insult, but Rose ran her leg against Dax again. "Why is that so hard to f-f-fathom? Like most jobs, ca-a-arpentry is a learned skill. You just have to give a person a chance and let them prove their w-w-worth. Are you so narrow-minded to think a w-w-woman can't build you a bigger and better stage? With that same logic, Lester couldn't possibly w-w-write songs you like because he's colored."

"What? Of course not." Frankie blinked his confusion, cocking his head back.

"Then hire Dax. She'll have a beautiful stage for me in a w-w-week or two."

Frankie rubbed his neck with more vigor. "How much?" he asked Dax.

Dax did the math in her head. Ripping out the old stage would take a day. Framing the new one would take a full day but adding the platform and trim work would take another day or two, depending on how intricate the design they wanted. Lumber and materials would cost about fifteen dollars. Add on her labor for four days. "I could do it for fifty dollars."

"Plus m-m-materials," Rose added.

Frankie split his gaze back and forth between Rose and Dax three times, but Rose never broke her stare. "Fine. She can start Monday, but I still want you to work on Thursday even if you're singing from the floor. See Jason for how it should look and the money to get her started."

"You won't be disappointed," Rose said.

"I better not. I can't afford you breaking a leg." Frankie walked away, looking as if Rose had bulldozed him.

Rose clasped her hand with Dax's beneath the table and brought it to her thigh. When she turned her head toward Dax, the look in her eyes was soft and filled with unmistakable love and well-deserved self-satisfaction. Dax had thought she could not love Rose more than she already did, but Rose had pulled off another beautiful, unselfish act. An act that filled and expanded Dax's heart to twice its size.

"Fifty dollars extra should carry the Foster House expenses for a month or two," Rose said.

"Thank you, Rose." Dax squeezed her hand and returned the look of love. "Spend the night?"

"I was hoping you'd ask."

CHAPTER TWO

Two days later

Standing behind the Foster House kitchen stove, Rose wiped the sweat from her brow, remembering the day after Riley King had vandalized the place and May had snapped her brace. Dax and May had needed help, so she had pitched in and worked side by side with May in the kitchen that entire day before singing two performances the same night. Her exhaustion made her voice husky, making it impossible to reach the high notes in several songs. As a result, she had sworn to never spend the day of a performance cooking over a hot stove. Today, though, was a special occasion. It was Charlie's birthday, and since she and Dax were best friends, May had invited her and her girlfriend, Jules, over for a late lunch celebration after the restaurant closed. The hour spent helping May prepare Charlie's favorite dishes was worth risking a gravelly voice.

Rose surveyed the results of their hard work. The biscuits and mashed potatoes were done, and now she and May had a lull while the chicken baked and the green beans steamed. She shifted her stare to the double-layer chocolate cake she'd covered in icing but had yet to decorate with Charlie's name. "Where do you keep your icing bag?" she asked, wiping another drop of sweat from her brow with a forearm before it stung her eye.

"Mine split yesterday, so Dax picked up a new one today at Edith's." May tested the beans with a fork and returned the lid to the steamer pot. "I think it's still in the box of purchases on my desk. Do you mind getting it? These are just about done."

"Sure thing, May."

Rose entered May's office, which also doubled as her bedroom. For either a bedroom or an office, the size would be adequate. But combined, the area was confining. Dax had done an excellent job maximizing space by adding wall shelves around the room's perimeter near the ceiling. However, there was no getting around the necessary furniture—a bed and desk. Suddenly, complaining about the stage size seemed petty, sending a twinge of guilt racing through Rose. How could she justify tearing down an entire stage to get an extra few feet of elbow space when May was forced to shimmy between her desk and bed every day?

Tucking away those selfish thoughts, Rose sifted through the contents of a cardboard box atop May's small desk. She pushed aside the half-dozen water glasses, utensils, and spices, eventually locating the icing bag with one of Edith's price tags. She snapped the tag off and went to toss it in the wastebasket on the floor at the end of May's desk when she noticed a ledger sheet on the corner of the desktop.

Rose never considered herself naturally nosy. However, the discussion with Dax and May at the Seaside Club the other night about the hard times besetting the Foster House had made her overly curious. She glanced at the columns of expenses in red ink and revenue in black for the week. The red exceeded the black by nine dollars. A few rows down, the names of May's three waitresses were annotated with their "wages due" in the first column and "wages paid" in the second. If Rose read the ledger correctly, each employee would be shorted three dollars this week. She wasn't sure how long the restaurant had been running a deficit, but based on their earlier talk, she was sure Dax and May had run through their savings. And here was May, cooking a free meal for Dax's friends for no reason other than it was the right thing to do.

The fifty dollars for the stage was nothing to Frankie but would go a long way for May. However, that money would not come through for a week or two. Rose had to do something now. She'd been blessed with a job that paid her more money than she needed every week and had built a small savings. She fumbled through her purse, pulled out nine one-dollar bills, and stuffed them in the left cup of her brassiere.

By the time she returned to the kitchen, her heart a little heavier, May had the beans in a bowl and was adding the butter and salt. She raised her hand with the icing bag. "Found it."

"Oh, good." May glanced at Rose and jutted her chin toward the oven. "Would you mind pulling out the chicken? Any longer, the cheese might burn."

"I'm on it, May."

A knock on the back door redirected May's attention. "I'll get that. It's likely Ruth coming to pick up the ladies' weekly wages."

While Rose removed the piping-hot chicken dish from the oven, she said, "Wait, May. Before you get the door, I have something for you." She placed the container on the stovetop and retrieved the folded bills from her brassiere. Cupping May's hands, she put them in her palm. "Now, don't get mad, but I saw the ledger in your office. I know you're short this week, and I hate seeing the ladies not get what they're due when the money Dax will earn from building the new stage is a week away."

May's eyes welled with tears. She squeezed Rose's hand. Her voice cracked. "You're the kindest, sweetest woman in the world for offering, but I couldn't possibly take your money. It's just not right."

"May, please. You've been so good to me and Charlie and Jules. Consider it a loan from one good friend to another until Dax gets paid."

May pressed her lips into a smile that spoke of profound gratitude. She squeezed Rose's hand tighter as if she were lost at sea and holding on to a life preserver. "I can't thank you enough, but you're not just a friend, Rose. You're family. You're like a sister to me, but this is definitely a loan. We'll pay you back."

May answered the door and let in Ruth. Following brief hellos, May collected the pay envelopes from her office and handed them to Ruth with a reserved grin. "You'll find full wages for you and the others."

Ruth formed her lips into a fine line. "Are you sure you can make the other bills to keep this place open? The girls and I talked. We're all willing to take a dollar or two pay cut to make it through."

"I'm sure." May rubbed Ruth's upper arms. "Let the girls know Dax is taking on a side job for a week or two starting tomorrow, so they'll have to pick up the slack while she's out. But the good news is that the work should bring in enough money to carry us through the winter."

"That's wonderful news, May." Following warm hugs, Ruth left.

May walked up to Rose with her arms wide open and pulled her into a giant hug. "It's like you're our guardian angel." She pulled back, the bond between them now as strong as steel. "I understand why you didn't accept Dax's offer to move in, but I get the impression that you wish you could say yes. Unfortunately, Half Moon Bay is full of busybodies. If it makes it easier on you, I can pass the word around town that we need a little more income and put flyers up, announcing a room for rent above the Foster House."

"Thank you, May, but it's not just the busybodies. It's Mr. Wilkes. I might not have a job if he knew I was living under the roof of his biggest competitor."

"Hogwash. I saw how he acted on Friday night." May waved her off as if she'd suggested the Seaside's biscuits were better than hers. "Frankie Wilkes needs you as much as you need him. You're why so many rich tourists come to town. Now, what's the real reason you're not living with us?"

Before Rose could finally tell someone why she had cold feet, the door separating the kitchen from the dining room swung open and Dax strode through. She'd ditched her customary bibbed apron since Rose last saw her and put on her suspenders. The black cotton webbing accented her dark blue dress pants and perfectly framed her rounded breasts beneath a crisp white men's button-down shirt. The sight drew in Rose's stare like a magnet.

Sexy. Sexy. Sexy.

Talk of food, money, and jobs no longer held importance. The contrast of a male presentation on Dax's solid female body was downright jaw-dropping. Rose wanted to devour every inch. Every day. The daily kisses in the residence upstairs barely kept her going. The twice-a-week sleepovers with the occasional third recharged her battery, but they weren't enough time with Dax.

Each step closer made her heart pound a fraction harder and faster until the thumping muffled every sound in the room. Dax finally stopped close enough to Rose that their breaths mixed. "Hi," she said and kissed her on the lips with the passion of a thousand entwined lovers.

The arms enveloping Rose were strong, yet their touch was as soft as a feather pillow. Losing herself in them was inevitable. "Hi." Rose let her breathy voice float like she was singing a sultry song on the stage to seduce unsuspecting patrons into buying another drink. Only today, she would seduce Dax into bed tonight before she had to perform.

The unmistakable look of desire filled Dax's eyes but receded quickly with a labored exhale. "Charlie and Jules are here. Why don't I help May plate the food while you finish writing Charlie's name on the cake?" Dax leaned closer and whispered into her ear, "I want to have my way with you as soon as they leave."

"You'll have to wait your turn. Those suspenders are driving me crazy," Rose whispered back.

"I wore them especially for you." Dax kissed her on the cheek before starting her task.

Minutes later, May, Dax, and Rose carried the food into the dining room and set it up at their center table, where Charlie and Jules were sitting. On the surface, those two looked like polar opposites. Charlie Dawson was quiet, tall, and thin with light brown hair cropped around her ears, and she wore men's clothes all day. Jules Sanchez, however, drove most conversations, was short with all the right curves, and wore dresses to complement her long brown hair. But Rose knew that below the surface, they were alike in what counted most. Both had hearts of gold and were loyal to a fault. Charlie repaired cars for a living, and as a nurse, Jules repaired bodies. They made the perfect couple.

Once seated, May raised her glass of water head high and said in a gleeful tone, "Here's to the birthday girl."

"Hear, hear," said Dax, Rose, and Jules, joining in the toast.

"Thanks, May," Charlie said. "Everything looks great, but you shouldn't have gone to all this trouble."

"Don't be silly. You turned thirty today. We need to celebrate your milestone."

"I couldn't agree more." Jules hooked her hand around Charlie's arm atop the table and leaned into her shoulder. "I can't believe I'm in love with a thirty-year-old."

"Well, next year, when you turn thirty, I will be too." After kissing Jules on the lips, Charlie returned her attention to the rest of the table. "Let's eat before everything gets cold."

During dinner, the conversation was light with Jules leading most of the lively banter. Before taking her last bite, Dax said, "I've been thinking about repairing the dock in the back."

Charlie had remained reserved until now. "What for?"

"Some of the fishermen mentioned that when the tides were right, they used to dock out back on their way to or from a catch and come in for a meal. If we brought back that convenience, one said he'd stop by more often."

"I haven't even looked," May said. "How many slots are there?"

"Six. The main dock is mostly solid, but the gangway needs lots of work."

"How much would it cost to make the repairs?" May asked.

Dax rubbed her chin, clearly doing math in her head. "About twenty-five dollars in wood and nails. I could use some scrap wood in the back to cut the cost."

"It's an excellent idea, but I wish we had the money," May said.

Dax slumped her shoulders, telegraphing her disappointment.

"I have wood scraps at the garage." Charlie leaned forward in her chair, showing enthusiasm for something for the first time since the awful night at Devil's Slide when she sent Riley King over the cliff with a swing of a tire iron to save Dax's and Rose's lives. "And the hardware store might let you pick through their scrap pile for free if you tell them what you plan to build."

"It's a pretty big project," Dax said with a wry smile. "With an extra pair of hands, we could reclaim the good wood in the basement that Riley King turned into scrap."

Rose remembered the night King had shown his true colors. He'd vandalized the Foster House and the secret speakeasy Dax had built downstairs, searching for a missing whiskey barrel. Charlie had hurt her head in the process and May had snapped her leg brace. It was an unforgivable act.

"Sure." Charlie shrugged. Her excitement faded instantly, and Rose suspected why. In the weeks since King died, Charlie had become increasingly withdrawn. Understandably so. She was the one who'd sent him tumbling to his death. But if she hadn't, Rose and Dax would have fallen to their deaths. Even so, ending his life, even in self-defense and defense of her friends, had come with tremendous guilt.

Charlie pushed her chair back and stood. "Excuse me. I have to use the bathroom."

After she disappeared down the corridor, Rose waited a minute, giving her time to conduct her business. She then excused herself and waited for Charlie outside the bathroom door. A flush, followed by the sound of running water and the squeak of the faucet closing, meant the door would open any second.

The door opened. Surprised, Charlie stepped out and moved to one side. "Sorry, Rose. It's all yours." She started to head down the corridor, but Rose placed a hand on her arm.

"Wait. Do you have a second?" Rose asked.

"Sure, Rose. What do you want?"

"I'm worried about you. It's your birthday. You should be happier, and I think I know why you aren't." Charlie lowered her head, and Rose continued, "Guilt is eating at you, isn't it?" Charlie looked up, her eyes glistening with unshed tears, but she remained quiet. "You didn't mean to kill him, and I'm sure keeping it a secret makes you feel you did something wrong." She placed both hands on Charlie's collarbones. "You did nothing wrong, Charline Dawson. Neither Dax nor I would be alive today if you didn't act quickly. You gave us a wonderful gift—life and each other. Because of you, we know what love feels like, just like the love you and Jules share. I'm so grateful to have experienced it. Riley King was a menace, so don't you shed one more tear over him."

"I've been trying, but I look at the tire rack in my garage every day, and I know what's hidden in the storage room behind it and how it got there."

"I have the perfect birthday present for you then." Rose snatched Charlie by the hand and pulled her down the hallway until they reached the table and their nearly finished feast. "Everyone, I know how we can make this day even more special for Charlie." Rose paused for the ladies to give her their full attention. "Charlie is still torn up about the night of the accident, and the whiskey barrels stashed in her garage are a daily reminder of the awful events of that night and what she had to do."

"Say no more." Dax threw her cloth napkin on the table, stood from her chair, and placed an arm over Charlie's shoulder. "How about you and I load up those barrels tonight and store them in our basement?"

Charlie nodded. Her shoulder slump revealed her relief.

CHAPTER THREE

Hot shower water sprayed Dax's tired back muscles. She turned to face the stream, lowering her head to let the needling massage her neck and upper shoulders while the water warmed her torso. Carrying the seven remaining whiskey barrels into the basement with Charlie earlier had reminded her it had been months since she'd lifted anything heavier than supplies for the restaurant. One thing was for sure. Until she rebuilt her muscle strength she would have to pace herself when she started demolishing the existing stage at the Seaside Club tomorrow.

The bathroom door creaked a familiar sound. It was opening. She would have to replace the hinges on it one day, but until then, it provided a delightful early warning. The timing of the visit brought on a smile. It was ten thirty. By now, Rose would have finished her last show, drunk warm tea with honey to coat her vocal cords, and walked the two blocks to the Foster House. She would have let herself in through the back door so as to not raise suspicion, using the key Dax had had made at Edith's Department Store. Finally, she would have tiptoed past May's room and up the stairs to the residence.

A rush of cool air hit Dax's backside when the shower curtain slid open. Her skin tingled at the temperature change, followed by the touch of Rose's hands as they slipped around her torso and cupped her breasts. Rose pressed their bodies together, instantly raising Dax's heart rate. Desire pulsed in her center, demanding attention, but Rose was presenting her with the opportunity to fulfill a fantasy that had sprouted after their previous night together.

Dax was still new to sapphic sex, but Rose had been a patient and skillful guide, testing boundaries but pulling back when Dax was unsure. Now it was Dax's turn to take the lead.

A boldness swelled, prompting her to twist around slowly, careful not to slip on the tub's wet surface. She captured Rose's lips in a searing kiss, and when their tongues collided, the temperature between them spiked hot enough to melt the wall tiles. Dax sent a hand between Rose's legs, discovering she was as slick inside as she was outside. She teased and pumped until Rose begged for her mouth. Dropping to her knees, Dax obliged. She threw Rose's left leg over her shoulder, steadied her by the hips, and turned fantasy into reality lick by lick until they left the shower and both lay sated in bed.

Rose settled snugly beside her beneath the covers. A leg was slung limply over Dax's thigh, and a hand cupped a breast. Dax ran her fingers up Rose's spine, her skin still damp from their long, water-wasting shower. If she could freeze time and spend eternity in a single moment, this would be it. Nothing in the world compared to the feeling of Rose's skin against hers with their legs entwined. They were connected from head to toe, from their minds to their hearts.

"I miss you when you're not here." Dax didn't intend to guilt Rose into moving in but holding back had become unbearable. Sleeping alone made her feel incomplete and ache for her other half.

"I miss you too." Rose lifted her head from Dax's chest and used a hand to nudge Dax gently by the chin to look at her. "But I can't risk changing things right now."

Dax sighed, understanding Rose's reasoning. Nevertheless, having to keep the town's busybodies at bay still stung. She prayed for the day when it would be better to let people think Rose was a loose woman than a lesbian. But for now she had to agree. A handful of people in town would not care, but from what she'd gleaned from conversations among customers, most would consider her and Rose's relationship abhorrent. They would stop coming to see Rose's show and stop eating at the Foster House if they knew the truth. While illusion was necessary, Dax was sure May's idea of announcing a room for rent could provide the perfect cover. Why hadn't Rose taken May up on her offer? It was perplexing. The sadness in Rose's eyes needed further explanation, too. She appeared more conflicted than ever about living together.

Dax eased Rose to her side and scooted to the head of the bed until her back leaned against the wall. She patted a section of the mattress next to her, inviting Rose to join her.

Rose snuggled next to Dax, pulling the covers past their breasts to keep them warm from the chilly night air.

"May said she told you about her idea to advertise a room to rent and that she wasn't buying your reason for not moving in." Dax intertwined their fingers, hoping to elicit the truth. "I sense you've been holding back. Please tell me why we can't be together. Is it that you don't love me enough?"

"God, no." Rose let go of Dax's grip and buried her face in her hands, exhaling soundly. She pressed her head against the wall and stared at the ceiling as if searching for the right words. "I feel so selfish."

Dax shifted to look her in the eye. "May told me what you did for us today, covering the payroll until I get paid. You are the most selfless person I know."

"But that's where you're wrong. The reason I'm afraid of losing my job isn't about money. It's about feeling normal."

"Normal?"

"When I'm with you or May or Jules or Charlie, I feel safe and comfortable because you're my family. And when I talk to any of you, I hardly stutter."

Dax clasped Rose's hand. She sensed the direction this conversation was about to take and wanted desperately to comfort her. Instead, she swallowed her words and replied with a silent nod, letting Rose get this off her chest.

"But when I'm with anyone else, my words always stick. When I worked at Ida's Café, I dreaded taking an order from a customer. Every time I had to talk to them, I stuttered. I got through it most days, but sometimes I'd hide in the bathroom and cry because I'd made a fool of myself in front of a group of rich tourists. And every time they'd stiff me after the meal."

Dax squeezed Rose's hand a little tighter. It broke her heart that Rose had been all alone for years. Dax should have been there to teach those thoughtless customers a lesson like she did with the school bullies who had teased her about her malady.

"But when I sing at the Seaside Club, my words never stick. When I'm on stage, I feel like everyone else. No other job can come close to making me feel that way." Tears escaped from Rose's eyes. "I can't chance losing it even if it means not being with you every night. God knows I want to, but I can't. I just can't."

Dax lifted Rose's chin with a hand. "I've loved you since the first day I laid eyes on you in seventh grade. I lost count of how many bullies I socked in the gut for making you feel you were anything less than perfect. I did that because your stutter didn't matter. You were perfect in my eyes. If singing at the Seaside Club makes you feel whole, then that's the way it has to be."

More tears fell from Rose's eyes, but a joyous smile trapped them in the corners of her lips this time.

"If two nights are all you can safely give me, we'll make the best of them." Dax gently eased Rose flat on the mattress and hovered over her, deciding whether she should taste Rose for her first climax in bed or wait for the next. "Starting right now."

CHAPTER FOUR

Five days later

After working her morning shift at the Foster House to get the staff through the breakfast rush, Dax was eager to resume her other job. Rose could sing to the Friday night crowd tonight from atop her larger, new corner stage if she scheduled her day right. It would be usable but not pretty. The trim work Jason wanted, including the words "Seaside Club" in painted, raised letters nailed to the stage apron, would take another day or two to cut.

She grabbed her coat from the wall peg near the back kitchen door and returned to the stove to kiss May on the cheek. "I'm heading out to the Seaside."

"How is it coming along?"

"It's some of my best work." Dax's voice was laced with obvious pride.

"I have no doubt. You have every reason to make sure it's the safest thing you've ever built."

"I do. Rose and Lester should be able to use it tonight, so I might stay late to watch her first show on it."

"If you don't mind, I might join you."

"I think Rose would love that."

Dax grabbed the sack containing a fresh apple and the sandwich May had made for her lunch and walked the two blocks toward the hotel. Instead of entering via the lobby today, she went to the back, where deliveries were made. The final shipment of wood she needed to build the surface of the stage had arrived. She would have to measure, saw, and nail down each piece by the day's end, but first, she had to bring them into the basement.

"Morning, Dax." The now-familiar voice had greeted her politely each day, a ritual Dax looked forward to. She never liked someone looking over her shoulder when she worked, but this job made it inevitable. As the club manager, Jason had to set up the lunch service and stay through closing at midnight. He remained politely on his end of the large room, though, only venturing to Dax's end when he had a question or curiosity had gotten the best of him.

"Morning, Jason. If things go as I plan, we should have a working stage tonight. It won't be pretty yet, but Rose and Lester will have a bigger platform for their show." Dax eyed the large stack of wood, calculating how many trips she would have to take up and down the stairs. After four long days of hard labor, she'd rebuilt her arm and back muscle strength and could easily lift the large pieces. However, the sheer size of the plywood sheets made it impossible to carry them down the narrow basement stairs alone without scratching the walls. "At least I hope so."

"That's great." He joined her stare.

Dax rubbed the back of her neck, thinking her estimate might have been too optimistic. She would have to make at least a dozen trips. "I better get started."

"How about we knock out this stack together? We can get it downstairs in half the time."

"Are you sure? Mr. Wilkes is paying me to do this myself."

"Well, he's paying me to manage the club, and this is club business." Jason removed his coat and hung it over the metal railing lining a set of exterior stairs leading to the basement—their destination. "How about it?"

Jason was the polar opposite of Riley King. He treated people with dignity and respect and expected nothing other than to be treated in the same fashion. Compared to Riley and Frankie Wilkes, he was a rare gem in the speakeasy world. His help could not have come at a better time.

"Only if you stop by the Foster House for some of May's biscuits tonight."

"You drive a hard bargain." He rolled up the sleeves of his work shirt despite the cool midmorning air. "Let's get to work."

By their final trip down, neither needed prompts from the other to avoid scraping the railings, walls, and doorjams at the crucial points. Within an hour, they had every piece of wood stacked against a wall of the club near where Dax had set up her sawhorses. In another two or three hours, she should have the subfloor of the stage down, just in time for Rose and Lester to arrive for rehearsal.

Rose had "rehearsed" every day this week, even on her off days without Lester. Each time she sang every song perfectly, making Dax suspect those rehearsals were merely an excuse to be in the same room with her. She blamed the glances and smiles they exchanged at every opportunity for slowing her down. It had taken her two days to complete the demolition when she should have done it in a day and a half. Though she was glad she'd taken her time. It was a miracle Rose hadn't fallen through and broken a leg. A relatively sound frame of aged two-by-fours undergirded the old stage. However, the surface was merely a series of thick wood slats. Several had bowed from the piano's weight and could have given out at any time. She planned on building a much safer platform by laying down a thick layer of plywood first and placing the new wood slats on top.

Dax grabbed a glass of water from the club kitchen and went to work. She started by laying out the subfloor pieces at the rear of the stage and worked her way toward the front. Staying focused, she developed a perfect rhythm of measuring, cutting, and nailing that didn't allow for breaks until she laid in the last piece. Having only a sheet and a quarter of plywood left over meant she'd estimated correctly and used the cut pieces expertly. She had always prided herself on not wasting materials, and this job confirmed she hadn't lost her touch.

A loud stomach growl signaled her lunch break was long overdue. Dax retrieved her lunch sack from her workbench before going to the kitchen. She waited for the head cook to finish pulling several pans of lasagna from the oven—today's lunch special. Dax knew better than to distract a cook while she was handling searing-hot dishes. One mistake, and she would have burns bad enough to keep her from work for a week.

Once the baking dishes were safely on the prep table, she stepped forward. "Excuse me, Sally. May I trouble you for a large glass of water with my lunch?"

"Help yourself, lass." The woman gestured her chin toward the racks of clean, stacked drinking glasses. While Dax filled her cup from the faucet, Sally asked, "Care for an end piece of lasagna? At the risk of sounding vain, the regulars say it's my best dish."

"That's very kind of you, but I brought my lunch." Dax raised her lunch bag as proof. But if she were honest and could spare the thirty-five cents, she would order a serving of it in a heartbeat.

"Maybe next time," Sally said before turning to chastise her assistant cook. "No, not the cream. The recipe calls for butter." She returned her attention to Dax. "Sorry, lass, but I have to save today's dessert."

Dax retraced her steps to her work area. The moment she stepped into the main dining room, she stopped in her tracks, unable to take her eyes off Rose standing in the middle of the stage. She was admiring Dax's hard work as if she'd created the *Mona Lisa*. Rose stepped forward where her microphone might be and held her arms wide open to measure the would-be distance between her and the piano.

Dax stepped toward her handiwork. "You'll have about an extra seven feet widthwise across the front and four more feet depthwise. When I'm done, you and Lester should have nearly double the space you had before."

Dax's voice caused Rose to turn toward her. A contented grin slowly developed on Rose's lips. "It feels higher."

"Almost an entire foot higher. We had enough head clearance, so I raised it to give the people in the back a better view."

"This is amazing, Dax. I never imagined a stage this grand when I tricked Frankie into hiring you to build it."

Dax ascended the steps to the new stage. She envisioned coming up behind Rose and wrapping her arms around her, molding their bodies together, but they weren't alone. Customers had rolled in for lunch and Jason was restocking glasses at the bar. Any show of affection would have to wait until they were behind closed doors.

"Tricked, huh? You are a devious one, Rose Hamilton."

"When I suggested rebuilding the stage"—Rose's expression turned sheepish—"I might have exaggerated its condition."

"But you didn't." Dax pointed to a few original floor slats from the demolition she'd leaned vertically against the wall. She'd kept them to prove to Mr. Wilkes that the old stage had been an accident waiting to happen. "Those warped slats over there tell me so. It was just a matter of time before they all broke."

Rose scanned the small lunch crowd. Stepping closer, she whispered so only Dax could hear, "You have a habit of saving me, and I love you for it."

Friday wasn't their usual night together, but when her stomach fluttered at the thought of having Rose next to her in bed all night long, Dax had to ask. "Tonight?"

Motion to her side prompted Dax to step a few feet away from Rose to avoid anyone suspecting something inappropriate between them. She glanced to her right, finding Jason had stopped at the foot of the stage. He had a concerned look on his face.

"Dax, I need you to come with me. Mr. Wilkes wants to see you in his office right now."

"Did I do something wrong, Jason?"

"I'm not sure, but he's fuming mad."

Dax didn't like the sound of that. Did Frankie Wilkes get a look at the stage and hate it? Had someone overheard her and Rose and put two and two together just now and gone running to him about it? One scenario would be fixable, the other devastating.

"Can it wait until after lunch? I haven't eaten since five this morning."

"I'm afraid not. I have orders to escort you to his office immediately."

Rose's face pinched with the recognizable sign of worry.

"It's all right, Rose. Whatever this is, I'm sure I can clear it up." Dax used a reassuring calm voice and handed Rose her lunch sack and drink. "Can you hold these for me? I'll be right back." She issued a furtive wink only Rose could see before walking off with Jason.

Once on the first floor, Jason rapped his knuckles three times against a door labeled "Owner's Office." He waited until a muffled voice from the other side told him to come inside, then politely held the door open for Dax to walk in.

The office was more ornate than Dax expected. The carpet was plush, the color of red wine, and fit for royalty. The bookcases were intricately carved with the ends shaped to resemble Greek columns. The desk was equally elaborate, something one might see in the governor's office. Frankie Wilkes was sitting behind that stately piece with his eyes narrow and nostrils flaring like her mother's used to do before the paddle came out.

"That will be all, Jason. I'll take care of this punk myself," Wilkes said.

"Sure thing, Mr. Wilkes." Jason closed the door behind him. An uneasy feeling flooded through Dax.

Wilkes turned his attention to her and sneered. "I bet you thought you'd gotten away with it."

"With what?" Dax said in an uncertain tone. Opening with an accusation meant something bad was about to happen.

"Thinking I was an easy mark by nicking my whiskey."

"You're still sore about the barrel I found on the beach? I didn't know it was yours until Riley and his sidekick broke in. He took it before I could sell it and smashed up the Foster House to teach me a lesson."

Frankie craned his neck and bellowed over a shoulder, "Come in, fellas."

A secondary door to the office opened, and two men in suits stepped through. Instant recognition twisted Dax's empty stomach into a thousand knots. The men were the Prohibition agents who had stopped her the night of Riley King's death. Besides Grace Parsons and Rose, they were the only two people who could place her and Charlie at the beach that night. And these two knew she was at the beach minutes before a load of smuggled whiskey barrels was brought ashore from the Canadian ship. A sinking feeling set in—she'd been caught.

The tall one with a square jaw and hollow, sunken eyes spoke, reminding Dax of the monster in a book by Mary Shelley that May had told her about years ago. Frankenstein's stature alone made him an intimidating man. Add a badge and a gun, and Dax had a healthy fear of him. "That's the one I saw at Shelter Cove the night Riley went over the cliff. There was someone else with her."

"I'm only going to ask you this once," Frankie said to Dax in a firm voice. "Where is my whiskey?"

"How the hell am I supposed to know? Riley King was your runner. Word has it the barrels went over Devil's Slide along with him. It couldn't have happened to a nicer guy."

"Tell her, Paxton." Frankie had a lopsided grin that said he wasn't about to buy any story Dax gave him unless it included the location of the missing barrels.

The shorter and less menacing-looking agent removed a well-worn toothpick from his mouth. He carried himself in a more businesslike fashion than Frankenstein, giving her the impression that he was the one in charge. "The sheriff didn't recover enough wood from the wreckage to account for a dozen barrels. Said two or three at the most went over the cliff."

Dax sensed she might not make it out of this office alive. Her survival instincts kicked in. About ten feet separated her and the closest door. She could dart that distance in about two seconds, but the closed door would require an extra second or two to open. The Prohis would surely catch her before she could get one foot out the door. Thankfully, the Seaside Hotel was teeming with guests and lunch patrons, so she doubted Frankie's muscle would use their iron. So that left using their hands and maybe some brass knuckles. She balled her hands into fists but kept them low at her thighs, preparing to defend herself against a beating.

Someone pounded on the door from the other side. A second later, the door flew open, and Rose burst in, a terrified expression on her face. "Are you all right, Dax?" Jason must have tipped off Rose about what was going on, so, naturally, her response was to come running.

"You need to leave, Rose." Frankie's demeanor changed from menacing to pleasant on a dime. "Your friend and I are having a friendly discussion."

"Friendly? You're never friendly when you're mad as hell." Dax blinked at Rose's statement. She never used cuss words. Never. And Rose looked furious enough to spit. If Dax weren't fearing for their safety, she would take more time to appreciate how cute she looked. "Why did you drag Dax into your office?"

"Business."

"If it has something to do with the stage, I'm thrilled with it and wouldn't change a thing."

"I have bigger things to worry about than a damn stage."

Frankenstein slipped his hand under his left suit jacket flap, presumably reaching for the same pistol he'd waved at Dax the night at Shelter Cove. Once bullets started to fly, there was no telling who they would hit. Dax had to get Rose out of there. "Rose, I'll be fine. We're just talking. Go back to the club."

"I'm not leaving without you." Rose stood extra straight, positioning herself between Dax and Frankie like a mama bear protecting her cub. "Now, unless your talk has anything to do with Dax's work, we're both walking out of here so she can finish the stage for my show tonight."

"We'll find someone else to finish the damn stage because this flimflam won't step foot in any of my businesses again."

Frankie's use of the word "again" was a sliver of hope that Dax might get out of this alive. Then again, it could mean she would not be stepping foot anywhere again.

"That's fine with me." Dax looked Frankie in the eyes. "I'll collect my pay for the work I've done. Thirty-seven dollars should do it."

Frankie laughed maniacally. "I'm not paying you one red cent."

"If you don't pay her what she's owed, don't count on me singing tonight." Rose planted her fists atop both hips, arms akimbo. It was a sexy look Dax didn't have time to admire.

Frankie's face and neck turned a hideous shade of red like he was about to blow. His voice turned sharp. "I've had all I can stand from you, Rose Hamilton. I don't care what Grace Parsons wants. You're fired. I'll find some other canary to put butts in those seats."

Dax snapped her head in Rose's direction. Her eyes widened in the same shock sweeping over Dax, plunging her heart to the lowest she'd ever felt. Rose had lost her job—all because of Dax's greedy idea to keep the whiskey barrels from that awful night at Devil's Slide.

Rose's breathing became audible. Her chin rose noticeably. "You're full of bad decisions today. You're sadly mistaken if you think people with the real dough will come here if I'm not the main attraction. The big money comes from Hollywood, and Hollywood means Grace Parsons. One word from her, and this place will dry up faster than the Sahara."

Frankie rose from his chair slowly, his brow creasing as if he were deciding whether to shoot Rose in the mouth or between the eyes. "I don't take kindly to threats, Miss Hamilton. You're lucky Grace Parsons is your benefactor, but don't press my patience a second time."

Dax had to act before Frankie changed his mind. "Let's go, Rose." She yanked Rose's arm harder than she should have, but she had to put distance between them and the danger. She pulled her out the door, down the hallway, through the lobby, and down the basement stairs.

Finally, at the bottom stair, Rose shook off Dax's grip. "Stop. You're hurting me."

Dax immediately halted, her heart thumping hard at the looming threat. "I'm so sorry, Rose, but you're not safe here. We need to get my tools and get out of here before those goons come after us."

"I'm not afraid of Frankie's thugs, even those Prohis. You heard him. He knows I have pull with Grace and the big money that comes here."

Dax scanned the corridor and stairwell to make sure no one else could hear, including the hulking guard at the entrance of the Seaside Club. "Those two goons are the ones who saw me at Shelter Cove, and they figured out the barrels weren't on Riley's truck."

"Dang." Rose cocked her head back. "What should we do?"

"I doubt Frankie suspects you had anything to do with it, but we can't be sure."

"Now I'm scared." Rose clutched the front of her blouse.

Dax bit her lower lip, considering the danger that might await them. "I don't want to let you out of my sight. You're staying with me until we're sure this thing has blown over. Let's collect my tools and your things from your dressing room and drop them off at the Foster House. Then I'll drive you to the boarding house so you can get whatever you might need for a few nights."

Rose nodded her concurrence. Timidly. Dax shared her uneasiness.

CHAPTER FIVE

Dread settled into Rose's belly as they walked to the Foster House. She'd seen Dax fight bullies, take on Riley King, and pull her from sure death at the cliffs of Devil's Slide. During all that, she had remained calm. However, the events in Frankie's office had left her rattled. She had seen the Prohis in the club several times but never knew who they were until today. That meant the situation was more dire than she had first thought, and she wasn't about to leave Dax's side. She would have to call Grace at the first opportunity.

After she dropped her things in the bed of Dax's truck, she followed her to the back door leading to the basement of the Foster House. Dax held her toolbox in one hand and her collection of saws in the other. She turned to Rose. "Stay here while I store my tools."

"What happened to not letting me out of your sight?" Dax may have said those words first, but Rose felt them just the same. "I'm going with you. Now, hand me those saws."

"Fine." Dax's shoulders slumped before she handed over her crosscut, hack, and coping saws. She unlocked the door before quietly leading Rose down the interior stairs. They took great pains to not make noise that would alert May and the other ladies working the last hour of lunch service on the main floor. Explaining things to Dax's sister would be much easier once she and Dax were safely settled into the residence above the restaurant.

Before they turned to go back up the stairs, Rose flipped over a corner of the tarp draped over the seven whiskey barrels that had put everyone she cared about in danger. She remembered the unsettling discussion she, Dax, Charlie, Jules, and May had had two months ago about those barrels. They'd agreed to hijack Riley's load and hold it hostage until he paid for the damages he'd caused. That night hadn't turned out as they'd planned, but they were in this together and needed to decide what to do next as a group.

Rose stared at the barrels and did the math in her head. Those wooden casks would garner over eight thousand dollars if someone sold their contents by the glass. Half of that was Charlie's and, by extension, also Jules's. The other half was Dax's, and that amount of money could float the Foster House for years. But those barrels could only help if they sold them or their contents.

The stumbling block was Frankie Wilkes. He'd clearly paid the Prohis to look the other way and allow the free flow of booze at the Seaside Club. If he got wind that Dax was selling whiskey out of the Foster House, he would likely sic the agents on her, and Dax would face years in prison.

"There has to be a way," Rose mumbled to herself. She no longer had a job, and business at the Foster House was slowly dwindling thanks to the recent economic crisis. She didn't know how long they could hold on, but she was sure the whiskey in those barrels could solve their problems. She carefully replaced the tarp. "Do you think we should hide this better?"

"That's probably a good idea." Dax shoved boating equipment in front of the barrels to camouflage them better. When she and Rose got into the truck, her stiff posture suggested she was still stressed.

"This will blow over soon, and we'll be fine." Rose briefly squeezed Dax's hand.

"I hope so." Dax started the truck and drove the mile to the boarding house in silence.

Rose opened the main door and walked in, Dax close behind her. Before placing her foot on the first stair, Rose recognized the prickly voice calling from the office next to the staircase.

"Miss Hamilton, I need to see you immediately." Mrs. Prescott had the worst timing.

Rose lowered her head and sighed before pivoting toward the open office. "Yes, Mrs. Prescott?"

Her landlady extended her arm, her hand gripping a small stack of dollar bills. "Eight dollars. I'm refunding your rent for the rest of the month. You have until the end of the day to move out."

"Move out? Why? I have violated none of your rules."

"Mr. Wilkes was clear. He no longer wishes to rent to you and will consider any belongings left in your room after five o'clock to be trash. After that, my son will haul it to the dump."

It made perfect sense. Frankie Wilkes owned half the town, including this boarding house. Rose had planned to let him pout for a night before making a call to Grace to put this ugly business behind them, but she was too late. Frankie was already taking his pound of flesh.

"Fine. Good riddance." Rose snatched the money and marched up the stairs, hoping she left a paper cut or two on the landlady's grasping hand in the process. Anger built, creating enough pressure to make her temples throb. She unlocked her room door and pushed it open with added force, not caring that she'd bounced it off the wall. That witch downstairs could send her a bill for damages, but that would be one bill she would never pay.

Rose stepped inside and stood in the room's center, untangling her thoughts and emotions. She wasn't homeless. Dax and May would see to that. But the idea of Wilkes kicking her to the street after she stood up to him was infuriating.

The door latched behind her. The next moment, Dax's arms enveloped her from behind, squeezing her tight. She rested her chin on Rose's shoulder. "I'm so sorry, Rose."

Rose closed her eyes, letting Dax's arms absorb her anger bit by bit. Soon, her muscles released the tension that had built since Jason suggested Dax might be in danger. She let her body sway and imagined music playing in the background. She sang one of Lester's slow, romantic songs. It told a story of would-be lovers, each longing from a distance until the day one summoned the courage to kiss the other.

Dax kept her arms around Rose's midsection when she finished. "Is that a new song? I love it."

"It's Lester's."

"It sounds as if he wrote it for us."

"He did."

Dax's arms stiffened. "He knows about us and is okay with it?" Her voice ended on an uptick.

"He knew about Grace and me and kept the secret for years. So, yes. He's okay with us. He was thrilled for me when I told him about our history."

"I wish we had more people like Lester and May in the world."

"I do too." Rose squeezed Dax's arm around her waist before escaping her grasp. "I better start packing."

She opened her closet door and dragged out her steamer trunk. The last time she packed it, she was escaping a life of servitude at her cousin Ida's café. She'd worked there ten hours a day, six days a week, for only tips—her punishment for loving Dax as a teenager. If Frankie hadn't overheard her singing there and made her an offer, she would not have discovered her true passion. Leaving when she did was the best decision she'd ever made.

But that was over now. Today, she would move into the Foster House with Dax, and tomorrow she would begin working in the kitchen with May. She loved Dax and May and wanted to do everything she could to help them get by, but working full time in a restaurant again had the distasteful flavor of punishment. It would take getting used to again, physically and emotionally.

"What furniture is yours?" Dax asked. "I can haul it down to the truck."

"The chair and vanity set are mine. The bed and dresser stay." Rose stripped her quilt from the mattress with the swoosh of a tornado. "But I paid a dollar for the bedding to replace the horse blanket Mrs. Prescott provided. She can have that itchy thing back."

Dax gently took the quilt from Rose's hand and laid it over her chair. She pulled Rose into a tight hug. "It will be okay, Rose. We'll get everything you own into the truck and take it to the Foster House."

"Then what? I have no job. I have some savings, but it won't last forever."

Dax pulled back a fraction to look Rose in the eye. "If we have to move to find work, so be it. Maybe we can head to San Francisco. I can try to get my old carpentry job back. And I'm sure someone there is itching to hire a singer with a voice like yours."

"You make it sound so easy."

"Because it is. We have each other and May, and that's all that matters."

Rose slung her arms over Dax's shoulders and let a seductive grin form on her lips. "I never knew you were such a romantic."

Dax pulled her tighter until their bodies molded together from hips to breasts. "You bring out the best parts of me." They kissed, not with lust, but with love. Their lives were transforming, but Rose wasn't afraid. She had Dax and was sure that would be enough.

While she packed her trunk, Dax prepped the vanity to load into the truck. She removed the mirror and carefully wrapped it with the quilt. After loading the drawers' contents into a small shopping bag, she opened the door but stopped.

"Dax! What are you doing here?"

Rose didn't have to turn to know who was at her door. It had to be her neighbor from across the hall. "Come in, Jules." She focused on her overstuffed closet, pulling out a giant bundle of stage dresses.

"I'll start taking things down, Rose." Dax hoisted Rose's chair in one hand and the vanity stool in the other before disappearing out the door.

"What's going on?" Jules scanned the room, her mouth agape.

"Close the door." Rose placed her batch of dresses on the bed, waiting for the door to close. "Frankie fired me and kicked me out of the boarding house."

"But why?"

"Prohibition agents—"

"Did you get arrested? Did they shut down the club?"

"Will you let me tell you what happened?"

"Fine." Jules huffed and shoved the dresses to the side several inches, clearing an area for her to sit on the mattress.

"The Prohibition agents who saw Dax at the beach the night Riley's truck went over the cliff were at Frankie's office. They've been on his payroll and figured out not all the whiskey barrels were on the truck."

Jules flew a hand to her chest. "Did they see Charlie? Is she in trouble?"

"No one is in trouble with the law, only with Frankie. But no. Dax said the agents didn't recognize Charlie."

"Thank goodness. What happened next?"

"Frankie called Dax into his office and confronted her. I was worried he might beat her to a pulp, so I barged into his office, hoping to stop it. But he fired Dax and refused to pay her for her work, so I threatened not to sing if he didn't pay her. My plan backfired, and he fired me too. So I threatened to have Grace dry up his business."

Jules gasped. "You didn't?"

"I sure as hell did." Rose felt heat build in her cheeks again.

Jules snapped her head in her direction. "You cussed. You must be steaming mad."

"And then some. That's when Dax dragged me out of there because she thought Frankie might do something to me. And he did. We got here, and Mrs. Prescott was happy to throw me out on my ear."

"I despise that woman."

"I'm happy to be done with her." Rose handed Jules the stack of dresses. "Now, take these down to the truck.

Once her things were gone, Rose folded the itchy wool blanket and placed it at the foot of the bed, where she'd found it the first day she'd rented the room five years ago. She rechecked the closet and dresser drawers and stood in the doorway for the last time. This was the place where she'd transitioned to adulthood. She could furnish it any way she pleased and had a decent paying job to make the monthly rent. She was on her own. If it weren't for Mrs. Prescott's ridiculous rules, she could come and go as she pleased. Besides living across the hall from Jules, that independence was the one thing she would miss about this place.

Once satisfied the room was in the same condition as the day she moved in, Rose closed the door and marched down the stairs for the last time with purpose. She slammed her key atop Mrs. Prescott's desk, making the old busybody jump. "You know where you can stick your rules." She curled her lip at her before striding out with her chin held high.

Five minutes later, Dax pulled the truck to the rear of the Foster House. She and Rose grabbed a handle on opposite ends of her steamer trunk and buddy-carried it through the back door into the kitchen. May was drying and stacking the last of the lunch plates and turned toward the ruckus they were making.

"What do we have here?" she asked, doing a poor job of hiding a smile.

"Rose needs a place to stay. We'll explain when we come back down." May's smile dropped in an instant, but Dax didn't break her stride, not stopping until she reached the hallway at the top of the stairs. "I don't want to presume. Which bedroom would you like your stuff?"

"Let's put it in one of the spare rooms for now."

Dax's expression grew long as they resumed their trek to the end of the hall and the room next to Dax's. The room, smaller than Dax's by a few feet, had a made-up bed, a rickety dresser with a chipped washbasin, and the same peeling paint as the rest of the rooms.

They placed the trunk below the window. Dax turned to walk out, but Rose grabbed her hand to stop her. She recognized the deep pout. "Get this straight, Dax. I'll be sleeping with you. I just need to go through my things to see what will fit in our room."

A smile bright enough to light up the entire bay sprouted on Dax's lips. "*Our* room, huh?"

"Yes, *our* room." Unsurprisingly, Rose liked its sound as much as she had liked the idea of living on her own. However, living alone now seemed like a lonely proposition. "I want to kiss you, but we have a truck to unload and a sister waiting for an explanation about the sudden change. If we start, I'm afraid we wouldn't make it downstairs for a while."

"I'm certain of it." Dax patted Rose on the bottom when she passed by. "Let's go talk to May."

After explaining the events at the Seaside Hotel and boarding house to May, the three sat around the center kitchen chopping block, sipping on cups of hot tea. "This is a mess," May said. "We need to get rid of those barrels in case those Prohis snoop around."

"I understand why you're afraid," Dax said, "but those barrels are worth thousands of dollars. We already can't make payroll, and the money we'd make from selling the whiskey could tide us over for a long time."

May pressed her lips into a straight line, shaking her head. "I agree we could use the money, but I don't want those things in this house longer than necessary. You need to sell them in San Francisco tomorrow."

Dax ran both hands down her face. "All right, May. I'll let Charlie know what's going on and see if she can come with me."

Once Rose stored her belongings in the spare room, she realized the day's wild swing of emotions, ranging from joy to worry to panic to shock to anger, had worn her out. Her appetite had bottomed out, and she could only nibble on the dinner May had prepared for her and Dax. She needed to make that call to Grace before exhaustion took over.

Rose pushed back her chair from the dining table and squeezed Dax's hand. "May I use the phone? I should call Grace and tell her what has happened. Maybe she can put Frankie in his place. I'll pay for the charges."

"By all means." Dax's smile was tight, making Rose think it was forced. The topic of Grace clearly still made Dax uneasy. She stood and gathered their dinner plates. "May and I will clean up."

"You've had a long day," May said. "I've got cleanup tonight."

"Thank you, May." Dax kissed her sister on the cheek before returning her attention to Rose. "I'll meet you upstairs."

Once May retreated to the kitchen and Dax went upstairs, Rose retrieved from her purse the paper on which Grace had jotted down the phone number to her house, her talent agent, and the movie studio. It was after seven. She figured she would likely catch Grace at home. She lifted the earpiece from the candlestick phone at the cash register near the restaurant entrance and clicked the receiver twice.

"Operator."

"Hi, Holly. This is Rose. I need to place a call to Hollywood."

"Sure thing, Rosebud."

Rose smiled. The nickname Edith, the department store owner, had given her years ago had stuck with many of the townspeople. After passing along Grace's number, Rose waited for the call to connect.

"Parson's residence," a woman answered.

"This is Rose Hamilton from Half Moon Bay. I need to speak to Grace Parsons."

"Yes, Miss Hamilton. Mrs. Parsons left your name. I'm sorry, but she is out of the country filming. I don't expect her back for another eight weeks."

"Eight weeks? It's important that I speak with her."

"I can send a telegraph, but I'm afraid her filming location is remote. It might be weeks before she gets it."

"Yes, please send it. I appreciate your help. Be sure to tell her it's important." Going into any more detail with someone she didn't know made Rose uneasy. With any luck, Grace would get the message and Frankie Wilkes would soon face the consequences of turning Rose's life upside down.

After completing the call, she ascended the stairs. Without the energy to consider anything other than sleep, she changed into her nightclothes and climbed into bed with Dax, hoping she was equally exhausted. Making love tonight was out of the question, but she welcomed Dax's warm, reassuring embrace when she slid into her side of the bed. She molded herself against her. "Can you just hold me tonight?" Rose brought the covers over them and hooked an arm beneath her pillow.

"Whatever you need." Dax rested an arm across Rose and kissed her on the back of her head. "What did Grace say?"

"Nothing. She's out of the country," Rose said. Grace's help would have to wait.

She tried to let sleep take over, but the scene in Frankie's office kept replaying in her head. She remembered bursting into the room, expecting to see Dax beaten and bloodied to within an inch of her life. Her pulse had been racing so fast that she had no self-control. What she said and did in Frankie's office wasn't planned, but they had one thing in common—protecting the woman she loved.

She hadn't considered the consequences until Frankie said those two life-changing words, "You're fired." The world around her stopped. Her anger returned as she recalled it, but she now directed it at herself, not Frankie. She'd gotten too cocky and now was paying the price for her arrogance. The money and a place to live were secondary to the most important thing she'd lost today—the ability to act out her life's passion.

Rose glanced at the Big Ben alarm clock on the narrow nightstand beside the bed. It was nine thirty. She should be on stage making love to the microphone with her voice, and Lester should be beside her at the piano, providing the mood music. Singing in front of an audience was not only her job. It was something she fed on. Unlike working at Ida's or helping May in the kitchen, she could not wait to start each performance. Once she'd stepped up to the microphone, the music would transport her to a place where only the people hanging on her every word existed. It was where everything wrong in her life had no hold over her, including her stutter. Knowing she would never go to that place again was devastating.

Rose trembled.

She wished she had that with Dax. She felt safe and loved when they were together like they were now, but a dark cloud hung over them. After each performance, she could share her joy from singing with anyone who would listen, but she could not do the same after a fulfilling night with Dax. Once the bedroom door opened, they had to hide the best part of themselves—their love for each other.

Rose wept for her loss.

Dax shifted her arm and held it tight against Rose's abdomen. "I love you, Rose."

Rose croaked between sniffles, "I love you too, but…"

"But what?"

"The thought of never singing to a crowd again hurts more than I'd imagined."

"I have an idea." Dax coaxed Rose to roll to her other side to face her. "How would you like to sing in the Foster House for special shows after hours?"

"But I'd need a piano and a player."

"May plays really well. I can pick up her piano from her and Logan's house when Charlie and I go to San Francisco tomorrow to sell the whiskey barrels. We can set it up in the corner by the kitchen and serve dessert with coffee and sodas while you sing. How about it?"

"You'd do all of that for me?"

"Of course, I would. But I'm also thinking about the survival of the Foster House. Business is bound to pick up once word gets around that Rose Hamilton is singing here."

Rose's instincts were right in seventh grade when Dax socked the bully teasing her about her speech for the first time. Based on that one heroic act, she knew Dax would always protect her. Would move heaven and earth to make her happy. Tonight's generous, heartfelt offer demonstrated that those qualities in Dax hadn't waned. If anything, they'd grown exponentially.

She traced Dax's jawline with a fingertip. "I'd love that very much."

CHAPTER SIX

Dax lifted an edge of the blind to peek out of the smudged door window of Charlie's Auto Repairs. Their plan to get out of town before the Prohis left their room at the Seaside Hotel had gone up in smoke two minutes ago. She and Charlie had successfully loaded the barrels at the Foster House and pulled into the garage for tarps and stacks of junkyard-bound tires to camouflage the load for the trip to San Francisco. They were about to leave when Dax spotted the Prohis' car parked across the street. Now they had to evade Frankie's paid watchdogs.

"We're cornered," Dax said.

"I have a plan." Charlie held up a buck knife in one hand and several soiled shop rags in the other. "I'll be right back." She stacked three crates against the back wall and crawled out the window there.

Dax resumed her perch at the door window while Charlie sneaked behind the Prohis' car, crouching low to avoid detection. She stuffed the rags into the tailpipe and stabbed the rear tires once each with the buck knife. Still crouching, she retraced her steps and returned through the back window minutes later.

"They won't get to the end of the block." Charlie's lopsided grin meant she was pleased with herself. "I'll get the door."

Dax hopped into the driver's seat and revved the engine. Charlie raised the bay door rapidly, tugging on the pull chain, hand over hand, as fast as a prizefighter pummeling a speed bag. She pointed an index finger at Brutus near her feet. "Stay, boy. I'll be back soon."

Once Dax pulled forward onto the driveway, Charlie stepped outside and released the chain, sending the door down in a loud, clanking thud. She hopped into the passenger seat before Dax rolled slowly onto the street. The Prohis' car angled into the traffic lane behind them.

Dax asked, "You're sure about their car?"

"Positive," Charlie said. "Hit it."

Dax pressed the gas pedal to the floorboard and shifted gears. Her Model T lunged forward, picking up speed. She checked her side mirror, watching the Prohis' vehicle gaining on them. Breakfast churned in her stomach. Had Charlie overestimated the impact of her trick?

"Charlieeeee?"

"Keep going," Charlie urged, looking as calm as if they were out for a Sunday drive.

Dax kept increasing her speed and checking her mirror. Her pulse revved as hard as the engine at the prospect of being caught with seven barrels of Frankie's stolen whiskey in her truck bed. Finally, she slowed to turn onto the main highway and rechecked her mirror. The Prohis' car wobbled. The distance between her vehicle and theirs grew. As she made the turn, the Prohis came to a sputtering stop.

Charlie leaned back in her seat with a satisfied grin. "Told ya."

Laughter filled the cab for the next mile. An hour later, Dax passed the San Francisco city limits sign. She weaved through surface streets, reaching the Cole Valley neighborhood. Rolling through this part of town brought back a grab bag of memories and emotions. She'd walked these streets for work and errands so frequently for nine years that she could close her eyes and recite to Charlie the color and architectural features of the next ten houses and the type of trees lining their yards. She'd been inside nearly half of the homes on this stretch of Stanyan Street, repairing stairs, floors, and cabinets after several powerful tremors had rattled the city. Not one house was the same.

She slowed the truck when two coastal live oak trees guarding a gray two-story Victorian house came into view. The back of her throat grew thick when she thought about stepping foot in that house for the first time. Mr. Portman had said tremors caused the stair railing to break, but by the second day on the job, Dax had figured out he'd lied and was a wife beater.

She'd fallen in love with Heather with her beautiful red flowing hair and timid demeanor. Their kisses were magical— until he'd beaten Heather to a pulp. He'd deserved the sucker punch she'd given him. That punch had triggered her forced move to Half Moon Bay, but she never regretted throwing it because Heather and her children had escaped his brutality, and weeks later, she reunited with Rose.

"Dax? Are we going to the speakeasy?" Charlie shook her from her memories.

"Huh?" Dax hadn't realized she'd brought their truck to a stop in the middle of the street. "Sorry." She downshifted, increased the throttle, and accelerated to the proper speed.

"Good or bad memories?" Charlie asked.

"Both. I'll tell you about it one day." Today, though, wasn't the day for examining old wounds. Instead, she had to focus on why they were in San Francisco.

Dax turned at the next corner and parked behind the building with the underground speakeasy. She eyed the load of illegal whiskey that lay hidden beneath tarps and stacks of old tires from Charlie's garage, thinking they were about to give away a goldmine. But that was the price she had to pay to keep May and Rose happy and safe. The money they would make today from the barrels could carry the restaurant for two years, maybe three. But what would happen if jobs around the state were still scarce? She had an idea of addressing that probability but was unsure how Charlie would react.

"Still thinking about those bad memories?" Charlie asked.

"Not this time. But I need to ask you something."

"What's on your mind, Dax?"

"I know May said to get rid of all the barrels, but I was thinking about holding one back and saving it for a rainy day."

Charlie shifted on the bench seat and ran a hand roughly across her mouth. "I don't know, Dax. We're taking a big chance now that Frankie and the Prohis are on to us."

"They're on to me. Not you. Now hear me out." Dax rotated to look at Charlie squarely. "We're selling these barrels for a quarter of what we could get if we sold it by the glass. We don't know how long money is going to be tight. We could easily hide one barrel and decide what to do with it later if we're still struggling."

"You have a point, but what would we tell May?"

"We wouldn't tell her. I have the perfect spot to hide one barrel—in the cinderblock wall of the basement of the Foster House."

"May might never speak to you again if she ever finds out," Charlie said.

"She'll never find it. The spot I have in mind is like a tomb. And if we ever have to break into the whiskey, she'll thank me for the foresight."

Charlie let out a breathy sigh. "I think it's a bad idea, but I won't stop you. I'll leave the decision up to you. Just prepare yourself in the event this idea backfires."

Dax patted Charlie on the upper leg. "You're a good friend. How about we get more work done on the dock after we get back?" After Charlie agreed, Dax said, "You should wait here with the barrels while I see if the owner is in."

Exiting the truck, Dax pulled her newsboy cap low to mask some of her girlish facial features and zipped her jacket high to camouflage her chest. She entered the deli at the front of the building, sounding the bell hanging above the door. The woman behind the counter had helped her before. She'd escorted her and Charlie to the basement speakeasy when they sold the first two whiskey barrels to get the money for May's brace.

"Hello, Mrs. Moretti." She removed her cap. "I'm Dax. I was here about two months ago for business with your husband. This morning, my sister called ahead, and I believe he's expecting me."

"Yes, of course," Mrs. Moretti said in a thick Italian accent. "How is May? Did she get her new leg brace?"

"Yes, she did, and we have you and your husband to thank. It's made all the difference in the world. She can even do a few stairs now."

"That's wonderful news." Mrs. Moretti rounded the counter and yanked Dax into a bone-crushing hug. She pulled back with a smile as wide as the San Francisco Bay. "Salvatore is expecting you." She kissed Dax on both cheeks and returned to the counter to press a hidden buzzer. The door marked "Janitor" opened, and a tall, brawny man stuck his head from around it. "Paolo will show you down."

"Thank you, Mrs. Moretti."

The speakeasy operation at Moretti's Deli wasn't as elaborate as the one at the Seaside Club, but it had the same bones—a bar with a mirror lining the back wall, a dozen round wooden tables with chairs, and a single bathroom to limit the coming and going of patrons. The only thing missing was a stage. Dax shook off the bitter memory of Frankie Wilkes stiffing her for the nearly completed stage she'd built for him.

"Dax." Mr. Moretti waved her over from behind the bar. A luxuriant mustache hid most of his jovial smile. When Dax approached the bar, he extended his hand and continued, "May said we have more business to conduct."

"Yes, sir." She shook his hand. "I hope you can accommodate us again."

"How many barrels are we talking about today?"

Dax paused for a moment. She would put this whiskey business behind if she told him seven. But if she gave him any lower number, she would leave the door open for an emergency fund if the need ever came.

She took a deep breath and said, "Six."

"How much do you want for them?"

"The last time we were here, you gave us six hundred for two barrels. So I guess eighteen hundred would do it."

Mr. Moretti placed a hand on Dax's shoulder briefly. "Your sister has been a loyal deli customer and a good friend to my Anna for years. So, for May, let's make it an even two thousand. Paolo will help you unload the barrels."

"That's very kind of you, sir."

His generous offer proved that May's example of thoughtfulness and compassion was infectious.

Soon the truck was lighter by six barrels and, after a trip to the junkyard, a dozen old tires. Charlie stored the remaining container on the bench seat between them under a blanket to cover it to free up the bed for May's piano. "How do you figure lifting the piano into the truck?" she asked.

"There are plenty of men out of work. If we offer four bits to four men at a soup line, we could get it lifted and tied off in minutes for only two dollars."

"Genius."

"Do you mean that as a good or bad thing?" Dax chuckled, handing Charlie her half of the whiskey money.

"Thanks. I guess we'll find out."

Two blocks from Logan's house, a church soup line was teeming with men eager to earn fifty cents for a few minutes of labor. Four of them jumped into Dax's truck bed with the promise of a lift back to the church if there was room in the back.

Dax pulled the truck curbside in front of Logan's house. She'd called this place home for nine years, but it no longer held that connotation. Her home was with Rose and May wherever they were.

"Wait here with the barrel, Charlie. It's our insurance policy."

Charlie draped a protective hand over the blanket-covered whiskey. "Do you think Logan will cause any trouble?"

"I doubt it. He's never been one to put up a fight."

The men jumped out, but Dax asked them to wait on the sidewalk. May had hidden a key to the front door on the porch, but she didn't want them to know about it because her sister still had belongings in the house that she might want to reclaim one day. She walked to the set of chairs and a small table where she and May used to sit for their regular Saturday Gin Rummy marathon. It was also where Dax would wait to watch Heather and her husband pass by on their way to the park to let their children play. Those few glimpses had been the best and worst part of her week. Each time Heather passed, they would lock stares long enough for each to convey their mutual longing. After Heather's second pass of the day, Dax had to wait an entire week to know she was safe from her husband's abuse. The days in between were agony. Finally, on that fateful Saturday, she had leaped into action to ensure that was the last day Heather had to be afraid of him.

Dax located the hidden key she doubted Logan knew about. The thick layer of dirt and leaves said the furniture and porch appeared to haven't been cleaned in months, likely since May and Dax left. She knocked on the screen door, only half-expecting Logan to be there, and waited a good minute before waving the men up to the house.

Just as Dax leveled the key at the lock, the door swung open. Logan appeared with a stubbled face, unkempt hair, and a wrinkled undershirt and pants. Before losing his job following the big market crash, he was always clean-shaven and well-dressed. The person in the doorway was a broken man.

"What the hell are you doing here?" he growled.

Dax wasn't afraid of him, not anymore. Logan had already done the worst thing he could to May by abandoning her, and the last four months had proved she and Dax didn't need him. They had survived just fine without him.

She stood taller. "I'm here to get May's piano."

"She doesn't need that old thing to run a restaurant. Go away." He grabbed the edge of the door to close it, but Dax slammed a hand against it to stop him.

"I'm not leaving here without May's piano, Logan. These four men are here to make sure I get it." Dax gestured her head toward the interior of the house. "Let's go, fellas. I'll double your pay if we get the piano in the next five minutes."

Before Logan could object, the largest of the men barreled his way through the front door, pushing Logan into the wall and out of his way. "Where is it?" The other men followed.

"In the parlor on the right," Dax yelled. Logan looked dazed, rubbing the back of his head. She looked Logan in the eye, pressing a palm against his chest. "I don't want any trouble. All I want is May's piano, and I'll be out of your way."

He shook his head as if clearing out the cobwebs. "Why is that thing so damn important to her?"

"It just is."

A chorus of grunts came from the parlor, and seconds later, two men shuffled toward the front door, each lifting an end of May's 1912 Sherman Clay upright console piano. Its Rosewood construction made for a heavy lift; it would require all four men to get it into her truck bed. Dax directed Logan farther down the entryway to give the men more room to work. While one man barked out directions on how to get it out the door, she retrieved the piano bench from the parlor. She returned to see the screen door slam shut behind the men.

"I'll be on my way now," she said and turned to walk out.

Logan grabbed her by the jacket sleeve and spun her around. His eyes were full of rage, and he'd formed a hand into a fist, ready to throw a punch.

Dax's instinct was to break the piano bench over his head, but May needed it. She dug deep for restraint and narrowed her eyes to telegraph the certainty behind her warning. "Don't even think about it, or I'll have those men beat your face into ground beef."

He lowered his hand, and Dax walked out with nothing but disgust for the man May once loved enough to marry. While the men loaded the piano and after she was sure Logan had gone upstairs, she returned the key to the hiding place. Once in the truck, she glanced at Charlie on the passenger side, still protecting the whiskey like precious cargo.

"How did it go?" Charlie asked.

"Just as planned." Dax took the men back to the church and paid each a dollar apiece for their trouble. Their business in San Francisco complete, she put the truck in gear and Logan Foster behind her and May, hopefully for good.

CHAPTER SEVEN

Rose washed, rinsed, and placed the last water glass on the drying rack. After swiping a sheen of sweat from her forehead, she wiped her hands dry with the dishtowel and tossed it into the nearby hamper. No stranger to working a restaurant's dining room and kitchen in Half Moon Bay, she considered the day's work light. Too light. If today was an accurate barometer of the average daily foot traffic, the Foster House was in trouble. Dax selling those whiskey barrels could not have come at a better time.

She scanned the kitchen, ticking off in her head the checklist she'd used to close Ida's Café for the night. Everything appeared to have been done. "Anything else I can help with, May?"

May sat on her stool at the center chopping block where she'd placed two forks and the last slice of chocolate cake from the day's lunch service. "Join me?"

"You know cake is my weakness." Without hesitation, Rose dragged over another stool and took a generous bite.

Once they'd polished off the slice, May returned her fork to the dessert plate. "I'm so glad to have you here, but I'm sorry about the circumstances. Dax told me why you hadn't accepted our offer sooner, and I completely understand."

"Thank you for understanding and taking me in when I needed a place to stay. You've been nothing but kind to me."

"You're family, Rose. You'll always have a home with me, but we have to discuss your work in the restaurant. I'm not sure how much I can pay you."

Rose reached across the countertop and squeezed May's right hand. "Like you said, we're family. You pay me nothing. Like Dax, I'll pull my weight and do whatever work needs doing."

May cupped Rose's hand with her left. "We're lucky to have you, but we need to establish who does what in the kitchen. If this chocolate cake is a sample of how you bake, you need to make the desserts every day. You're so much better at it."

Rose laughed. "I'll be happy to be your pastry chef."

While May went to her room, Rose sorted through the clothes upstairs. She hadn't realized how many dresses she'd collected for work over the years. A dozen were cut low on the chest, tight at the waist, or slit high in the thigh. None of those was fit to wear off the stage. Thankfully, three dresses were appropriate for daily wear. She stored the entire lot in the spare room closet, which was, surprisingly, twice the size of the one she had at the boarding house.

After hanging her day dresses beside them, she opened her steamer trunk and organized the rest of her clothes. She had no plan to peek into Dax's dresser drawers, so she stacked items atop the six-drawer dresser in the spare room before deciding which pieces went where. As she grabbed the first stack, she saw motion from the doorway. Dax was leaning against the frame with her arms crossed in front of her chest and a smile warm enough to heat the room.

"You're back early," Rose said.

"I wanted to make sure you were safe." Dax pushed herself from the frame and walked inside, looking at the bed with a box of Rose's bathroom necessities. She shifted her stare to the dresser. "I don't have much stuff in my room. I can combine drawers and give you half the dresser."

Rose eyed her stacks of clothes, silently chastising herself for buying things she didn't need, merely wanted. She should have saved more during the tourist seasons when she earned twice the money needed to survive. Instead, she'd splurged on makeup, dresses, and shoes for work and pretty blouses and skirts for her time off. Now her spending seemed frivolous. That wasted money could have carried the Foster House deficit for a year or more.

"I'm afraid I have too many things. I'll have to pare them down."

"You'll do no such thing. Just keep everything in here." Dax stepped to the dresser and opened the top drawer. "What do you want in here?" A grin sprouted on her lips when she finished stowing Rose's clothes. She extended a hand. "I have a surprise for you."

"I like surprises."

Dax led her down the stairs. Reaching the bottom, she said, "Close your eyes." She guided Rose down the corridor with her eyes shut, taking her deep into the main dining room and angling her just so. "Open them."

Rose snapped her lids open, a warmth instantly radiating in her chest. The window blinds had been drawn closed. The tables had been repositioned, clearing a ten-by-ten-foot corner section of the room, where Dax had positioned May's upright piano against the wall. May was on the bench in front of it, and Charlie and Jules were seated at the nearest table, all of them beaming.

An extra ceiling light had been hung, highlighting the area. An upside-down produce crate with a broom handle sticking vertically out of the bottom had been positioned a few feet from the piano, facing the dining room tables. Rose gasped, taking it all in. Dax had painstakingly re-created the environment Rose loved the most, down to a makeshift stage with a pretend microphone stand.

Rose flew a hand to her chest, her heart swelling with love. "This is wonderful. How on earth did you get it in here?"

"Charlie and I stopped at Edith's Department Store and asked her husband and two other men to help us."

"How about you sing us a little song, Rose?" May spun to face the piano. "I learned this one last summer." May tinkled the black and white keys, producing an upbeat tune.

After eight notes, Rose recognized the song. She waited for May to begin the verse again and belted out the words to "I Wanna Be Loved By You."

Dax offered her hand to dance, pulled Rose closer, and joined in the next verse, smiling and bouncing to the music. Dax spun her around and pecked her on the lips. Charlie and Jules joined them on the small dance floor, singing and swaying to the music. And when the song finished, Dax wrapped Rose in her arms and lifted her off the floor, spinning her around once more.

"I'm so glad you like it, Rose."

"I love it." Rose pulled Dax into a hug, still soaking in her grand gesture. "And I'll show you how much later tonight."

"All right, lovebirds," Jules said. "Join us for a Coca-Cola."

Everyone grouped around the table, sipped their soda drinks, and chatted about the possibilities with a piano in the restaurant. Being able to entertain opened a whole new way to market the Foster House. It was no longer merely a place to eat. Besides providing singing for tourists on the weekends, the restaurant could be a destination for special parties and weddings.

The conversation continued, and for the first time in her life, Rose felt safe enough to display her affection for the woman she was with in front of others. It felt natural to link arms with Dax and kiss her on the lips. She was among friends of the same persuasion or of the mindset that same-sex relationships didn't matter. Moments earlier, Jules had hit Charlie with a kiss hot enough to make May blush. The freedom displayed in the room nearly made Rose forget that the type of love she shared with Dax was illegal and widely considered immoral. Almost.

A knock on the main door made everyone freeze and pull apart to a socially acceptable distance. May put her glass down and said, "It's all right, ladies. I'll get rid of whoever it is."

May opened the door, but Rose could not see who it was from her vantage point. But when she moved to the side to let the person inside, Rose instantly recognized the attire and suspected foul play. Her mother's cousin, Rose's former tyrant and virtual prison matron, stalked over the threshold. In the nine years she had known Ida, she'd never stepped inside the Foster House. Why would she? It was her competition.

After May closed the front door, she and Ida remained near the entrance and talked in hushed tones. Unfortunately, Rose could not make out a word from her location. But when May placed her hands on her hips in clear defiance, Rose knew what Ida was up to.

"I'll be right back, ladies," Rose said to her tablemates. She pushed herself from her chair and strode toward the door with purpose and confidence. Ida no longer had a hold over her and could not shame her into doing what she wanted. However, Ida could make trouble for May and the Foster House. While Rose approached, she could not make out what they were saying, but Ida shut her trap when she got within hearing distance. An explanation wasn't necessary. She was here to make trouble.

"You need to leave, Ida," Rose said.

Ida stiffened. "You might not care what your presence here could mean for the Foster House, but May would."

"And you told her what? That my questionable morals would be bad for business? They certainly weren't bad for you for the four years you treated me like an indentured servant."

May's lips turned up into a clearly forced grin. "Ida was kind enough to convey her concern that rumors about you and Dax might percolate in town if I allowed you to live here."

Rose turned toward Ida. "And I'm sure it's merely a concern of yours, not a warning." Anger fueled her words, and they came out as smooth as silk. Rose paused when Ida harrumphed and raised her chin. It was time to put this horrid woman in her place. "Need I remind you about your own secret? I can percolate some rumors of my own. I'm sure this town would be thirsty for something juicy concerning the biggest hypocrite Half Moon Bay has ever seen."

May stepped toward the door and opened it. "You are always welcome to eat here, Ida, because I never discriminate, even against a busybody like you. But don't you ever come here again, threatening me, my family, or my business. I turn the other cheek only once. After that, God help you."

"Well, I never." Ida sniffed and turned on her heel.

"And that is the source of all your problems." May slammed the door at Ida's back and turned toward Rose. She straightened her posture, pouted, and placed both hands on her hips. "Well, I never," she said, using a high-pitched voice and bobbing her head.

Rose broke out into a full belly laugh, and May joined her. She'd mocked Ida a hundred times in private, but it was a thousand times better to see someone else do it. And witnessing May simultaneously defend Rose and craftily threaten Ida was priceless. May and Dax were alike in their protective instincts, but May's approach was more subtle.

Their laughter came to a gradual stop. Following a moment of silence, May's expression turned serious. "I'd never let anyone dictate who I let stay in this house, but I'm worried that woman could cause trouble for Dax too."

Rose understood May's concern. For years, she'd lived with the possibility of Ida telling the whole town why her parents had sent her there, but Ida never had. That gave her the impression her cousin was embarrassed about what the townspeople might think about her for employing and housing a woman with "immoral appetites." That and what Rose knew about Conroy guaranteed Ida would not talk.

"You have nothing to worry about, May. Ida is all bark and no bite. She doesn't want her own deep dark secret coming out."

"Are you sure? Dax has enough on her plate."

"I'm sure. Let's get back to the fun." Rose hooked an arm around May's and guided her back to the group.

Dax kissed Rose on the cheek when she sat. Charlie remained quiet, sipping on her cola. Surprisingly, Jules didn't pepper her with questions, though her fidgeting and spoon spinning on the tabletop were clear signs she was bursting at the seams for the details of her and May's conversation with Ida. Charlie had likely preempted the immediate interrogation with a stern warning.

"Go ahead and ask," Rose said.

Jules squirmed and leaned forward, elbows on the table. "What did the old biddy want?"

"To make trouble for Dax and me."

"But Rose gave it to her with both barrels," May said.

"Me?" Rose wagged her thumb in May's direction. "This one packs a verbal wallop. I recommend never crossing her."

Jules shook her head. "Ida was crazy for coming over here. She clearly thinks you were bluffing about Conroy." Rose kicked Jules in the shin under the table. Her friend may have been the magnet for all the gossip in town, but Rose steered clear of it. Now she didn't have a choice.

"What about your brother?" Dax asked.

"This has to stay between the five of us. Are we in agreement?" Rose waited for everyone's confirming nod. "Ida gave birth to Conroy. I don't know who his father was, but she was forced to give him up, and my parents took him in and raised him as their own."

"That poor woman," May said. "No mother should ever be forced to give up her child. No wonder she's angry all the time."

"But it doesn't justify her threatening to tell the town about Rose and me," Dax said, folding her arms across her chest. Compassion for the woman who took advantage of Rose for years clearly wasn't in the cards for her.

"I agree, but it explains why she's so judgmental," May said.

"How so?" Dax asked.

"If she was young when she had to give up her baby, that experience taught her bucking society was one of the worst things she could do. That's why she's so put off by what you and Rose share."

Rose hadn't considered Ida's experience in those terms, but maybe she should have. She'd grown up with the son Ida had been forced to abandon. That alone was enough to make any woman resentful. Add on the layer of Rose being an outcast without paying a steep price, and it was no wonder Ida took out her anger on her. Rose had never thought this possible, but her icy impression of Ida thawed a fraction.

CHAPTER EIGHT

Dax fluttered her eyes open to moonlight-fed shadows dancing on the far wall of her dark bedroom. May's knitted wool blanket kept the cold night air from pricking her skin, but she realized something else was keeping her warmer. The snugness against her breasts and the tops of her legs reassured her that last night was not a dream, and neither were the previous four. Rose was next to her in bed and had been all night. Dax had dreamed of waking next to her every day for nearly a decade, and now that dream was reality. Five consecutive nights were a magnificent beginning, but Dax hoped for five decades, and with May running things at the restaurant, it was a possibility.

She craned her neck enough to see Big Ben would not bray its alarm for another twenty minutes, the signal that it was time to wake and prepare the Foster House for breakfast service. That should be enough time to give Rose a proper start to her day.

Dax caressed the length of Rose's thigh, dragging her nightclothes up from the knee, but Rose placed a hand as a roadblock, stopping her ascent. "It's my time," she whispered. "I started overnight."

"That doesn't matter." Dax recalled the care Rose had taken with her several weeks ago when her time of the month coincided with one of their weekly visits.

Rose kept her hand in place. "Cramps are bothering me this time. Maybe in a few days."

Dax drifted her hand to Rose's lower abdomen, discovering it was bloated. "Would you like me to make you a warm compress?"

"No need. I'll be fine once I take a shower." Rose wriggled and rolled over until their faces were an inch apart. They entwined their legs and pushed their bellies together. "But I will take a kiss."

Dax ran a fingertip down Rose's cheek. "Your wish is my command." Pressing their lips together, she kept her passion in check, but her insides didn't cooperate. They quivered at the sensation of Rose's body against her. *Every time*, she thought. Whenever they kissed, her body needed more. Another kiss or a caress would do if they were in the kitchen with only May around, but her body craved more intimacy in bed. Not even their monthlies could quell that instinct, but an extra-long cold shower could.

"Ready for your first performance tomorrow on the Foster House stage?" Dax had spent the last few days after the restaurant closed building a small platform in the dining room to give Rose the feeling of performing on a real stage, not a corner afterthought.

"I guess." Rose's lackluster response was not what Dax had hoped for and it broke her heart.

She squinted. "What's wrong? I know the stage isn't what you're used—"

Rose placed an index finger over Dax's lips. "The stage is beautiful, and I love you for building it. But without offering liquor, I doubt anyone will come."

Dax didn't know how to respond. Tourists went to the Seaside for booze and to see Rose sing, but even the locals might not come if they could go a few shops down the street to enjoy a snort while being entertained. Dax pulled Rose closer, holding her tight until they were ready to start the day. She and Rose finally dressed and entered the kitchen before May emerged from her room. This was a first. The lights had been turned on, though, which meant May had showered and would be out soon.

Dax retrieved her coat from the peg near the back door and kissed Rose on the cheek. "I'm off to the grocer." Last month, she and May had decided to pick up their daily order to save the fifteen-cent delivery charge. Every penny still counted, even after selling the six barrels of whiskey. She and May needed to stretch that money as far as possible.

She started the truck and let it warm up before putting it in gear. It didn't sputter once in the cold ocean air, a sign Charlie had the engine in top running condition. If her friend lived in San Francisco, she would have work lined up for months.

Turning on the headlights, Dax rumbled down Main Street, going deeper into town and parking in front of the Spanish Town Store. She pushed the main door open, which chimed the bell hung high on the frame and alerted Mr. Thompson that a customer had arrived. The store was mostly dark but lit enough for employees or business owners to pick up their morning orders, which were staged in rows near the front door.

Dax located the four boxes marked "Foster House" and loaded the first one into her truck bed. When she turned to go back inside, another set of headlights appeared in the dark, growing larger until the vehicle parked next to Dax. The sign on the passenger door said the truck belonged to the Seaside Hotel.

"Great," Dax mumbled to herself. She had nothing against the employees who worked there, but Frankie Wilkes had left a nasty taste in her mouth with his threats to her and Rose. Now that Rose was no longer working in his club, she half-hoped their business would shrivel up or migrate to the Foster House. However, the size of the Seaside order stacked near the front door suggested that wasn't the case.

Dax returned inside for her second box, propping the door open with a produce crate, but stopped when someone called her name.

"I thought that was you, Dax." Jason stepped through the open door, bundled up in a winter coat and fedora. "How is Rose doing? I hear she's living and working at the Foster House with you."

If Dax had any doubt that Jason's interest in Rose was more than professional, the concerned tone in his question erased it. He clearly had a crush on her, but Dax was convinced he would never let on that he did.

"She's fine, Jason. I'm just glad we had room for her."

"I can't believe Frankie fired Rose and kicked her out of the boarding house. What in the hell happened in his office? All Frankie would say was that he'd had enough of her."

"She defended me." An incomplete version of the truth seemed appropriate for the man who had likely saved her life. "I can't get into specifics, but thank you for tipping off Rose. I wasn't sure if I was going to walk out of Frankie's office in one piece."

"Well, I'm glad it worked out." Jason scanned the surrounding area as if making sure they were alone. "Rose should probably know that Frankie hired a new singer who's supposed to start tomorrow night."

"Is she any good?"

"She's okay." Jason shrugged. "But she's no Rose Hamilton. I doubt she'll draw as many out-of-towners as Rose did."

"Good." Dax silently snickered. She hoped Frankie Wilkes had shot himself in the foot by letting Rose go.

"I get the feeling," Jason said. "Please tell Rose that if she ever needs anything, she only needs to ask. And the same goes for you."

"Thanks, Jason. Your kindness means a lot. I'll pass along your message." Dax shook the hand he'd offered and finished loading her groceries. During the drive home, she debated how much to tell Rose. The way she'd acted the last few days, Dax could tell the sting of losing the job she loved had yet to wane.

She could not bring herself to add to it first thing this morning. Maybe she would tell her tonight if Rose felt better.

As the day progressed, Dax was in and out of the kitchen, hauling dirty dishes and keeping May and Rose stocked with clean ones. Thankfully, Rose's cramps seemed to be bothering her less and less. By two thirty, the lunch crowd had died down, and Dax estimated foot traffic was up, giving her hope this downward trend in business might be short-lived.

While the servers completed their cleanup and closing routine, Dax tallied the receipts at the register. She was almost finished when a car pulled into a parking space in front of the Foster House. With the sun's blinding rays filtering through the plate glass window, Dax could see only the back half and didn't readily recognize the vehicle. It was likely a traveler passing through.

"We might have one, Ruth," she yelled over her shoulder.

A car door slammed, followed by footsteps clomping across the wood-slat sidewalk. The main door swung open, and Dax looked up. Her muscles froze. She'd thought her heart could not sink lower than when Rose was fired, but she was wrong. The perfect life she, May, and Rose had built was about to come to a grinding halt.

"Where's May?" Logan had the same stubbled face and was in the same wrinkled clothes he'd been wearing when Dax saw him last week at the family home in San Francisco. He appeared as gruff as he sounded, and the question was arrogant, without an ounce of compassion about May's leg and how she was getting along.

"Where else would she be?" Dax instinctively shoved the money she was counting in her front pants pocket and closed the register as she spoke. "She's exactly where you abandoned her."

Heat bubbled in Dax's belly at the biggest blunder she may have made in years. She'd picked up May's piano to make Rose happy, but all the resulting smiles she'd put on Rose's face with the makeshift stage could not make up for bringing Logan into their lives again.

Without another word, he walked toward the kitchen.

Dax's mind spun, weighing the meaning of his return. Could he have found a job and be here to take May back? If so, that would mean he would put the Foster House on the market and Frankie Wilkes would snatch it up in a flash. Or had Logan sold the house and was here to stay? Either scenario signaled disaster.

Dax flipped the sign on the main door and locked it, closing the restaurant fifteen minutes early. Logan had taken long strides, so Dax had to double her usual pace to beat him to the kitchen. She passed him and burst into the kitchen where May and Rose were cleaning the day's cooking.

"May"—Dax's heart beat wildly at the prospect of their lives changing at her next words—"Logan is here."

"What?" May turned to face Dax when Logan stepped through the swinging door from the dining room. She dropped the grill scraper in her hand to the floor with a loud clang. She remained still instead of lunging toward the husband she hadn't seen in nearly four months. She didn't even call out his name. His two dispassionate letters, which gave no insight into his return, clearly dictated her equally unemotional response.

"What? No hug?" Logan's question was as insincere as his sudden appearance, and clearly, no one in the room was buying it. He approached May, kissing her on the forehead.

"What are you doing here?" May's face turned ashen, and her shoulders were stiff.

Logan looked at Rose—with no hint of recognition, thank goodness—and returned his attention to May. "Let's go upstairs to talk."

May rolled her eyes and patted her right leg. "I haven't done that many stairs in years." Her claim wasn't entirely true. With Dax's help, she had used the stairs to the Seaside Club twice after receiving her new brace. But Dax figured that was May's way of remaining within hearing distance of her and Rose if their reunion wasn't cordial.

"That's right. Send your girls home, and let's talk."

May wiped her hands on the dishtowel hanging from her shoulder. "The ladies and I have to finish our work. They should be gone in a half hour. You can wait in the dining room. I'll have a sandwich and some coffee brought over and join you when I'm done."

"Dammit, woman." Logan's face turned fire-engine red. "I drove over an hour to talk."

"And after leaving us here for four months, the least you can do is wait another half hour so my staff can put the Foster House in order because I can't do it after they leave."

Logan sucked in his anger, his neck muscles cording. "Fine. Ham with extra pickles." He walked out stiff-legged, pushing the door so hard it strained the hinges with a loud squeak. It flapped several times until it settled, separating him from the lot he'd left behind months ago.

"Dang, May." Dax could not form a more coherent sentence after her sister's display of bravado. Four months of laboring until she could not stand. Four months of sacrificing to pay her bills and employees before herself. Four months of surviving while the town bully had her in his sights. All had transformed her sister from a mouse into a lion.

May plopped down on the stool at the chopping block, running her hands through her hair. "What in tarnation is he doing here?" She snapped her focus to Dax. "What did you do to him last week?"

May's words came out more like an accusation than a question, which hurt. Having her sister mad at her was uncomfortable, but Dax could not bring herself to lash back. She merely sat on the stool across from May and reached out a hand until she took it. Rose came up behind Dax and rested a comforting hand on her shoulder.

"I'm sorry." May squeezed Dax's hand before letting it go. "What did he say when you saw him last week?"

"He said you didn't need the piano to run a restaurant and asked why it was so important. I told her it just was and that I wasn't leaving without it. When the men I hired pushed their way past him, he had no other choice but to let me take it." A sinking feeling took root. If Logan stayed in Half Moon Bay, Rose's return to the stage, albeit a small corner in the Foster House dining room, would have to be put on hold.

"So he's angry, curious, and, by the looks of him, flat broke." May ran a hand across her mouth. "I don't like this one bit."

"I don't either." Dax gripped Rose's hand atop her shoulder and squeezed it, filled with foreboding. She craned her neck toward Rose. "Make sure he doesn't see you going upstairs. The fewer questions asked, the better." When Rose responded with a nod, she redirected her attention to May and pulled the cash register money from her pocket. "You better put this in the strongbox. After the ladies leave, I'll take his food to him and get the rest of the change."

Once Rose tiptoed upstairs and Dax had locked the door behind Ruth and her crew, May entered the dining room, carrying the restaurant ledger and a pencil, prepared for questions. Logan had finished his sandwich and was reading the copy of the *Half Moon Bay Review* a customer had left on the register counter. He appeared unrushed and engrossed in the minutia of local news. Dax joined them at the table.

"It's good to see you, Logan." May's greeting had a sweet lilt but sounded forced to Dax. She kissed him on the cheek. "Why didn't you call or write to say you were coming?"

"That's unimportant. Thanks to your sister, Mr. Portman blames me for losing his family, so he put the word around the city that I'm a troublemaker. No one will hire me." Logan scowled at Dax.

Dax rolled her eyes. She could not care less about what Mr. Portman thought and its repercussions for Logan.

"Can't you look across the bay for work?" May asked. "We could sell the house and buy a smaller one closer to your work."

"Impossible. A house that size requires a buyer with deep pockets, and Portman has steered away everyone with that kind of money. Making it worse, the bank won't agree to a sell at a loss and is set to take the house next month." Logan shook his head. "I'm glad we didn't buy the car on credit. Otherwise, the bank would have it too."

Dax's stomach soured at the tenor of the conversation. Fearing where it was going next, she locked gazes with May. Her narrowed eyes and heavy breathing suggested she had come to a similar conclusion.

"I'm moving in. I've brought as much as I could in the Chrysler, but I'll need Dax and the truck to fetch my bed and other large items."

May cracked her pencil in two with a loud pop, and Dax's eyes snapped shut. Their lives had just changed for the worse.

"Dax, I need you to help get my bags upstairs."

Dax's breathing shallowed at the thought of Logan finding Rose in Dax's room. She and Rose had been sharing it for the most part, with Rose still storing most of her clothes in the spare room. She needed to stall. Dax removed her work apron and started toward the stairs. "Let me change my shirt. You go unload things onto the sidewalk, and I'll be right there."

Not waiting for an answer, she bounded up the stairs two at a time. She skidded to stop at her bedroom door. The room was unoccupied. "Rose," she called out softly.

"In the other room," Rose called.

Dax darted down the hall again, stopping at the room where Rose had stored her clothes. Rose was placing more of her things in a dresser drawer. "What are you doing?"

"I didn't want to chance Logan coming up here and finding any of my things in your room. The fewer the questions the better, you'd said."

Dax relaxed her shoulders. "Thank goodness. Logan is here to stay. He's moving in." She pulled Rose into her arms, pressing their bodies together tighter than she thought possible. Her throat swelled at the ramifications of Logan's return—separate beds, separate rooms, acting like friends again, not lovers. They would have no place where they could be alone. "This changes everything."

"I know." Rose squeezed tighter. The impending step back to loneliness manifested in every quick breath between them. She pulled back and kissed Dax with a rushed passion, but pain laced their long goodbye.

It became too painful to continue. Dax pushed Rose by the arms, forcing their lips apart. Her heart felt as if it was 1920 again and her mother had ripped Rose away before she could touch her hand one last time. Like then, she felt she would never see Rose again. The smothering thought she might have to wait another nine years to kiss her again made it hard to breathe.

"I have to go. Logan is expecting me to help him move in."

"We'll find a way, Dax." Rose kissed her again and pushed her toward the door. "You better go before he suspects something."

Dax stepped toward the door but stopped before turning toward her room. She glanced over her shoulder and whispered, "I love you, Rose."

"I love you, Dax." She shooed her with her hands. "Now go."

Dax dug through her closet for an old shirt and dashed downstairs. May had disappeared, likely to escape to her room to absorb the ramifications of Logan's arrival. If Dax could, she would do the same and curl up with Rose on their bed until they had a strategy to get Logan out of their lives for good.

Outside on the sidewalk she discovered a steamer trunk larger than Rose's and several boxes. She figured the trunk would require them both to haul up the stairs, so she moved to start on the boxes. She struggled to lift the first one, estimating it weighed over thirty pounds.

"Geez, Logan. What's in these boxes?"

"Books. I want to make an office out of the third room."

Dax froze. There were only three bedrooms upstairs. If Logan insisted on a private office, either she or Rose would have to sleep elsewhere. More than likely, he would kick Rose out to reclaim the space. Dax could build an office in the living room or basement, but she doubted he would wait the week needed to get it done.

Out of time and options, she had to say something. "We don't have room for a private office. May took in the cook. We give her a room upstairs and three meals a day in lieu of pay. We could set you up in the living room. It's plenty big."

"Why in the hell did May hire a cook? She was supposed to do all the cooking."

"If you bothered to visit, you'd know that May's leg brace broke, and she could barely stand. We were lucky Rose was available and willing to work for only a place to live."

"Hogwash about the brace. May was walking fine today."

"That's because we…" Dax paused. She could not tell him they'd bought a new brace because he would ask where they got the money for it. She had to bend the truth more than she already had. "We found her a used one, and I earned money for it with carpentry work."

Logan mumbled under his breath, emphasizing several cuss words. "Let's just get these things inside." More cursing ensued while he ascended the stairs, carrying a suitcase and two suits. He walked through the door of the biggest room—hers.

Dax left the first box of books against a wall in the living room and caught up with him. "I suppose you'll want the biggest room."

Logan placed his suitcase on the floor. "This was my father's room. So yes, I'm taking it." He opened the closet and snatched the five items Dax had hung on the rod there before hanging up his suits. He shoved them into her hands. "You can take whatever room the cook doesn't have after we get the rest of my things."

"Fine." Dax dropped off her clothes in the third room, mulling over the extra work facing her. She hadn't kept that room clean and had used the closet and a corner to store Logan's father's old papers. May had the bed from that room downstairs, so Dax would have to sleep on the couch until they retrieved Logan's bed in San Francisco. The dresser was accessible, but she would have to move the boxes and loose stacks of papers to the basement.

She helped bring up the rest of his things, moved her belongings to the third room, and dusted off a bookshelf in the living room for Logan to stack his books. While he unpacked, she quietly ushered Rose downstairs and located May in her bedroom. She closed the door with them inside.

"Is he settled in?" May plopped on her bed. Her tone was flat, without emotion, as if she'd already resigned herself to their new reality.

"He took over my room."

"Figures."

"I couldn't argue about it."

"You should take the bed in the spare room until you get Logan's in the city," Rose said.

She clasped Rose's hand, pulling it close to her chest. "I'll be fine on the couch for a few nights. So far Logan has said nothing about kicking you out, and I don't plan on giving him a reason to consider it an option. I told him you're the cook and living here in lieu of a salary. Once he sees how much you contribute to the Foster House, I'm sure he'll keep you on and let you keep your room." If he didn't, Dax would face the hardest decision of her life—staying with May or leaving with Rose.

"I won't let him do otherwise." May gave Rose a reassuring nod. "The hardest part will be juggling the books. We'd planned to dip into the whiskey money to make ends meet. Logan is a banker by trade. He'll know something is up when I give the ladies their full salary and the books don't balance."

"I can pretend to do some odd jobs," Dax said.

"What if Logan finds the money?" Rose asked. "We have to hide it."

"I'll cut a section of baseboard and trim back the wall slats under May's bed. We can hide it there."

Rose reached into her brassiere's left cup, pulling out a wad of money, a look of worry etched on her face. She placed the cash in May's hands. "Hide mine too."

CHAPTER NINE

A week later

The muffled clang of Big Ben sounded through the door from down the hall, rousing Rose from a twilight sleep. She sighed because her nightmare was just beginning. Slinging her legs to the edge of the bed for the seventh consecutive day without Dax next to her was crushing. She showered without the possibility of Dax joining her and dressed without giving Dax a kiss hot enough to heat the entire floor.

Heading downstairs, she took stock of the past agonizing week. When the Foster House was open, Rose had been kept busy cooking and preparing orders with May. Though Dax coming in and out of the kitchen had provided frequent mouthwatering distractions. And once a day, she and Dax had sneaked into May's room for a not-so-quick kiss while Logan was still asleep upstairs. Those were five glorious daily minutes Rose would not trade for anything, but she craved more.

At night, Dax was down the hallway, a tiptoe distance away, yet she might as well have been on the other side of the world. Logan's room between them kept her out of reach. Falling asleep had become nearly impossible. She'd spent hours lying in bed, replaying in her head the nights she'd fallen asleep in Dax's arms, most after making love. Her physical needs had roared stronger with each passing night. She'd considered satisfying them herself but dismissed the idea, opting to wait for their first Half Moon Bay weekend off together.

When the Foster House was closed the previous weekend, Logan had Dax help him. On Monday, they put together his office in the upstairs living room. And on Tuesday, they drove to San Francisco to retrieve more furniture from the home the bank would soon take. Then it was back to work on Wednesday. But this weekend, she and Dax planned to sneak to Charlie's garage for several uninterrupted hours together. If the weather held, they would also drive to Shelter Cove to take in the ocean over lunch.

When Rose reached the bottom step, she closed her eyes, imagining what tomorrow's lunch might be like. The cold, winter ocean breeze would nip at her cheeks and flutter the short wisps of Dax's hair at the trailing edge of her newsboy cap. They would huddle in the rock outcropping that hid them from the beach on three sides. They would sit atop one of May's hand-knitted quilts, bundled in winter coats and boots with their arms linked to keep warm. Lunch would be an afterthought between kisses, and when their fingers were too numb from the cold to caress the other, they would consider heading back to the Foster House.

The sound of clomping on the stairs brought Rose out of her daydream. Dax's steps were slower than Rose expected. Recalling Dax's groggy "good morning" when they'd passed in the hallway, she thought sleep had likely eluded her too.

"You're running late today." Rose brought out her most expansive smile, hoping it would perk up Dax when she turned around, but she froze.

"Morning, doll." Unshaved and with mussed hair, Logan lumbered to the bottom stair. He'd thrown on a wrinkled plaid robe but left it untied, exposing his knee-length flannel drawers and U-neck undershirt.

Rose instinctively gave him a wide berth, taking a step back and cringing at his pungent morning breath when he passed her. The demeaning greeting didn't escape her, either. Countless drunk Seaside Club patrons had addressed her as doll while offering to buy her a drink. They usually expected her to swoon at their feet but comparing her to a child's toy gave her the creeps. Logan was no exception.

Before following him into the kitchen, she counted to ten, crossing her fingers that Dax or May was there. She pushed the door open, witnessing Logan snatching an orange slice from the counter and swatting May on her bottom as she chopped onion for the breakfast service.

"Stop that." May's tone teetered on disgust. She waved her utility knife toward the dining room door. "Unless you're here to help us get ready to open, get what you came for and go upstairs." May's feistiness was both called for and reassuring. It demonstrated her resistance to Logan's intrusion and refusal to let him control her.

Logan may have owned the restaurant, but he needed May, Dax, and her to run it to keep the money rolling in. And May had taken every opportunity since he arrived to remind him of their new power structure. Neither had all the power, neither would relinquish any, and neither could walk away.

He poured himself a glass of milk from the refrigerator and grabbed the last double slice of apple pie left from yesterday's lunch service. "Send someone up later to get the dishes. I'm heading back to bed."

"When should we expect you today?" May asked. "It's inventory day, and we could use the extra help."

"I need to finish going over the books. There's no reason this place should be in the red if you run it correctly."

Rose and May mumbled under their breaths. He knew nothing about running a restaurant and even less about this town. Making a profit became impossible once Frankie Wilkes opened the Seaside Club for lunch service and divided Half Moon Bay's off-season lunch crowd between three establishments, not two.

Logan placed his items on a serving tray and snatched a fork from the bin of clean utensils. "You were supposed to keep this place afloat, not run it into the ground."

May slammed the knife on the chopping block, and Rose swore she saw steam coming from her ears. "And how have I run this place into the ground?"

"For starters, you're overstaffed. You don't need two cooks." Logan eyed Rose up and down as if she were the day's special. "Since the doll works for room and board, one of you should wait tables. Then you can let a waitress go."

"You don't know what you're talking about." May's face reddened. "Frankie Wilkes is why business is down. He blames us for ruining his plan—"

"May." Rose had to stop her from opening the biggest can of worms the town had ever seen. If Logan learned Frankie had wanted to buy the Foster House since his father died—or since he was killed, if Jules was right—he would sell this place in a heartbeat. She had to come up with a story fast. A version of the truth would hopefully work. "There's no reason to air my dirty l-l-laundry."

"Now, what kind of dirty laundry could a pretty girl like you have?" Logan asked.

"I used to sing at the h-h-hotel. F-F-Frankie h-h-hired Dax to b-b-build a new stage. I had her change how it looked, and F-F-Frankie hated it, so he f-f-fired her and refused to pay her. That's when I got mad, and he f-f-fired me."

"I don't get it. What does Wilkes blame May and Dax for?"

"The singer he h-h-hired to rep-p-place me is c-c-costing him a bundle."

"It sounds like you have a hot temper." Logan leered at her up and down as if deciding if she was worth the trouble.

"She has no such thing," May said. "She's—"

The back door swung open. Dax walked in, carrying a crate from the grocer with the rest of today's fresh produce and dairy. She hoisted the box on the chopping block. "Isn't it a little early for you, Logan?"

"And that's why I'm heading back to bed." Logan lifted his tray of pie and milk. He gave May a long, hard stare, making Rose think he didn't buy their story, and disappeared into the dining room.

May remained silent, locking stares with Rose. The look on her face suggested she realized they'd dodged a lethal bullet.

"What did I miss?" Dax asked.

"Nothing," Rose said, but she mouthed, "I'll tell you later." The details would have to wait until she was sure Logan could not hear.

CHAPTER TEN

Dax wiped down the last dirty dining room table with extra vigor, mumbling her outrage. "Run this place into the ground, my ass. Let go one of the ladies? Not on your life." She threw the damp dishrag into her busser's bucket with a resounding thwack. "And that's the last time he calls Rose 'doll.'"

Logan had abandoned her and May, expecting them to take a restaurant that had been closed for a month and get it running well enough for them to survive on, and they did. They cleaned up the place, bought supplies with the paltry money Logan had left them, and hired staff.

He gave May no credit for making a tiny profit each month until the Seaside peeled off a swath of the lunch traffic by starting lunch service. All he saw were red numbers for the last few weeks. Dax knew they could hold on by using the money from selling the whiskey barrels, but Logan didn't. And his brilliant solution was to let go of a hardworking employee.

They would need all the experienced help they could get when the weather warmed and tourist season arrived. According to Ruth, they'd likely have to bring on another two servers to handle the load. But what were May and Dax to do in the meantime? They could not tell Logan they had a plan without revealing they were sitting on a bundle of cash. He would take it for sure.

"You're sure you don't need help with the inventory?" Ruth approached from the beverage station area at the old bar. The other two servers were wrapping up their cleaning for the weekend.

"Rose and I can handle it, but thanks for offering." Dax gestured her chin toward the other servers and returned her attention to Ruth. "You ladies enjoy your days off. We'll see you on Wednesday."

Dax locked up and carried the last dirty dishes into the kitchen. May, pencil in hand, was jotting down some notes after inspecting her spice rack. Rose had the pantry door open and was counting various items. "Where do you want me to start, May?" Dax asked.

"Can you help Rose inventory the pantry and tackle the basement? I'd like an accurate list and assessment of the condition of the supplies we have down there and whatever else was untouched by Riley King when he broke up your little speakeasy."

"Sure thing, May." Dax entered the ten-foot-long, narrow pantry and guided Rose to the back until her heels hit the wall. She removed the pencil from Rose's hand and placed it on a shoulder-high shelf before pressing their bodies closer until their breaths mixed. "I've missed you."

"I think about you all night." Rose's husky tone was the invitation Dax wanted.

"That makes two of us." Dax kissed Rose. She neither rushed it nor deepened it. Instead, she focused on the tingling sensation their linked lips and bodies radiated through every muscle and nerve. Her body temperature inched higher, but not so fast that she could not control herself. Having control didn't equate to wanting to exercise restraint, though.

Dax rotated her hips and rocked against Rose in a slow rhythm guaranteed to raise the heat in the pantry high enough to bring every fruit and vegetable on the shelves to a full bake. Rose joined in, hooking a leg around Dax's thigh, inches below her bottom. Thoughts, vivid but impractical, of dropping to her knees and hiking Rose's skirt up to take her into her mouth took over. Instead, she licked Rose's tongue as if they were in bed and she was between Rose's legs. A moan escaped. Dax could not be sure if it was hers or Rose's.

"A little more inventorying and a little less whatever in there, please," May called out.

When Dax pulled back, she and Rose broke out in quiet snickers. "Yes, ma'am," Dax said loud enough for May to hear before giving Rose a brief kiss. "We'll pick this up tomorrow at Charlie's. She won't open the garage until noon, just for us."

"Charlie is a great friend." Rose straightened her clothes and picked up her pencil before giving Dax a wink. "We better get back to work."

After jotting down the quantity and apparent age of the items in the pantry, Dax and Rose descended the basement stairs. The plywood wall partitioning the storage area from her and Charlie's ill-fated speakeasy was still up. She'd replaced the cannibalized sheets she'd used to board up the broken windows upstairs months ago, but there was no need for it now that Logan was back. Selling the hidden whiskey from there was out of the question. Maybe she could repurpose the wood to finish rebuilding the dock.

Dax eyed the stacks of restaurant supplies and furniture. Unfortunately, she'd done such a good job saving space that it would take time to move things around to count accurately what was there. Working in unison, she and Rose began shifting boxes, crates, and boating gear. When they reached the area beneath the stairs, Dax paused.

"Wait. I saw some liquid at the foot of the stairs for the second day in a row. I want to see if the barrel is leaking." She moved a crate and an old tackle box before tapping her toe on the false wall she'd built beneath the lowest part of the stairs. A three-foot-high by two-foot-wide section angled outward from its resting place. She moved the handleless door out of the way, exposing the ten-gallon barrel she and Charlie had agreed to hold back from the sale.

"I get why you kept it," Rose said, "but I still think May will blow her top if she finds out."

"She won't find out. We'll only sell the whiskey if we run out of money." Dax picked up the false door and moved to put it back in place, but a voice startled her.

"You're sitting on a barrel of whiskey?" Logan appeared at the cut-through of the plywood wall. "How big?" He strode faster than he had all week, his eyes widening with expectation.

Dax could not speak. Could not move. She gripped the false door tighter while her heart thudded so fast it might explode. A sinking feeling enveloped her so ferociously she felt the earth pull her under. She'd been careless. She should have checked to ensure she and Rose were alone, and now her sloppiness could cost everyone she cared about dearly.

Logan bent at the knees and tilted the barrel to measure Dax's once-hidden treasure. "It looks to be about ten gallons. This is worth a lot of money. We need to sell it."

"It's illegal," Rose said. "That's why it's hidden."

Logan waved Rose off as if she were absurd. "No one enforces the Volstead Act out here. Federal agents only raid a place as political payback." He turned his attention to Dax. "Where did you get it?"

She could not tell him the truth, but she could tell him a plausible cover story, though. "The beach."

"Something like this doesn't wash ashore." Logan stood taller, stiffening his posture. "Now, where did you find it?" His eyes narrowed as if expecting another lie.

"My friend and I took the Model T out for a spin after she got it running. We went walking along the beach and came across it. We think it was part of a smuggled load from one of those Canadian trollers and was accidentally left behind." Everything Dax said was the truth about the first barrel she and Charlie had found. It just wasn't the truth about this one.

"Is anyone looking for it?" Logan rubbed his chin as if weighing his options.

"I don't know." Dax shrugged. "My friend and I were holding it for a rainy day."

"Well, it's pouring on me. I could sell this somewhere and keep the bank from taking the house for a year."

"You wouldn't be in this mess"—Dax glared—"if you hadn't taken out a mortgage on a paid-off house to invest in the market."

"I would have made the payments if you hadn't interfered in a man's business."

Dax formed her hands into fists. Every man was the same, acting as if a woman was something to possess, not cherish, and thinking he could do with her as he pleased. "A man's business? He used my friend as a punching bag. No man should ever beat his wife. I'm glad she and the kids got away from him."

"And I'm sure your friendship was purely innocent. From the day she took you in, I told May that you were a freak and would be nothing but trouble."

"Well, this freak took care of your wife after the accident when you wouldn't. And this freak worked and contributed to her own keep, including running this place with May for nothing but food and a place to stay."

Logan snapped his stare at Rose. "Is that why you're here? Working for free? You're a freak too?"

Dax positioned herself between Logan and Rose, forming fists again and grinding her fingernails into her palms. "Leave her out of this. This is about getting your grubby hands on the whiskey to save your house, but May will never stand for it. Trust me. She would rather pour it into the sewer than have it in this house."

"Then she doesn't have to know. We can offer a shot to customers in coffee cups for a dollar."

Dax put her hands up in surrender. "Not me. I'm not taking the risk."

"Fine. I'll do it. I have three weeks to make a payment on the house to keep the bank from taking it. I can make ninety dollars by then."

"Half of that barrel belongs to my friend. You'd be stealing from her."

Logan pointed toward Dax's hidden compartment. "That thing is in my house, so it belongs to me."

CHAPTER ELEVEN

Dax warmed up the Model T, revving the engine longer and faster than necessary. Rose had already left. May was up, leisurely sipping a cup of coffee in the kitchen and reading the newspaper on her day off. So, the only one she might wake was Logan. She hoped he was cussing into his pillow.

Within minutes, she was rolling through the central part of town. As usual on Monday mornings, the start of the Half Moon Bay "weekend" for locals, the roads were nearly void of cars. Arriving at Charlie's garage, Dax pulled her truck around to the back where it would not be visible from Main Street. Extra caution was needed if Logan came looking for her.

Dax shivered when she knocked on the back door, not from the cold but because of what awaited her inside. Soon she would share a bed with Rose, skin to skin, with no chance of anyone, especially Logan, interrupting them.

The door swung open to the overpowering smell of grease. Charlie gestured for Dax to come inside. "Rose is upstairs already."

"Yeah. Logan might suspect something is up between us if we left together, so we took off a half hour apart."

"Rose mentioned as much." Charlie cupped her hands together, brought them to her mouth, and blew into them before stuffing them into her coat pocket to counter the cool air.

"What else did she tell you about Logan?" Dax asked.

"Just that you had something you needed to tell me."

Warmth expanded Dax's chest. Rose never spread gossip and had to be pushed against a wall before passing along a story that wasn't hers to tell. Logan and the whiskey was a topic for Charlie and Dax. "Let's sit."

"I've already poured the coffee." Charlie invited Dax to the break table near her office. Tendrils of steam rose from two chipped ceramic coffee mugs from the Foster House that Dax had given her. A sugar bowl sat between them.

After adding two spoons of sugar, Dax took a seat and sipped her coffee, considering how to tell her best friend she'd likely lost her five hundred dollars. She looked Charlie squarely in the eye. "I messed up. I checked on the barrel without making sure Logan wasn't in the basement, and now he knows about the whiskey. He plans to sell it to customers and give the money to the bank to save his house."

Charlie sipped on her coffee. Her expression remained constant without a hint of anger or disappointment.

"Aren't you mad about losing the money?" Dax asked.

"A little, but this could be a good thing." Charlie returned her mug to the table.

"How do you figure?"

"Logan will be busy finding takers for his whiskey, which means he'll have less time to watch you and Rose."

"Or blame May for running the Foster House into the ground," Dax added.

"That's crazy talk. Did you tell Logan that Frankie Wilkes was on to us about the whiskey?"

"No, and I don't plan to. But if Frankie gets wind of whiskey flowing in the Foster House and sends in the Prohis, only Logan should be in their crosshairs. Our customers and staff can attest that not a drop of liquor was sold there until Logan showed up. That way, he's the only one going to jail."

"I don't think you have any other choice." Charlie downed her coffee and stood up from her chair. "I'm heading out to pick up some parts in San Mateo. I'll be back around noon."

Dax walked her to the door. "Thanks for letting us use your place. It means a lot."

"Happy to do it."

"Maybe we can finish repairing the dock soon. We're almost done."

"Sure thing, Dax. Lock up after me." Charlie patted Dax on the back of the shoulder before walking out with Brutus trailing behind her.

Sliding the deadbolt closed, Dax closed her eyes and let out a breathy sigh—one less worry off her plate. Thankfully Charlie had taken the news about Logan and the whiskey in stride. Her primary concern was now for her and Rose, not the lost money. She pushed thoughts of Logan, whiskey, and the Foster House to the side and ascended the stairs to the only room above the office.

Dax opened the door to Charlie's bedroom and found herself unable to move. Unable to breathe. She stood in the doorway, taking in the most beautiful, alluring sight. Rose was lying in bed on her side, looking like a Greek goddess. She'd propped her head up by an upturned palm and bent arm, and the covers had been pulled up only to her waist, exposing her bare upper torso.

Perfection. From afar or up close, Rose's imperfections, visible and hidden from the world, had made her perfect to Dax since she laid eyes on her in seventh grade. Head to toe. Inside and out. Dax would not change a thing about her.

"Come to bed," Rose said slowly, lowering her tone and flipping the covers back, revealing nothing but skin to her knees.

Every nerve ending fired at once, making the room spin. Dax worked the buttons on her jacket as fast as her fingers would move. Her shoes and clothes flew off in a whirl. The cold air in the room was a welcomed counter to the heat rising inside her.

It cooled her enough to remember that making love to Rose should not be rushed. They might not have many moments like this with Logan living in the house, so today should be relished. Each touch and kiss should be explored to its fullest to make a lasting memory.

Dax slowed her movements and slipped onto the mattress, noting the sheets felt smoother than she expected. They smelled freshly washed, and their pale blue tint looked familiar. She ran a hand across the soft cotton. "Are these your sheets?"

Rose nodded unhurriedly. "It seemed like the thing to do."

Dax shifted to her side, entwining their legs and caressing Rose from hip to thigh. Her fingertips tingled, sending a radiating wave of desire on a swift course. "Considering what we're about to do, that's very considerate."

Easing Rose to her back, Dax moved on top of her, breast to breast, center to center, skin to skin. This was the woman she was meant to grow old with. Nothing in the world could alter that fact. Not Logan with his prejudices. Not the town's busybodies and their self-righteousness. Not the state and its unjust laws. This was where Dax was supposed to be, and she would move heaven and earth to be with her again and again.

They kissed and touched and tasted until exhaustion took over. Rose fell asleep minutes after finishing, nuzzled against Dax's side with a hand covering a breast. Meanwhile, Dax willed herself to stay awake. With one arm draped across Rose, she soaked in the warmth and comfort of their entwined bodies. Individually, they were strong, but together they were invincible. Their connection fueled Dax's resolve; she was convinced nothing could keep them apart for very long. They would find a way to create moments like this until one took her dying breath. Even then, Dax was sure their connection would survive, carrying the other until her dying day.

Dax woke with a start and bounced to a sitting position. The door had swung open, rattling when it hit the wall. Logan stormed through with the look of a madman. The dim light illuminated his bloodshot eyes, and the veins strained against the skin of his neck.

"Freaks!" He released a guttural roar and pointed a pistol directly at Rose as she slept.

"No!" Dax acted as a shield, positioning herself between Rose and the gun. When he cocked the hammer back, she flung herself atop Rose to absorb the bullet.

A shot rang out, and the room went black.

"Dax. Dax," a voice called. Something shook her. "Wake up."

Her body twitched with force, and her eyes sprung open to the room lit by the midmorning sun. Heart pounding to a deafening beat, she tried to make sense of her surroundings. "What?"

"You were having a bad dream." Rose caressed Dax's cheek. Soothing. Calming. "Are you okay?"

Dax's heart slowed, allowing her to recall the horrible scenario her mind had conjured up. "I'm fine," she said, but she wasn't. A bad feeling seeped into her pores, and Logan was at its center. She feared danger would follow them until he was out of their lives. She smoothed Rose's hair and coaxed her closer to hold her.

"Do you still want to have lunch at the beach?" Rose asked.

The prospect of huddling between the rocks at the cove with their bodies pressed together to keep warm and seeing Rose's hair flutter in the ocean breeze was tempting. However, the dream was a disturbing reminder that private moments like this would be hard to come by. She wanted to enjoy it for as long as she could. "I'd rather stay here. Go back to sleep."

CHAPTER TWELVE

A week later

For what felt like the hundredth time today, Dax entered the dining room with a freshly emptied dish bucket. She eyed the tables in the center and along the room's perimeter. While most were still occupied, the table in a booth along the street window, recently vacated, was covered with scattered lunch plates, cups, and condiment bottles haphazardly aligned. She headed there.

As she stacked the dirties into her bucket, the residual smell of whiskey was pronounced, evidence Logan had made several sales at this table. Dax had to give him some credit. Since he busted open the barrel two weeks ago, word spread quickly among the regulars that whiskey had become an unofficial "daily special" when Logan was there. He had a rule: the "special" was only available with the purchase of a meal.

Lunch business had picked up so much that May had brought on another server part-time and agreed to keep the restaurant open until four, an extra hour, to accommodate the crowd. And yesterday, Logan had brought up the idea of offering dinner service until eight. "With two cooks and a few more servers," he'd said, "we could easily open for dinner."

May had resisted, exercising caution. "We'd have to expand the menu selections and train an additional shift of waitresses and a busser. That's a lot of work on an assumption. What if this lunch surge is because Ida's Café or the Seaside are temporarily closed? We should ask around to see if the surge will last."

Logan had no response to May's logic because he already knew why business was up—whiskey. And making things worse, Dax had not offered an explanation, keeping silent when he gave her a warning look. The omission, she feared, would soon come with a heaping serving of regret.

She placed the dirty cups carefully in the bucket and arranged the condiments properly. She was removing the damp rag from her shoulder to wipe down the tabletop and booth seats when a loud bang startled her. She snapped her gaze to the road through the window as gasps filled the room. Two cars had T-boned in front of the Foster House. It looked severe enough to expect injuries.

She tossed her rag in the bucket and darted out the main door. The crushed metal of the car and pickup truck in the street brought back memories of the accident that had maimed her sister—May's misshapen and bloody leg and the horror she'd felt, thinking she would never walk again. Dax feared the same fate for these passengers.

Reaching the tangled mess, she recognized the signage on the passenger side door of the pickup. It belonged to the Seaside Hotel. She circled to the driver's side and wrenched at the door, but the bent hinges fought and creaked against her pull. Summoning a rush of strength, she gave one hard yank and created an opening wide enough for entry.

"Are you hurt?" Dax shouted, her pulse beating wildly at the sight of the male driver slumped over the wheel. She shook him by the arm. The man groaned but didn't move. She eased his upper torso to an upright position, instantly recognizing him. "Jason!"

He moved slowly, becoming less groggy. Blood trickled down a cheek from a gash on his forehead. "He pulled right out in front of me. I didn't have time to stop."

"You have a nasty cut on your head." Dax wished she had her dishrag to stop the bleeding. "Are you hurt elsewhere? Can you move?"

Jason tested his arms and legs and felt his chest. "No, I think I'm fine otherwise."

Dax eased him out of the truck's cabin and waved over two men who had dashed onto the street from the restaurant. "Fellas, can you help him inside and tend to his head?"

"Sure thing," one said before both men guided Jason through the front door of the Foster House.

Dax glanced at the car Jason had hit. His truck had pushed in the driver's door considerably. Two men were at the passenger side, dragging the driver out that door. She circled the car while the men placed the man on the pavement. "Can I help, fellas? How bad is he?"

"He's dead," one said.

Dax grimaced. She'd never seen a dead body up close, and the thought of standing over a man minutes after he'd taken his last breath was unnerving. His face was bloody, but he appeared to be merely unconscious.

"Are you sure?" She knelt beside him and rested a hand on his chest to check for a sign of life, but her hand remained still. He wasn't breathing, but the potent smell of whiskey wafted up from his lifeless body. Who would be drunk this time of day? She studied the man's face again, this time recognizing him from the restaurant. He was a man from the booth she had cleaned minutes before the accident. A man who Logan had served his daily special to. Too much, apparently.

Seething erupted in Dax. The man was a local trawler who had eaten at the Foster House nearly daily since she and May reopened it. She knew little about him, whether he was married or had a family, but he was always polite and left a tip for his server. Now, he was dead because Logan had seen fit to make a profit off him.

She scanned the newly gathered crowd on the sidewalk and picked out Logan a few feet from the Foster House front door. Her seething grew into a rage. Two men she knew were now hurt or dead because of Logan's desire to make a fast buck. She stomped toward him, balling her hands into fists. Pressure built so fast that she was sure her nails had drawn blood in her palms.

When she got within striking distance, she let a punch fly, hitting Logan squarely on the jaw. Her knuckle cracked instantly, but the pain was worth it. She'd caught him off guard and sent him stumbling backward. Before he could regain his balance, she connected a softer second blow with the other hand, landing it on the opposite side of his jaw and sending him to his knees on the wooden sidewalk slats.

She hadn't thought beyond exacting her pound of flesh from Logan. She towered over him while he gathered his bearings, debating whether to continue the beating. However, a glance at the crowd determined all eyes had turned on her. Given Logan's illegal side business, a public spectacle was the last thing the Foster House needed. "Come around back," she ordered.

She marched to the end of the sidewalk at the corner and looked over her shoulder to make sure Logan had gotten up and was walking in her direction. She didn't wait for him. Instead, she continued to the back out of earshot and eyesight of bystanders and prepared for a fight.

Logan appeared around the back corner of the Foster House, madder than when she'd laid out Heather's husband for beating her. Five feet away, he formed fists and wound an arm backward, but Dax put up a hand in a stopping motion. "That wreck is your fault." Anger seeped through her gritted teeth.

Logan withdrew his punch, cocking his head back. "My fault? What are you talking about?"

"The man driving the car reeked of whiskey, and you were the one who served him. Now he's dead, and a friend of Rose is hurt."

"That's on him." Logan shrugged without a sign of guilt. "I gave him what he paid for. He was the one who got behind the wheel of a car. Not me."

"How much did you sell him?"

"Five shots."

"You should have cut him off after two or three."

"You're kidding, right? I made five dollars in an hour. At this rate, I'll have enough money in a few days to get the bank off my back for a few months." Logan's lack of compassion turned up the heat on Dax's fury.

"Well, unless you want May to find out about your side business, you're going to limit how much you sell to a customer in one sitting. We can't have them leaving falling-down drunk."

"Fine." Logan agreed too quickly for Dax to trust him. Keeping a close eye on him would be tricky unless she had help. Thankfully, she knew exactly who could assist her.

CHAPTER THIRTEEN

Minutes earlier

Rose removed the potato slices from the deep fryer, hooking the basket on the rung a foot above the grease level. *Did the order say roast beef on white or a roll?* She reviewed her twentieth order in the last hour, confirming white bread with extra lettuce. May was just as busy to her left, working on three orders simultaneously. Rose wondered if two people in the kitchen would be enough to handle the robust lunch crowd that had developed since whiskey had become an unofficial menu item in the afternoon. The breakfast service had thinned some, and according to the waitresses, several early regulars had shifted to the afternoon—a logical reaction to Logan's personal service.

Plating the order and placing it on the staging table beneath the warmer lights, Rose rang the tabletop bell once, the signal to Ruth that her order was ready. She wiped her brow and noticed May was working from her stool again. That made the fourth time this hour.

Rose peeked at May's orders. "I'll get the fries going and slice the apple pie."

"Thanks, Rose." May patted her leg with the brace. "This thing is slowing me down today."

"At least it's for a good reason. More business means we'll make payroll again this week and post a little profit."

The door to the dining room swung open, and Ruth stepped in and grabbed her order. She inspected the food. "Thanks for getting the potatoes extra crispy. Horace is a stickler. He doesn't leave a tip if any part of this order isn't perfect."

"So I've heard," Rose said.

A crash sounded, followed by a high-pitched scream and loud rumblings from the dining room. "What the dickens?" May said, glancing at Ruth. "Can you find out what's going on out there?"

The murmurs didn't let up after Ruth disappeared into the dining room, giving Rose the sense that something was seriously wrong. She helped May finish cooking the orders on the grill and plated them moments before Ruth returned. "There was a car accident out front. It looks pretty bad."

"These orders are ready. Help me take them out," May said.

Ruth, Rose, and May grabbed an order each and hurried to the main dining room. Half their customers, including Logan, had filed to the sidewalk to watch the chaos. After dropping off their plates at the tables, whether occupied or empty, the women stood near the front window, taking in the scene outside. Dax was helping a man out of the Seaside Hotel pickup truck, and two other men were entering the other car from the passenger side.

The T-boned vehicles looked horrifying, yet Rose could not take her eyes off them. Cars traveled up and down that street every day at all hours, and she had never paid them any attention unless one was flashy or driven by someone she knew. But seeing these two in a tangled mess, colliding by happenstance, made her think of May and how being in the wrong place at the wrong time could change a life forever.

Rose threw a hand to her chest when two men helped an injured man inside. She gestured to an unoccupied table in the room's center. "Put him over there." When Rose got closer to him, she gasped. "Jason! Are you okay?"

"I have a whopper of a headache, but I'm fine." Jason's speech was slower and his face paler than usual. The blood trickling down the side of his face emanated from a deep wound on his forehead.

"You have a terrible gash above that eye." Rose grabbed clean paper napkins from nearby place settings, folded them together, and pressed them against the wound. "You might need stitches."

"I can take him to Doc Hughes," one good Samaritan said. "My car is down the street."

"Thank you," Rose said before turning her attention to Jason. Blood had soaked through the napkins already, indicating they had no time to waste. She helped him from the chair. "Ask for Jules. She's the nurse on duty today. She'll take good care of you."

When the men guided Jason outside, Rose returned to the window to look for Dax, but she and Logan had disappeared. Customers filtered back in, returning to their tables, cueing Rose to get back to work. "We better head back to—" Rose stopped in midsentence when she glanced toward her right and discovered May sniffing a coffee cup in Dax's busser's bucket. "What are you doing?"

May smelled another mug. "These cups smell of whiskey. I don't know if I like the idea of customers sneaking liquor into our restaurant." May lowered her voice when Rose stood beside her, inspecting the cups. "Frankie Wilkes might make trouble."

"I don't know what you can do about it. I'm heading to the kitchen." Rose snatched the bucket of dirty dishes and hightailed it out of the dining room before May could ask questions. Getting rid of the evidence and going back to work might distract May enough for her to drop the subject. Rose didn't want to choose between hurting Dax by telling the truth or lying to the woman who had been nothing but kind to her. Placing the bucket in the left sink, she drowned the proof of Dax's lies in soap suds.

The moment May limped through the dining room door, the back door flew open. Logan marched through the kitchen like a petulant child throwing a tantrum, fists and arms held straight at his side. He mumbled something about rules and stomped out the other door. The distinct sound of clomping feet on the creaky stairs followed.

Moments later, Dax appeared at the back door, repeatedly flexing and curling the fingers of her right hand.

"What's got him in a huff?" May asked.

"When isn't he huffy?" Dax's indirect reply implied she was the source of Logan's exaggerated gruffness, which raised Rose's curiosity. Logan was all about money these days, so why would he disappear upstairs when he could still sell a few shots of whiskey before the restaurant closed? No matter the reason, Rose had to warn Dax about May. That meant getting her alone.

"Hey, Dax, can you help me find the extra cooking grease? I want to change it out after we close today."

"Can it wait? I'm a little wound up right now." Dax placed her hands on her hips, lowering her head and letting her shoulders sag. She looked exhausted. "The driver of the other car died."

Dax's pain was palpable. Rose placed a hand on her back and rubbed in gentle circles. "I'm so sorry. Who was it?"

"Walter, the fisherman from the marina. He'd been drinking."

"Was he just in here?" May continued at Dax's affirmative nod, "So the whiskey I found in the coffee mugs must've been his."

Dax angled her head toward the ceiling as if begging the heavens for forgiveness. "I should have done something."

"It's not your fault, Dax," May said. "It's not like you knew he'd brought the liquor into the Foster House."

Dax hunched over and placed her hand atop her slightly bent knees. "It is my fault. This wouldn't have happened if I'd sold all the barrels like I was supposed to."

"What do you mean?" May twitched her head back. "I counted the money."

Rose leaned in closer to Dax and whispered. "Are you sure you want to do this?" Rose continued at her nod. "Do you want me to leave?"

Dax straightened and clutched Rose's hand. It was cold and trembling. "Stay." She looked May in the eye. "I lied. The Morettis gave me a better price per barrel, so I held one back for a rainy day."

"I don't appreciate being lied to, Dax." May sat on her stool at the center chopping block, rubbing her lips with a hand. "Does Charlie know?"

"Yes, but I convinced her. We could make four times selling the whiskey by the glass than by the barrel. I told her this downturn might not be a blip and we might need more money, so she agreed to hold one barrel back."

"But what does that barrel have to do with Walter? Did you sell him some whiskey?"

"No." Dax shook her head with the vigor of truth. "But Logan did. He saw me when I checked the barrel in the basement last week. He's been selling it by the cup to customers ever since and pocketing the money. He says it's for making a payment on the house before the bank takes it."

"That lying cuss." May rubbed her temples tiredly. "The bank foreclosed on the house last week. They gave us until the end of the month to claim our belongings."

"Why didn't you say anything?" Dax asked.

"Because Logan said he was embarrassed. That's the last time I believe a word from his mouth."

Rose's loathing of Logan Foster grew exponentially. If she could harness that negative energy, she could circle the world in Charles Lindbergh's plane. "I'm ashamed to say that I've known about this since the day that sneaky cuss discovered the barrel. I was there and can tell you he's had Dax tied in knots since."

"We need to confront him and make him stop," May said. "I couldn't take it if another customer died because my husband served him too much booze."

"I already gave him a beating for it," Dax said before explaining the ultimatum she'd issued, including the limits she insisted he impose.

"That's a good start," May said. "But what I really want is him out of our lives."

"Which is why I refused to help him," Dax said. "If Frankie Wilkes or the Prohis get wind of what he's doing, he'll be the only one selling and going to jail."

"Maybe we need to make sure Frankie Wilkes finds out," May said.

"We need to be smart about this," Rose said. She'd seen how Frankie operated for years. He never got his hands dirty, but he always got his way. The only exception was the Foster House. She suspected he would do anything to get his hands on it. "Frankie has too many friends in high places. He could make it look like we were part of the operation and put us and the entire staff in prison."

"Then what do we do?" May asked.

"We follow Dax's plan. We watch Logan like a hawk and make him think he has more to lose than he really does. That way, he'll keep his side business low key and out of Frankie's sight."

"Under one condition," May said.

"What's that?" Dax asked.

"No more lies and no more secrets." May shifted her stare between Dax and Rose. "All of us."

CHAPTER FOURTEEN

Two weeks later

The marina waves lapped against the thick pilings of the nearly renovated dock behind the restaurant. The rising tide meant Dax had to work faster to finish nailing up the cross-steps leading from the water. She and Charlie had been out there for hours, replacing the rungs in all six dock ladders. Some looked sturdy enough, but she didn't want to chance it. The weight of one heavyset fisherman could result in him plunging to the bottom of the marina.

Though she'd bundled up sufficiently to repel a Sierra snowstorm, Dax's fingers had gone numb. While replacing the first two rungs, she'd discovered her bulky gloves had made handling the nails awkward, so she'd tossed them aside to speed up her work. She hammered in another nail and moved up one more step. "Ready for the next one," she yelled to Charlie on the main platform.

"Coming down!" Charlie replied.

A second later, another two-foot-long two-by-four tethered to a length of rope appeared over the edge of the dock. Dax untied it and looked up. "Got it." Charlie gave her a thumbs-up and retracted the rope.

Dax placed four five-inch nails in her mouth, positioned the plank across the studs, and hammered two on each side. When she rested for a moment, her fingers stiffened against the cold. She considered calling it a day but looked up again and counted the remaining steps. Two more, and they were done. "Ready for the next one!"

This time Charlie peeked her head over the edge with a look of concern. "Logan is coming."

"Wonderful. It must be after twelve. Give me the plank." Dax repeated the process and got the first two nails in before Logan leaned over the dock far enough to see her.

"I need to talk to you," he said.

"I'm a little busy here, Logan. I'll be inside in about twenty minutes." Dax hammered another nail, this time with extra vigor.

"I'd rather talk out here. Alone."

Dax had an inkling of the topic. Talking outside meant he didn't want May to hear. And alone meant Charlie should not hear either. Coupled with the findings of her last check on the barrel hidden beneath the basement stairs, she suspected he was out of whiskey.

"Unless you're willing to come down here, you'll have to wait until I'm done." Her fingers hurt too much to stop and start back up again. And she especially would not accommodate Logan. He'd made the last three weeks miserable. Between roaming the house at all hours and demanding food anytime he pleased, he'd made it impossible for her and Rose to sneak a kiss here and there.

"Fine," Logan said before disappearing.

Dax hammered another nail before Charlie popped her head over the edge. "He's waiting at the top of the walkway. What do you think he wants?"

"More whiskey. I think he's out." Dax whacked the nail flush.

"That went fast." Charlie handed her the final plank.

"He's been drinking up the profits for a week," Dax said. Every evening she would find him half-drunk at his upstairs desk.

"Figures."

Dax nailed in the last rung, hooked her hammer into her tool belt, and climbed to the main platform. She'd been so focused on her nearly frozen fingers that she hadn't realized her back had become as stiff as the boards she'd been nailing up.

"Geez, I'm getting old." She stretched out the kinks enough to help Charlie pick up the extra planks, rope, and bucket of nails. She paused to admire the culmination of the hard work they put in on their one day off together each week for the last month. The Foster House now had a safe, operational dock. The only things left to do were to post signs warning customers about using the dock at their own risk and pass the word around the marina.

"We did good, Dax," Charlie said. "A month ago, I would not have believed this old dock would ever be used again."

"We sure did." Dax motioned for them to make their way up the gangplank. "Can you take these to the basement while I talk to Logan?"

"Sure thing. I'll let Rose know you'll be right in." Charlie took all the supplies and peeled off toward the house when they met with Logan.

Dax shoved her hands in her coat pockets, hoping a little warmth would take away the icy sting. "What do you want to talk about, Logan?"

"I finally sold out of whiskey yesterday. Where can we get more?"

"What happened to making enough to keep the bank from taking your house? I would have thought you'd made enough weeks ago."

Logan ran a hand across his mouth. "I'm still working on it, which is why I need more."

She expected a lie and wasn't disappointed. "Maybe if you didn't drink so much of it, you'd have more to sell."

"Look, I'm not in the mood for your smart mouth. Tell me where I can get more whiskey to sell, or your friend Rose is out on her ear."

"You wouldn't."

"Try me." Logan stood his ground, unflinching. Uncaring.

Dax's distaste for Logan turned to pure hatred. No matter how hard she, May, and Rose worked, Logan would have a hold over them. She imagined living a life without Rose under the same roof, a life where May had to go back to sweating in a kitchen for ten hours a day without help. It was a dismal future, but it was also one she could avoid with the following words.

"I have an idea, but we'll have to wait until Sunday."

CHAPTER FIFTEEN

When Sunday night rolled around, Dax still could not bring herself to regret making a deal with the devil—not if it meant Rose would still be in her life. She knew she was rationalizing, but having Rose's and May's concurrence with her plan made working with Logan palatable. Almost.

The headlight beams of her pickup bounced off the low-hanging fog as she downshifted its gears to begin the climb up the cliff of Devil's Slide. Dax wasn't sure which devil was worse—the geological one in front of her or the biological one sitting beside her. May's accident had revealed Logan's selfish side years ago, but losing his job and house had fully exposed his true self. He loved money more than his wife and didn't care about whose life he ruined to get it.

That dynamic was about to change. Dax gunned the engine and shifted again, gripping the wheel extra tight. Their speed steadily increased, higher and higher. She rounded the first turn in the road but kept the throttle level. The force pushed Logan into the door with a thump.

"Are you trying to kill us?" Logan extended a stiff arm, palm against the dash.

The fog had obscured the next turn, but Dax was ready for it. She took it at the highest speed she thought she could control and sent Logan sliding across the bench seat, nearly hitting her.

"Slow it down, Dax," Logan growled.

"Only if you agree to split the profits between Charlie and me." A third high-speed turn sent Logan thudding into the door again.

"You're nuts. I'm not sharing a penny."

Dax opened the throttle more. "You better decide quickly. The most dangerous turn is next."

"All right. All right. But I get half."

Dax didn't let up. "An even three-way split, or we take our chances on the next curve."

"Fine. A third each."

Dax let up on the throttle and let a half-cocked smile form. "I'm holding you to it. If you renege, you better check your car's brakes every time you hop into it or you might end up at the bottom of Devil's Slide like Riley King." The threat was a cryptic one, she knew, but better Logan considered her a mortal threat than the powerless girl he had once walked all over.

Navigating the truck around the cliffs and down the incline, Dax coasted to the stretch of gravel running the length of the beach at Shelter Cove. She parked close to the hillside to camouflage the pickup as much as possible and turned off the engine. When she doused the headlights, the area turned black, but her eyes soon adjusted enough to discern the ebb and flow of the waves crawling on the shoreline.

"How do you know this is where smugglers drop their cargo?" Logan asked.

"I just do."

"So what's the plan?"

"We wait." Dax put on her warm winter gloves and watch cap and set her focus on the waterline. If the Canadian ship kept to the same schedule as it had on the night she and Charlie heisted Riley King's load, they had about a two-hour wait or as much as four if Jason was right. Thankfully he still had a soft spot for Rose and told Dax that the captain varied the ship's arrival time to keep the Coast Guard on their toes. She prepared herself for a long night.

Dax's hands and feet remained warm and toasty as the hours passed. Logan, however, hadn't come prepared and had to resort to blowing on his fingers at regular intervals to keep the ocean chill at bay.

"You should have warned me it would be this cold," he griped.

Dax snickered. It served him right. "Everyone knows it's cold enough to freeze your eyes shut on the beach at night." Motion at the waterline caught her attention. One, two, and then six small motorboats appeared and beached themselves on the wet sand. If they were as quick as the last time, she and Logan had less than five minutes to make their move. "They're here. Let's go. And for goodness's sake, be quiet."

This risky plan might rile up Frankie Wilkes, but it was the only way Dax could think of to keep Logan in check. She grabbed her fourteen-inch brass Eveready flashlight and exited the truck, easing the door against the frame before walking toward the boats. Logan followed her lead. She kept a sturdy pace in the dry sand, her feet sliding slightly to the side with each step. A glance backward confirmed Logan was struggling to keep up, his slipping feet making him resemble a toddler learning to walk for the first time. She gave another chuckle.

Stopping well short of the dozen men unloading the barrels to the beach, Dax silently thanked Jason for the inside information regarding the smuggling operation. She flashed her light three times—the smugglers' signal that she was friendly. The men stopped their well-practiced movements, and she flashed the sign again. One waved her forward. She moved down the beach and approached the one who had beckoned her. Logan followed silently behind.

"Can you get a message to Albert Burch?" she said to the one who appeared to be in charge. He eyed her up and down in palpable skepticism. "Jason from the Seaside sent me. We have an offer for your captain."

"What's your offer?" He kept a stiff posture.

"I'm Dax. This is Logan. We own the Foster House at the far end of the marina in Half Moon Bay. We just finished repairing the dock there this week. It has six slips and enough deck space to accommodate your load. The Seaside would like their shipments delivered to the dock to avoid having to go over Devil's Slide. The last time their truck went over the cliff, it cost them thousands. If you talk to your other customers, I'm sure they'd prefer it too. We'll—"

"We'll let you use the dock weekly for one free barrel each time you make a drop-off," Logan interrupted. Dax cocked her head toward him briefly. His bold suggestion was four times the monthly payment Jason had suggested, and it might get them shot.

The smuggler jutted his chin with a grunt. "I'll pass it along. If he's interested, he'll send a man to the Foster House in a week." The men, having finished unloading their cargo, disappeared into the night without another word.

CHAPTER SIXTEEN

One week later

Dax carried another full bucket of dishes into the kitchen and instantly directed her eyes to the beautiful woman dumping potatoes into the fryer basket. Depositing her load at the sink, she sidled next to Rose and whispered, "Charlie said we can use her place tomorrow."

"I know. Jules told me," Rose whispered back. "Though I don't think you can top yesterday."

"I plan to try." Dax released a contented sigh. Without Logan coming down to sell his whiskey during the day, she and Rose had more opportunities for a few minutes of privacy. Yesterday's escape into the pantry after the restaurant's closing had escalated quickly from kisses to unbridled passion within minutes. It was raw, sweaty sex, nothing like they'd shared before. She had had Rose in a frenzy, bucking uncontrollably against her hand. Bringing out an animal instinct in Rose gave her more pleasure than all the times they'd made love. It was something she wanted to re-create, again and again, starting tomorrow.

The door to the main dining room swung open, and Ruth stepped through. She picked up her order and said, "Dax, a man is asking for you and Logan."

"Who is it?"

"I've never seen him before. He must be a tourist."

"Thanks, Ruth. Tell him I'll be right there." When Ruth walked out, plates in hand, Dax considered the timing of the stranger's visit. If her instincts were correct, Captain Burch was ready to accept her and Logan's offer. She called May over and huddled with her and Rose. "I think this might be Burch's man. I know we discussed this before, but I want to make sure we're still okay with this. What should I tell him?"

"We do whatever it takes to stay together," May said.

"That means making a deal that might change our lives forever," Dax reminded them.

May glanced at Rose, and they gave each other a nod. "Make the deal," Rose said, giving Dax a brief, yet passionate kiss. The kiss erased any doubt Dax may have had. Staying together was paramount.

Dax entered the dining room and asked Ruth to point out the man. She gestured toward a booth along the wall occupied by one man. She'd expected him to be large, unshaven, and dressed as if he'd come ashore from pulling in a day's catch, but this man was dressed in a pressed suit and sporting a fresh barbershop cut.

She approached him with caution. "I'm Dax. I understand you're looking for Logan and me. How can I help you?"

He drank the remaining coffee in his cup, wiped the corners of his lips with a paper napkin, and placed it on the empty breakfast plate. "Mr. Burch sent me. Is there someplace we can talk in private, including Logan?"

"Come with me." Dax led the man past the bathrooms and up the stairs to the second-story residence and gestured for him to wait in the living room where Logan had set up his office. "Wait here. I'll get Logan."

Dax walked to the door of Logan's room—her old room— and knocked. She only half-expected an answer, so she didn't wait to rap a second time before opening the door and entering. As she suspected, Logan was asleep on the bed, face down. With no whiskey to sell or skim from the stock, he slept during the day and visited the Seaside Club at night. Dax wasn't sure how much he spent there to get his drink on, but it wasn't enough for him to steal from the Foster House till. Dax counted every penny deposited there and handed it to May for safekeeping to pay the bills and the staff salary.

She gave Logan's shoulder a healthy shove. "Logan, wake up. Burch's man is here."

"What?" He stirred and moaned, shifting his head to one side. "What time is it?"

"It's nearly one." She snatched the covers and yanked them to the foot of the bed. "Get up. Burch sent a man."

"Shit." Logan bounced from the bed in his underthings and scrambled to put on his pants, shirt, and shoes. "How's my hair?"

"Like you stuck your finger in the wall socket." She handed him one of the four half-empty glasses of water from his dresser. "Slick it back."

Logan dumped some water into a hand and ran it through his hair until he looked as if he was fresh out of the shower. He strung his suspenders over his shoulders and led the way to the living room and his makeshift office. He extended his hand to the well-dressed man. "I'm Logan Foster, proprietor of the Foster House. Please have a seat." Logan guided him to the couch and chair. "With whom do I have the pleasure of speaking?"

"My name is not important. I'm here to broker an arrangement between you and my employer, Mr. Burch. You offered the use of your dock in exchange for remuneration. Is that correct?"

"Yes. We've spent the last few weeks shoring up our dock and plan to let customers tie up there while lunching with us. The slips will be empty at night. By making your drops in the marina, your clients can avoid the dangerous route past the cliffs that have already cost them money and lives."

Logan had tossed around the word "we" as if he'd worked his hands to the bone to make that dock usable again. That could not be further from the truth. He'd only stepped on it once to extort Dax into getting him more whiskey.

"My employer checked with his clients, and they are amenable to the change of venue," the man said. "But one barrel per shipment is too steep." Dax had predicted Logan's opening offer would be rejected and hoped it would not earn them a bullet to the head.

"What is your offer?" Logan asked, leaning back on the sofa, looking relaxed and confident. He was in his element, negotiating the terms of a deal.

"One barrel a month."

"That won't do. Besides fixing the transportation issue, you'll expose us to great risk of federal prosecution by using our dock. That deserves proper compensation."

"We recognize the risk and can go up to one barrel every other shipment."

"That's acceptable." Logan's expression remained unchanged. Dax had to give him credit. He was adept at bartering.

"We currently make deliveries on Sunday night to the beaches, but the marina has heavy foot traffic on the weekends. So we'll have to find a more suitable day. Do you have a suggestion?"

Logan rubbed the back of his neck and stammered, "Umm." He had no clue about Half Moon Bay culture.

"Monday or Tuesday morning," Dax said. "Those are the slowest days of the week. The tourists are gone, and most of the town shuts down for our version of the weekend. I recommend Tuesday."

"Tuesday it is. We'll start next week. Expect our boats between one and two o'clock. Our clients will park their trucks behind the building, load them, and be gone within fifteen minutes of delivery. Your barrel will be marked with a red X."

Logan stood and extended his hand. "You have a deal."

CHAPTER SEVENTEEN

Two weeks later

Grace's husband turned their Packard Roadster into the parking lot of the Seaside Hotel and parked in the spot labeled "VIP." He turned his head, looking at her with unmistakable concern. She reached across the front seat and squeezed his right hand. "I'll be fine tonight, Clive. Spend the night with Jason. He'll be disappointed if you don't."

"But I'm worried about you."

"I'll find another distraction when I'm ready."

Clive shifted on the bench seat to look Grace squarely in the eye, signaling the discussion was about to turn more serious than she might care for. "How long have we been together?"

"Eleven years."

"And for all those years, I've seen you through many distractions, so you could avoid grieving. You and I both know Rose was not a distraction. You love her as much as you loved Harriet."

Clive knew her better than anyone and had never been more right. After Harriet, she had sworn to never let herself love like that again because she would never survive another loss that deep. Rose was no exception, at least at the start. The way the lovely young singer had clung to the hope of reuniting with the love of her life, however, had made Grace consider that love was not a lost cause. Visit by visit, bit by bit, she had lowered her defenses and let herself feel again. And just when she was ready to admit as much, Dax reappeared, her reunion with Rose breaking her heart all over again. Grace considered fighting for Rose, but it took only one conversation with Dax to realize it would be a losing battle.

"And what if I do? I can never have Rose because her heart was never mine. It always belonged to Dax."

"Then why torture yourself by coming here?"

"I have business here. Besides, Rose left a message months ago. I need to find out what was so important."

"The business runs itself and a phone call to Rose would have sufficed when we arrived home."

Clive was right, but she could not help herself. When they returned to Hollywood two days ago after months of filming in Morocco, her housekeeper asked about the telegram she'd sent following Rose's call. "It was important," she'd said. Grace had rejected the thought of calling Rose at such a late hour and decided a personal visit was needed to explain why she never responded.

"I trust Frankie Wilkes about as far as I can throw him, which makes it necessary for me to be here to remind him who is in charge of our mutual venture."

"And going to Rose's show tonight? What purpose will that serve?"

"Besides explaining my absence? I'm not sure."

At ten minutes 'til seven, Clive offered Grace his arm at the door of their suite. "Ready, my sweet?"

"I have been since the last time Rose and I said goodbye."

Each dressed immaculately in a black tux, they descended the stairs to the basement and entered the Seaside Club without delay from the guard—the privilege of ownership. Jason's eyes instantly locked on them. He gave them a curious, nervous headshake.

Grace leaned into Clive, whispering, "Don't disappoint your man tonight."

He patted the hand that was linked around his arm. "After closing."

They settled into their traditional front-row table and ordered their first bottle of champagne—the first bottle from the case she'd brought with her from Hollywood. Grace admired the new stage. *Rose must love it*, she thought. Higher and larger than the old one, it provided double the space for her to make every man and woman in the place swoon.

Moments after the waitress poured their first glass and left, the lights in the club lowered. Lester emerged from the swinging door to the right of the stage and took his position at the piano. He leaned into the microphone and said, "Ladies and gentlemen, the Seaside Club is proud to present Miss Sarah Martin."

The room broke out in applause, everyone but Grace and Clive.

A blond woman came through the door, climbed the stairs, and stopped center stage behind Rose's microphone. She was pretty enough to star in one of Grace's films, but her voice didn't rival Rose's. It wasn't even close. Sarah Martin was like an extra in a movie whose acting had no soul. Her singing was technically correct, but it lacked the ability to seduce a listener into believing she was the only one in the room.

By the second song of the evening, Grace wondered what had happened to Rose that prevented her from performing tonight. Singing was her passion, something she loved nearly as much as she loved Dax. Was she sick? Injured? The presence of a stand-in singer meant she'd been out for at least a few days.

By the end of the performance, Grace's questions had turned into downright worry. She whispered into Clive's ear, "Can you ask Jason to come to our table? I have some questions."

"Of course, my sweet."

Minutes later, Clive returned with Jason. They made a handsome couple, but Clive claimed he was too broken to give Jason what he deserved. The damn war had been brutal to so many, leaving most participants hollow and a shadow of themselves after witnessing the horrors. Grace wished she knew the prewar Clive, the one his cousin said always smiled and brought light into a room merely by entering. That Clive was dead, though. The Clive who had found her was a quiet, wounded soul. They both were, actually, though, able to provide each other with the comfort and understanding they needed. She'd hoped Jason would be his Rose and draw him out of his dark hole.

"Jason, you're looking well." Grace patted the chair to her left. "Please sit." He did. "Is Rose ill tonight?"

Jason instantly frowned and leaned closer. "I would have told you earlier if I'd known how to contact you." He glanced at Clive, sending Grace's heart into a wild rhythm as she feared the worst. "I'm sorry to be the one to tell you this, but Frankie fired her nearly two months ago."

Grace let out a sigh of relief, thankful to learn she was still alive. The next second, anger took over. She ground her back teeth and felt every muscle tense. Wilkes had overstepped and gone against her explicit instruction regarding Rose. She pushed aside her anger long enough to ask, "What do you mean that you didn't know how to contact us?"

Glancing at Clive again, Jason sighed. "Your husband has yet to pass along a way to reach either of you."

"I see." Grace was disappointed. Clearly, Jason was more invested in the fling between him and Clive than Clive was. Knowing how broken her husband was from the war and his inability to commit to a man or a woman other than herself, she hoped Jason wasn't setting himself up for heartache.

Jason looked left and right before lowering his voice to a near whisper. "Frankie also kicked her out of the boarding house he owns. Rose has been staying at the Foster House and working in the kitchen there."

Grace slammed a fist on the table, drawing the attention of patrons from all ends of the room. She should never have agreed to film in Morocco. Otherwise, she would have checked on Rose earlier. Her sweet Rose was meant to grace the stage, not sweat over a hot stove. The pounding in her ears was so loud it drowned out the music playing through the loudspeaker. Frankie Wilkes had gone too far. He would pay the price for his insolence.

"Thank you, Jason. We'll make sure you have a way to reach us when we're not in town." She covered Clive's hand with hers before glancing at him. "Come with me." She didn't have to ask if he'd brought his pistol because he was never without it. Her next meeting likely would not escalate to the point of needing it, but she could not rule it out.

"My pleasure." Clive stood first, pulling out Grace's chair for her. "Later tonight, Jason?" His impish smile telegraphed his apology.

"We'll see." Jason turned on his heel but not before Grace saw the hurt in his eyes. Clive had some repair work to do.

Grace marched out of the club with purpose, an increasing rage fueling her fierce strides. Her first stop was at their suite— to pack up their things. They would not be staying or returning until the dynamic had changed. Until Wilkes understood who had the real power in their partnership. Before leaving the privacy of their room, she said to Clive, "Frankie won't be happy when I'm done with him."

"I assumed as much."

"I'm afraid this will mean Jason might have to look for other work if Wilkes draws this out." Grace cupped Clive's hands, pulling him forward. "But I'll take care of him."

"Thank you, my sweet." He kissed her on the forehead.

After they reloaded their Packard, Grace twisted the knob to Wilkes's office door and stormed in, foregoing the courtesy of knocking. Perhaps she should have. She discovered Frankie sitting in a guest chair with his pants around his ankles. A naked woman was kneeling in front of him, her face in his crotch.

Frankie pushed the woman off and pulled up his pants, shooting Grace an incredulous stare. "Christ, Grace. What happened to knocking?"

Grace drifted her stare to the woman on the floor, who was struggling to cover herself with her arms. She recognized her as a hotel maid. "Get dressed, dear. Your employer and I have much to talk about."

The woman retrieved her slip from the desk and put it on, covering herself enough to not warrant a ride in the police wagon. When she moved to put on her maid's uniform, Clive gathered the rest of her clothing and shoes, gripped her by the elbow, and tugged her to the door. "Outside." He slammed the door shut behind her.

Grace gave Frankie a stare cold enough to freeze the oceans. He deserved to be taken out to sea, slashed a thousand times, and thrown into the water as chum. "You have gone too far."

"With what?" He circled behind his desk and tucked his shirt in.

"Rose."

"Ah." He plopped in his chair, smug as a playground bully. "Firing your lover is worse than murder. A murder I can tie to you."

"I see you've figured things out, but your threat has no teeth. You cannot implicate me without endangering yourself. And firing Rose was the last straw. We are done."

"Then leave and forfeit your share because I'm not walking away."

"I have something better in mind." Grace flicked over the nameplate on Frankie's desk, the one labeling him as the proprietor of the Seaside Hotel. "This is not my primary venture. However, it is yours. The club downstairs funds everything you own. I'd rather see this place shuttered than have you profit from it, so I'm putting the Seaside off-limits to my friends, and you know what that means. When it withers, so will you."

"You'll bankrupt me." Frankie rose from his chair and leaned on the desktop, his fists knuckle-down.

"And when this hotel goes on the auctioning block, I'll grease the right palms to pick it up for pennies on the dollar, rebuild it, and run it the way I see fit."

"You bitch." Frankie's eyes were afire. Clive stepped forward, his right hand stuffed beneath the left panel of his tux jacket. If he weren't there, presenting the possibility of gunplay, Grace suspected Frankie might have reached across the desk and tried to strangle her.

"Good day, Mr. Wilkes." Having had her say, she prepared to leave.

"Watch your back, Grace."

Clive drew his pistol, fast-marched across the room, and pressed the muzzle against Frankie's temple. He cocked back the hammer, sending those once fiery eyes darting in every direction. "Say the word, my sweet."

Unless Grace interceded, the four words Frankie Wilkes had just said would be his last. "This man deserves to suffer, but his death tonight would deny me that satisfaction." She rested a hand on her husband's shoulder. "Let's leave him to his misery."

Minutes later, Clive pulled the Roadster to the back of the Foster House. When Grace asked why he didn't park in front, he said, "We've stirred a hornet's nest, my sweet. I don't want to come back to find the tires flattened."

"You're always thinking ahead, my dear. I agree. It's best to enter through the back." Grace knocked on the back door. Moments later, it opened to reveal a plain woman with a kind face and a leg brace. "I'm sorry to bother you, but I'm here to see Rose Hamilton. She's a friend of mine."

The woman eyed her closely. "You're Grace Parsons," she said before pulling her into a tight hug. "Thank you for saving Rose's life."

Grace pulled back. "It was all instinct, but Dax was the one who pulled her to safety. I should thank her."

"Where are my manners? I'm May, Dax's sister. Please come in." She escorted Grace and Clive into a well-kept kitchen. Signs of recent baking remained on a chopping block in the center of the room.

Once inside, Grace shook May's hand. "I'm pleased to meet you, May." She gestured beside her. "This is my husband, Clive. I understand Rose is staying with you. May I see her?"

"Of course. We were baking pies tonight, and she stepped into the bathroom a moment ago. I'll get her."

May disappeared behind a swinging door and returned a minute later. The door swung inward again, revealing the woman for whom Grace had discovered she would sacrifice everything. "Rose," she whispered with a breathy sigh. This beautiful songbird was not meant to wear a greasy apron nor have her hair tied back into a stringy ponytail. No. Rose was destined to live in the spotlight, adorned by sequined gowns and with imported makeup and hair immaculately brushed to frame her angled jawline.

"Grace, you came." The sadness in Rose's eyes likely meant Grace's arrival was too late. That she'd suffered for months.

"Of course I did. I just heard. Your message never reached me in Morocco. Why didn't you call again?"

Rose dipped her head to a deep sigh. "There was nothing you could do."

"That's where you were wrong. Is there somewhere we can talk in private?"

Rose rolled her eyes. "May's husband is upstairs. We can't chance him overhearing."

Grace turned her attention to Clive. "Would you mind?"

"Say no more." Clive kissed Rose on the cheek before walking out to the adjoining room. "It's good to see you, Rose."

"It's good to see you, Clive." Rose turned to May. "Would you sit with him and tell us if Logan comes down?"

"Of course." May poured two cups of coffee and made her way to the other room.

Rose and Grace pulled stools up to the center block and sat. "Please, tell me what happened," Grace said.

Rose explained about the Prohibition agents and Dax and their suspicion about Riley's whiskey shipment, including Dax's suspected involvement. She added, "I was sure he would beat the truth out of her if I didn't get her out of there, so I threatened to not sing if he didn't give Dax what he owed her for building the new stage. That was when he fired me. And when I got to the boarding house, Mrs. Prescott kicked me out on his orders."

Grace reached across the countertop and squeezed Rose's hand. She should have protected her better or at least checked on her sooner. "I'm so sorry you had to go through this."

"It was my fault. I overplayed my hand. He owns both places, so there was nothing you could have done."

"Yes, there was. Frankie owns only half. I own the other half."

"You what?" Rose's mouth fell open.

Grace felt exposed. She hated putting herself in a vulnerable position. Other than Frankie, the only other person who knew she was a silent partner was Clive. He'd repeatedly proved his loyalty, and she trusted him with her life. He put no one's needs above hers, including his own. Grace would always put her needs above Rose's. But she knew she could not say the same about Rose—because she rightly put Dax's needs first. But all that didn't matter. She loved Rose too much to let this situation continue.

"I'm Frankie's silent partner. I gave him the seed money to buy up the properties in the marina."

Rose recoiled, her lip curling. "You owned the hotel and club all this time and said nothing?" She rose from her stool and paced in front of the stove. "So I was essentially having sex with the boss? I feel like the slutty maids who go into Frankie's office nearly every night."

Lord. What had Grace done? She expected Rose to be angry at her for holding back the truth, but not this self-denigration. What had occurred between them, what Rose had done, was nothing like what the women had done who whored themselves to Frankie Wilkes for a raise or a tip. Grace had to remind Rose of that.

She circled the chopping block and intercepted Rose's path, stopping her with both hands on Rose's upper arms. "What we shared was nothing of the sort, and you know that. We may have begun as physical distractions, but our affair evolved into something deeper and stronger. Can you deny that?"

Rose's eyes softened a fraction and glistened. "No, I can't, but I can't help but think Frankie kept me on because of you."

"I can honestly say that your job security was because of your talent and ability to draw a crowd. My friends from Hollywood come here to hear you sing. But"—Grace lowered her head, averting her gaze—"I made keeping you on a condition after the story I told Frankie about a traffic accident at Devil's Slide. I didn't want him blaming you for Riley's death."

Rose raised Grace's chin with a hand. "I believe you. And thank you."

"I'm relieved you're no longer beholden to Frankie. I've cut ties with him as well. He's a dangerous man."

"We know. He has the Prohibition agents in his pockets," Rose said.

"He's not only involved in graft," Grace said. "He's a killer."

"A killer?"

Grace cupped Rose's hands in hers. "I swear to you. I knew nothing about either of these things until that night at Devil's Slide. Frankie brought Riley King and his friend Jimmy Gibbs to Half Moon Bay specifically to threaten Mr. Foster into selling, but it got out of hand. Then, when Dax started asking questions about Foster's death, he had Riley kill the only witness."

"That 'accident' makes sense now," Rose said. "Riley was cleaning up loose ends. We suspected he had something to do with Mr. Foster but not Gibbs." She slumped on the stool. "And to think I let that man kiss me."

"We've both made bad choices." Grace returned to her stool. "Mine was trusting Frankie Wilkes to run things without resorting to violence. But I'm about to make him pay for his misdeeds." She reached across the countertop and squeezed Rose's hand again. "Especially for hurting you."

"What's your plan? We've been walking on eggshells for months, waiting for Frankie to act on his suspicions about Dax."

"I'm putting the Seaside Club off-limits to my friends. Without the deep pockets of Hollywood, Sacramento, and San Francisco, the hotel and club will wither and die."

"But so will the town. You can't do this, Grace. People I care about will lose their livelihood. The Foster House was barely staying afloat until Logan started selling whiskey to the customers on the sly. Charlie's garage. Edith's department store. They'll all go under if you go through with this."

The fear in Rose's voice sent chills through Grace. She hadn't thought through the ramifications of plucking the enormous thorn from her side. Shuttering the businesses of the hardworking people of Half Moon Bay was not an option, she decided, but there had to be another way. Then it came to her. Whiskey was the key.

"I have an idea. Would you like to sing to an audience again, my sweet Rose?"

"I do miss it, but May and Dax need me here."

Grace looked around the kitchen. It seemed larger than the one at the Seaside Club. "How big is the Foster House? Is there a basement?"

"Yes. Why?"

"Perhaps we should bring May and Dax in for my proposal."

CHAPTER EIGHTEEN

Rose tiptoed upstairs, hoping Logan was asleep or passed out from tapping the barrels in the basement. Since striking a deal with the Canadian smuggler, he hadn't sold the whiskey as quickly as he had with the barrel he'd stolen from Dax and Charlie. She suspected Frankie had something to do with it. He had power in this town, and he'd likely put the word out that drinking at the Foster House was a risky proposition. As a result, Logan now had more whiskey than he could sell—and he spent most nights drinking it.

She got to the top landing and turned toward the hallway without looking toward the living room and Logan's office, hoping if he was there, he would keep his nose in his glass or ledger book.

"There's our little canary." Logan's slurred words made Rose cringe. At least he'd stopped calling her doll or dollface. She considered continuing down the corridor, pretending she didn't hear him, but that would likely set him off. She decided a little reverse psychology was in order.

She stopped and turned. Logan was at his desk, glass in hand, half-filled with whiskey. "Evening, Logan. How good are you with plumbing? We h-h-have a clogged sink in the kitchen, and it's a stinky, u-u-ugly mess."

"You better get Dax." Logan flipped a page in the ledger. "I'm balancing the books."

"All righty." Rose spun around and headed down the hallway, smirking. He'd been balancing the books every day for a month. His aversion to manual labor should keep him upstairs until Dax returned.

As she knocked on Dax's door, Rose felt her heart start thumping a little faster. It had been exactly three days and four hours since she had last been between Dax's legs, bringing her to the edge. In another three days, the bed above Charlie's garage would become their private oasis again for a few hours. In the meantime...

The door swung open, and Rose's breath caught in her throat. Dax still had on her dark work trousers but had exchanged her button-down shirt for a man's white sleeveless undershirt. Dark suspenders rode the outer edge of each breast, drawing Rose's stare in like a magnet.

"Wow," Rose mouthed.

A devilish grin sprouted on Dax's lips, teasing her until heat crept into Rose's cheeks. "How can I help you, Rose?"

"Umm, I... we...the sink is backed up in the kitchen. Can you help us unclog it?"

"Sure." Dax moved to step into the hallway, but Rose raised a hand chest high in a stopping motion. Dax looked positively appetizing, and she didn't want to share her with anyone else.

Rose whispered, "Put on something over those." She let her gaze drift to Dax's chest again. "Or I'll devour you right here."

Dax issued a slow, seductive wink before grabbing a light jacket and zipping it enough that only the skin at the lowest part of her V collar showed. It was torture. Pure torture. "Let's tackle that sink."

At the bottom of the stairs, Rose gave Dax the "shh" sign with an index finger over her lips. She leaned to whisper into her ear, but Dax angled her head and stole a dizzying, tongue-filled kiss. She could lose herself in Dax's embrace for hours, but Grace was waiting and they needed to talk before Logan got curious.

Rose summoned every ounce of strength she had and pushed Dax back. "Grace is here. She wants to talk to you and May."

"About what?"

"Frankie."

Dax gave an unreadable nod and turned the corner into the main dining room. Clive was sitting near a wall with an unobstructed view of the front door, the kitchen, and the corridor leading to the bathrooms and stairs. His sniper training, something Grace had told her about during one of their pillow talks, had kicked in, giving Rose a sense of comfort. He was positioned at the perfect vantage point from which to repel a sneak attack from any direction.

"What is he doing here?" Dax asked.

"Making sure Logan doesn't eavesdrop."

Pushing open the kitchen door, Dax found May and Grace sitting at opposite sides of the center chopping block, engrossed in conversation and sipping coffee. They'd only met tonight, but this scene made them appear like old friends. Dax hadn't considered Grace's age until now but estimated she was older than May and near Logan's age, closer to forty than thirty. That would put about ten years between Rose and Grace. No wonder she always seemed more worldly. She'd experienced a decade more of life.

Both heads swung toward the entryway when Dax stepped inside. Grace stood, greeting her with open arms. "It's good to see you, Dax. Thank you for taking care of our Rose in her time of need."

Dax gave her a brief hug. "Of course. There was never any doubt that Rose belonged here." She'd chosen those words carefully to stake out her territory. Grace had enough money to shower Rose in diamonds and furs for life, but Dax had only her heart to give, which she had done ten years earlier.

Two extra stools had been gathered at the chopping block, and Grace gestured toward them. "Please sit. I have something important to discuss."

Dax remained quiet while Grace explained the truth about her relationship with Frankie Wilkes. The news didn't surprise her. In fact, considering everything Rose had told her about Grace, it made sense. The cases of champagne she'd brought from Hollywood on each trip weren't for private use. They were for the club. And the off-menu fine cuts of beef Grace ordered at the club were not because of her celebrity but because she was an owner.

But when Grace said she intended to force Frankie out by making the club and hotel wither, Dax's concern intensified. No hotel meant no tourists. "If the hotel dries up, so will the town. The money from tourist season keeps Half Moon Bay running the rest of the year. We reopened the Foster House after the summer and didn't have a chance to build up a savings like the other town businesses had. Instead, we've been relying on whiskey money."

"Which is why I asked to speak with you and May," Grace said. "I can put the Seaside Hotel and the rest of Frankie's shops off-limits but make sure everyone knows the rest of the town is open for business."

"I'm not following." Dax squinted in confusion. "The Seaside is the only club in town. Where would your friends go?"

"Right here. The Foster House is a perfect venue. It's on the waterfront with a restaurant on the main floor, and the basement is ideal for a club."

Had Grace thought this through? Dax could not see how the Foster House could substitute for the Seaside. The restaurant was larger, but the basement was raw and smaller. "We don't have the space like the Seaside."

"How many guests can it hold?" Grace asked.

"One hundred upstairs and about half that downstairs. It could be more in the basement, I suppose, if I add a storage shed outside and take out the overflow items."

"That should be plenty of seating for the short term," Grace said.

"But we don't have tables or chairs or a bar. Riley smashed it all." Dax shook her head at the memory of Riley and Jimmy's baseball bats splintering everything she and Charlie had built. They'd destroyed weeks of blood and sweat in minutes.

"I could ship the furniture and equipment needed to convert the basement into a top-notch speakeasy and club. Hire whatever staff you might need to help build and run it. Of course, my friends will need to be entertained." Grace glanced at Rose with unmistakable love in her eyes before returning her attention to Dax. "I'll need your skills to build a stage big enough for Rose to sing from."

"That I can do, but where would we get the alcohol? And not only whiskey."

"I understand you already have a creative arrangement with Captain Burch to use your dock. He's a friend. I can get us any amount of whiskey, gin, and vodka we might need."

"What about hotel rooms? We're only a restaurant. Where would your friends stay?"

"Most don't stay overnight and opt to stay in the city. But some might on opening night. I can rent several row houses a few blocks from here for special VIP accommodations."

"What about the Prohibition agents?" Rose asked. "Frankie will send them after us."

A faint smile formed on Grace's lips. "Who do you think pays them? Their loyalty is to the money, not Frankie."

"This will certainly whip Frankie into a tizzy," May said. "The only problem is that Logan owns the Foster House. He would have to agree to all of this."

"From what you told me, May, Logan responds to money. I could offer him a cut of the profits for as long as we use the Foster House."

Grace had an answer to every misgiving about her plan to take down Frankie Wilkes except for one—his temper. He'd already fired Dax and Rose on the assumption about his lost whiskey. Once he learned about the Foster House's grand transformation, he might go off the deep end.

Dax stepped closer to May and placed a hand on her shoulder. "Are you sure you want to do this? Frankie could make a lot more trouble for us."

May patted Dax's hand and asked, "Do you know who Grace is doing this for?" Dax knew the answer. Grace had said it herself. Firing Rose was the last straw. It was crystal clear that Grace loved her. "She's doing it for you, Rose, Charlie, Jules, and people like you. She wants to make a safe place for people who love like you to enjoy themselves. But, to do that, she must first force out Frankie."

If that were true, she and her friends would not have to always live in the shadows. They could gather and dine and show affection in safety, just like they had the night Dax had brought home the piano for Rose. That was a cause worth fighting for. "Then, you're sure?" Dax asked.

May stared into her eyes with the certainty of what was right and just. "Aren't you?"

CHAPTER NINETEEN

Six weeks later

Truckloads of furniture and equipment had arrived today. Delivery men hauled the things to the basement of the Foster House, and Rose ensured each one was fed before they left. The same went for the electrician who installed the lighting. The painter who camouflaged the cinder block walls. The plumber who built two small toilet closets and improved May's shower. And the carpenter from San Mateo who helped Dax lay down the beautiful wood floor. But an extra slice of apple pie went to the men who carried May's piano down the basement stairs and placed it in the corner of the stage Dax had nearly finished.

The basement was void of workers for a few minutes, and Rose was finally alone with Dax and able to take in its transformation from a musty, damp space into an intimate club. She climbed the steps leading up to the stage and stood in its center, looking out to the main floor. The lights were turned up enough to brighten the area for Dax to finish the trim on the stage facing. She imagined them dim and the spotlight hanging from the ceiling shining on her. She imagined seventy-five patrons filling the tables, each set with a candle lantern, casting an amber glow. She imagined smoke tendrils emanating from cigars and cigarettes and floating to the ceiling to form a cloudy layer.

Glancing at the piano ended her dream state. Grace had scheduled the grand opening in two weeks and lined up a piano player for Rose to audition. "William is very popular in San Francisco," Grace had said during her last visit. "I'll send him down next week. If you like him, he's yours." William was due any time.

Arms wrapped around her torso from behind. She didn't have to guess, didn't have to look, to know they belonged to Dax. They'd become as familiar as her own hands. Their shape. Their firmness. Their strength. Those arms were on Rose's menu of daily cravings.

"I have a surprise for you," Dax whispered, pressing their bodies together and warming Rose instantly. "Close your eyes." She released her hold and said, "Keep them closed," seconds later. Her voice sounded as if she was across the room.

"You have me curious." Rose fidgeted.

"No peeking." Dax sounded closer. "Okay, open them." Rose did. Dax had placed a beautiful, never-before-seen RCA ribbon microphone on an adjustable stand in front of her. She gasped. "Grace said I should be here when you see it for the first time."

Rose threw a hand over her mouth. "How in the world did Grace get her hands on one of these? This isn't supposed to be for sale until next year."

"When she mentioned she would ship a microphone soon, I remembered the article you read in the *Chronicle*. You'd said you'd give anything to sing through that microphone, so I told her about it, and the next thing I know, it shows up special delivery."

Rose ran her hand across the metal casing, caressing it with her fingertips like she was making love to Dax. She inspected the label that read Microphone Type PB-31. "This must be one of the ten prototypes. It's supposed to provide incredible clarity."

"So you like it?" Dax asked.

"Like it?" Rose glanced around the room. Two delivery men had entered and descended the stairs, each carrying a case of drink glasses for the bar. Of course, a proper response to Dax's question would require privacy. She tugged Dax's hand and led her into one of the new toilet closets. Closing the door, she cupped Dax's cheeks and mashed their lips together in a searing kiss. Thudding Dax against the wall, she pressed a knee into her crotch, urging her legs apart. Maintaining contact, she alternated pressure to turn up the heat.

It worked.

Dax pushed her backward in the small space until her back hit the opposite wall. Rose bumped her knee out and kept it steady while Dax bucked wildly against it. Erotic moans. Roaming hands. Charged breathing. Dax suddenly tensed and jerked, releasing a muffled groan into Rose's neck and wobbling against her arm for support.

"I love the surprise," Rose said.

Once Dax regained her strength and steadied her breathing, she replied, "I *guess* so."

When they returned to the stage after straightening their clothes, Dax resumed nailing up the trim, and Rose sat at the piano, reviewing a set list and placing the sheet music in the correct order for the audition. They exchanged glances periodically, each round birthing thoughts of repeating their dressing room tryst, causing Rose's breaths to be shallow. Knowing she would never get prepared for William at this rate, she turned her back to Dax and continued her work.

"Excuse me. I'm looking for Rose Hamilton." The smell of oakmoss preceded the man's voice like an early warning system. "I'm William Hackett. Grace Parsons sent me."

Rose turned. Her eyes focused on his blond crew cut. His voice sounded deeper, his shoulders appeared more muscular, and his face was more chiseled than she remembered. Time may have faded the signs of youth, but it hadn't erased the memory of humiliation scarred in Rose's brain. "Oh, hell no."

"Excuse me?" William asked. He may have been ignorant of his cruelty, but he was by no means innocent.

Anger built in Rose. "You don't r-r-remember me, do you?"

"I'm afraid I don't." His eyes inspected Rose, but no sign of recognition came.

"Well, I do, and you need to get the hell out of here, you halfwit," Rose bellowed, causing Dax to stop her hammering and stand between her and the annoying twit who had caused her countless nights of tears when she was younger.

"What's going on, Rose?" Dax asked.

Rose pointed an index finger at William, wishing it was a sword that could cause him as much pain as he'd caused her. "Billie."

Dax's brow instantly furrowed, her lips pressing into a rigid line. She pushed up her sleeves and balled her hands into fists before spinning on her heel. "Back for more punishment, Billie?"

A flash of recognition crossed William's face. He stepped backward when Dax inched forward, chest heaving like she'd run a mile. "The babbler from high school?"

The insult was enough to send Dax into protective mode. When they were kids, she'd chased one bully after another for tormenting Rose about her stutter. But this particular scoundrel had made fun of Rose in class after the teacher forced her to read aloud from a book, embarrassing her more deeply than anyone had before. It was so traumatic that Rose ran from the classroom and didn't stop until she reached Sweeney Park, where Dax had found her. She recalled feeling inadequate, incapable of speaking smoothly—a skill even a toddler could master. That feeling returned just as strongly, something that hadn't happened in years.

But if Rose read Dax correctly, William, or Billie as he called himself in high school, was about to receive a second dose of Dax's wrath. Without warning, she let fly a punch to his face and sent him tumbling into table and chairs. She stood over him while he struggled to regain his wits, ready to toss a second blow. "No one makes fun of Rose."

William tested his jaw before looking up at Dax. "You. You're the one who broke my foot in school."

"And I'll do it again if you say one more mean thing about Rose."

William rose to a sitting position and shoved Dax backward. The stage broke her fall, but her head clunked against the microphone stand, sending it teetering. Rose steadied it before it could crash to the hardwood floor. *Phew!*

William rose and started for Dax, but the two delivery men cut him off, snatching both arms. "Trust me, you don't want any trouble here, Mac," one said before they dragged him up the stairs and tossed him out the door.

Rose flew down the stage steps and went to Dax's aid. "Are you all right? Did he hurt you?"

Dax sat on the edge of the stage, rubbing the back of her head. "I think that's going to leave a knot."

"Are you dizzy? Should I get Jules?" Unable to contain her worry, Rose checked Dax's head. Seeing Riley King pummel Dax and the bruises he'd left had been enough for one lifetime. She would never forgive herself if Dax got hurt defending her honor from that high school bully.

Dax clutched Rose's hand, pulling it from the back of her head to her chest. "I'm fine, Rose. I've hit my head a hundred times." She released Rose's hand. "What in the heck was Billie doing here?"

"He's the pianist Grace sent for the audition."

"You've got to be kidding."

"I wish I were." Rose sat beside Dax on the stage, sliding close until their thighs touched. "We're supposed to open in two weeks, and now I don't have anyone to accompany me on piano."

"I'm sure Grace can find someone." Dax made it sound as if a pianist who knew the songs Rose wanted to sing would magically appear at their doorstep.

"Someone willing to play the songs I like in time for him to learn them for opening night? I doubt it." Disappointment built. Opening night was supposed to be a who's who of Hollywood stars, and Grace had billed Rose as the main attraction to get them there. It would be a disaster if Rose didn't have a well-prepared piano player backing her up.

"What about Lester?" Dax asked. "I know he has a contract with the Seaside Club for another six months, but maybe he's willing to play for you if Grace guarantees to cover the cost of breaking it."

"The last time I spoke with him, he worried more about Frankie than the money." Singing with Lester again would be ideal, but putting him in danger was out of the question.

"But that was before Grace was involved."

"You have a point." Rose still felt uneasy about putting Lester in Frankie's crosshairs, but she was out of options.

CHAPTER TWENTY

Rose pulled the last pie of the day from the oven and set it out to cool on the rack by the pantry door. She eyed what else had to be done between the breakfast and lunch rushes, but May had everything covered. She did the math in her head. The second cook Grace hired wasn't expected to start until next week when they started serving dinner, so Rose had another six shifts before she could hang up her apron for good. She never once resented the long hours and hard work—May had taken her in when she had no place to go—but singing was her passion. And with Lester's cooperation today, it could be a reality again.

Dax entered the kitchen. "Hey, May, I'm heading to Edith's to pick up our order before the lunch rush." She hung her apron on a hook by the back door and grabbed her coat and truck key.

"Why don't you take Rose with you?" May said. "I can handle things here."

Rose checked the clock. She still had a half hour before Lester should arrive for their talk. "Are you sure?"

"Go." May shooed her. "For the life of me, I don't know why you're still helping me in the morning. We don't get crazy busy until lunch."

Rose took off her apron and kissed May on the cheek. "Because we're family."

Dax pulled out of the parking area in the back and rested her hand on the seat bench, palm up. Rose pressed their hands together and entwined their fingers, wishing she could entangle their bodies. Logan had been up at all hours since agreeing to Grace's offer. He secretly sold whiskey during the day, drank in his living room office in the evening, and roamed the hallway upstairs at night when he could not sleep. That left precious little opportunity for her and Dax to be alone.

"Two more days," Dax said. She didn't have to explain further. In two days, Charlie would vacate the garage in the morning and not return until noon to open for the day. Dax would use the spare key, and Rose would follow twenty minutes later to avoid suspicion. They'd spend the next four hours making love and napping in each other's arms.

"Two more days," Rose said in return.

Releasing Rose's hand only to shift gears, Dax drove through town and parked in an angled space in front of Edith's Department Store. She squeezed Rose's hand again before opening the door and stepping inside the store.

While Dax inventoried the items in the box left near the front door for the Foster House, Rose went to the jewelry display counter where Edith was stocking new arrivals. "Good morning, Edith. What new goodies do you have this week?" Her eyes drifted toward the upper right corner of the display, where she'd seen a ring that had caught her eye the last time she'd visited, but the space was empty.

Edith popped her head up from behind the glass counter. "Well, hello, Rosebud. We got in a few necklaces this week that you might like." She pointed to a collection of silver and gold baubles in the case.

"Those are nice, but I was looking for that rosebud ring I saw last week. It was beautiful." And expensive. But it was exactly what she was looking for to wear for her return to the stage in front of a VIP crowd.

Dax sidled up to the counter next to Rose.

"I'm sorry, Rose, but a tourist came through a few days ago and bought it," Edith said.

"Bought what?" Dax asked.

Rose pouted her lips. "A beautiful silver rosebud ring. I thought it would look good with the dress I bought for opening night." She directed her attention to Edith. "Can you get another one?"

"I'll have to check my supplier in San Francisco. When would you need it?"

"Next Friday."

Edith rubbed her chin. "I'm afraid that might not be possible, Rosebud. This last shipment of jewelry took three weeks to come in."

"Well, darn. That's okay, Edith. I'll go through my things and find something to pair with my dress." Rose turned toward Dax. "Ready to go?"

"Yep. Everything is there." Dax pulled money from her pants pocket and counted out eight dollars and fifty cents. "This should make us even, Edith. It's much appreciated. Oh, and May made a peach cobbler today. Stop by any time. A slice for you and your husband is on us for getting these supplies so quickly."

"That's so kind of you. Can we stop by after closing?"

"Of course. May should be awake until eight."

"Perfect. Tell her to expect us after six."

After driving back to the Foster House, Dax brought the supplies into the kitchen while Rose excused herself to meet with Lester in the main dining room. She filled two cups with coffee from the beverage station and retreated to a corner booth for privacy.

Minutes later, Lester appeared at the main door. His bright, friendly expression made Rose's heart smile. Besides Jules and Charlie, she considered Lester one of her dearest friends in Half Moon Bay. She missed seeing and working with him seamlessly for two shows a night. They'd performed together for enough years to have a shorthand of cues to address anything that might happen during a performance. But mostly, she missed her friend.

He sat across from her, squeezing her hands. His dark skin was the polar opposite of Rose's. They were like the black and white keys on his piano. "It's so good to see you, Rosebud." She welcomed the nickname he'd begun using with her after their first week together. The department store owner had called her that, and Lester liked it so much that he carried on the tradition. "You said you had something important to discuss."

"I do." Rose slid a mug of coffee closer to him. "What have you heard about the goings-on in the Foster House?"

"Most of the town knows you're expanding to include dinner service to compete with the Seaside," Lester said. "And that Logan is selling whiskey on the side."

"That's only half of it. I'd like to show you something." Rose exited the booth and wagged her head toward the kitchen. "Bring your coffee if you'd like."

She led him into the kitchen. He dipped his head in greeting. "Hello, May. Hello, Dax."

"It's good to see you, Lester," May said. "I'll have some fresh hot biscuits for you on the way out."

"I'm going with them, May," Dax said.

Dax took the lead, descending the stairs to the basement. The first area contained a generous changing room for Rose and storage for club and restaurant supplies that should not be exposed to the elements. The rest of the equipment and supplies were now in a storage shed on the side of the building.

Dax pushed through the new swinging door leading to the renovated area and held it open for the others. The club was fully lit, and the bar was being stocked. Lester issued a robust whistle in appreciation. "You really are competing with the Seaside."

Rose gestured to her right and the new stage. Dax peeled off to turn on the stage lights and the ceiling-mounted spotlight. "That's not the best part." In two loud clicks, lighting fit for an opera performance washed the stage. Rose led Lester up the steps to center stage. "You know what this is, don't you?"

Lester inspected the microphone. His mouth fell agape. "No way. How did you get your hands on one of these?"

"Grace Parsons." Rose outspread her arms as if surveying the land. "She's funding the entire club to drive Frankie Wilkes out of business. His days of running Half Moon Bay will soon end. And I want you to perform with me, Lester. It will be like old times. You and me on the stage, performing the blues songs you wrote."

Lester sat at the piano bench and started playing one of his songs. Rose stepped up to the microphone and gave Dax the signal to turn on the sound system and club loudspeakers. Rose sang the words to the song Lester had written to memorialize her and Dax's teenage love. She'd sung it to Dax once before, but not to accompaniment. They locked eyes. Each note flowed as a caress across the room. And when the song ended, Dax turned off the spotlight, returning their love to the darkness for only her and Rose to see.

"That was beautiful, Rosebud," Lester said.

Rose came closer and leaned an elbow on the piano. "So, what do you say? We open next Saturday with a private party. Grace has invited an enormous crowd from Hollywood, and I need you to play for me. Grace will pay you twenty-five percent more than what Frankie is paying you, and she'll pay whatever it takes to buy you out of your contract."

Lester leaned closer and murmured, "I thought you were with Dax. Is she okay with Grace doing all of this?"

"I am and she is. Grace is being very genteel as she is with everyone."

"Except with Frankie Wilkes if she's doing all of this."

"He's a special exception." Rose sat next to him on the piano bench. "I know you're concerned about making him angry. Grace plans to bankrupt Frankie and buy up the Seaside. Are you willing to be part of that? Would you like to?"

"It looks like the writing is on the wall." Lester tinkled the piano keys again contemplatively before looking Rose in the eye. "I'd love to, Rosebud."

CHAPTER TWENTY-ONE

In the six months Dax and May had operated the Foster House, Dax never had seen her sister this nervous about preparing a meal. She wasn't even this worked up before the restaurant's opening day when Riley King sabotaged their grocery order. May's anxiety was uncalled for in Dax's opinion. The Foster House was closed to the public for the night's special event. Grace had brought in extra staff, the seventy-five guests had preselected their meal preferences, and the ingredients had been assembled. The only thing left was to prepare the meals when the customers requested them.

May double- and triple-checked the cuts of meat in the chiller, counting each variety and jotting down the numbers. She'd said she could fudge on the sides but not the entrée.

Dax approached and placed both hands on her upper arms. "It's all there, May. You and Sheila have accounted for everything."

"I know."

"Then what is it?" Dax rubbed May's arms before letting go. "What has you wound tight as a spring?"

"I don't like customers traipsing through my kitchen."

"That's only for tonight." Dax adjusted the bow tie topping off her black tuxedo. "It's great that some of Grace's friends wanted to dine upstairs so they could experience the restaurant too. That could mean they'll return for the food, not just the club and booze."

"I know. I know." May lowered her voice when the new cook entered the kitchen. "I'm not sure if Sheila is up to the job."

"She'll do fine. She's been helping you with the lunch crowd for days."

May's shoulders drooped. "Yes, but Rose and I had a system. We didn't have to guess what the other needed, and I certainly didn't have to tell Rose what to do."

"Sheila is being respectful and not overstepping."

"But she does things so differently."

"Do her ways make the kitchen run better or worse?" Dax asked.

May rolled her eyes. "Better, I guess."

"Then change is good," Dax whispered and kissed May on the cheek. "I'm going to check on Charlie. Another wave of guests is expected." She left the kitchen confident May and Sheila would pull off flawless food service tonight.

Once outside, Dax breathed in the early evening spring air. The bone chill it carried had prompted her to let guests who dined upstairs use the interior stairs to get to the club for tonight only. Being a Hollywood VIP came with certain privileges.

A shiny new Cadillac coasted up to the front of the Foster House. Charlie, dressed in a tailored black tuxedo that matched Dax's, both supplied by Grace, went to the driver's side, where the driver rolled down the side window. "Good evening," Charlie said. "Welcome to the Foster House. Parking for the club is around back. Or if you'd like to dine upstairs instead of the club, I can take it around for you."

"Grace did mention the joint has a quaint full-sized restaurant," a woman from inside the car said. "I'd love to try it."

"Anything for you, Karen," the driver said. Both car doors opened, and two women stepped out, immaculately dressed in furs and the tallest heels Dax had ever seen. The driver handed Charlie the key.

"Thank you, miss. We'll pull it around back. Your key will be with the bartender in the club," Charlie said. The ladies walked through the door, and Charlie's stare followed them like a bloodhound onto a scent.

Dax playfully slapped her on the back of the head. "Jules would kill you if she saw you staring at another woman like that."

"I'm not looking at *them*. It's their shoes. How do women walk in those things?"

"Beats me. I've seen some pretty fancy clothes tonight, but those two take the cake." Dax shoved her hands inside her coat pockets, gripping a small box with her left. "How are you holding up? Are you keeping warm?"

"Warm enough. Ruth keeps bringing out hot coffee."

"How many more cars do you expect?" Dax asked. "Grace said some friends were driving up together but to expect twenty-two cars."

"Then there should be one more after this. Once it arrives, I'll come downstairs to keep things flowing."

"Thanks, Charlie. I really appreciate the help tonight."

"Have you given Rose her gift?"

"Not yet. That's where I'm headed next." Dax patted her on the shoulder. "I'll take this one around back since I'm heading down."

"Thanks, Dax." Charlie flipped her the key and returned to the dining chair she'd positioned near the front door.

Dax hopped into the front seat of the Cadillac, inserted the key, and took a moment to admire the luxury of the interior. She'd never been in a vehicle with leather and polished wood. *So this is how the other half lives*, she thought.

Dax hadn't believed that two dozen cars could fit in the back of the Foster House, but Charlie had done an excellent job of lining up the cars in two rows, all facing taillight to taillight, so no one had to back out when they left. She headed to the end of a row and pulled through, lining up the Cadillac with the car next to it.

She ran both hands smoothly around the steering wheel, thinking that one day she would have a car like this of her own and take Rose for a drive down the coast to see Hollywood, if only to prove a point. Maybe it was how they grew up, but Rose didn't believe she was worthy of the attention of the starlet crowd. She could not have been more wrong. Sure, the people who had come tonight had expensive cars and clothes. And some women had jewelry fit for Cleopatra, but Rose outshone every one of them. She was Hollywood on the outside, but hometown on the inside, and Rose had made it clear every day that Dax was her home.

Dax went to the back door. It was being guarded by two men Grace had brought in for the special event. Both were shivering in their tuxes. "Evening, fellas. Thanks for being here tonight. I'll send out a thermos of coffee and a few cups."

"Thank you, ma'am." One tipped his fedora. Dax cringed at the moniker. She'd never considered herself a "ma'am" before. "If it wouldn't be too much trouble, can we have a few more of May's biscuits too?"

"Of course, fellas. And be sure to take turns in the dining room on the main floor. May set aside some of her meatloaf for you." One or both of them would stay on after tonight to act as security for the club. Grace had yet to decide on the number. Based on how much their faces lit at the mention of May's cooking, she guessed there would be some elbowing to see which one got the job.

The other guard pressed a newly installed button near the door, alerting the bartender that the door was about to open and the coast was clear. If he'd pressed it three times, a series of red lights would turn on inside. Another press of a button inside would roll a fake wall mounted on hidden casters into place, shielding the bar from the rest of the room.

Dax entered and stood at the top stair landing to take in the transformation that had taken place in less than two months. It was nothing short of spectacular. The Foster House basement now rivaled the elegant speakeasy she'd scouted in San Francisco during the construction of the new club and far outstripped the Seaside. Seeing the place filled with men and women like them, paired up in same-sex couples, made the name Rose asked her to carve into the side of the stage very poignant. She had said this place would serve as a beacon for others like them. That they would come for hundreds of miles just to be among friends.

Dax entered the Beacon Club, recalling her path getting here. Six months ago, she was sitting on May's porch in San Francisco, waiting for Heather, the woman she loved from afar, to stroll past the house. That day, when she'd confronted Heather's wife-beating husband, she knew her life would change, but she never had envisioned this. Her life had centered on carpentry and caring for May, and Rose had been a distant but persistent memory that had occupied a corner of her heart. But everything she'd endured—from Logan abandoning her and May in a strange town to Rose returning and Riley King's death—had led to this moment. She was now the manager of the poshest speakeasy in the state.

Descending the stairs, she stopped at the bar and waited for the bartender to finish with the three customers at the other end. She gestured him over. "Another set of car keys for you, Jason. They belong to a shiny new Cadillac and two ladies in very tall heels."

"Ah, Susan and Karen." Jason wrote their names on paper, wrapped the slip around the keys, secured it with a rubber band, and placed it in a box under the bar.

After the incident that killed the drunk fisherman in front of the Foster House, Dax insisted on securing car keys as the price of admission. If a patron was too intoxicated, she would make sure they had plenty of coffee and sobered up before driving away. When Grace objected, Dax had said, "I won't have another death on my conscience. If you want me to manage the club, this is how it will work."

"How are the servers doing? Any problems?" Dax asked Jason. She was happy Grace had convinced him to tend bar for the Beacon Club. He was experienced with the speakeasy environment. She was more pleased to learn that he was like them and quickly dropped the suspicion that he had a crush on Rose. Instead, she attributed his special attention to "family" looking out for one another.

"They're great. Though I haven't seen the busboy in a bit. I'm going to need another rack of glasses pretty soon."

"I'll check on it after seeing how Rose is doing."

Dax made a path through the main seating area. She and Grace had settled on thirty-eight tables for two. Any number could be pushed together with topper boards and tablecloths added to make for fewer gaps and smoother surfaces. Grace had called her a genius for that idea. Tonight, they'd arranged the room for two tables of six, ten tables for four, and a dozen tables for two, which kept the three servers hopping.

Before Dax passed the front row of tables, Grace gestured to her. Dax calculated she had only fifteen minutes before Rose would begin her warmup routine for her show and hoped whatever Grace wanted would not take much time.

"Yes?" Dax leaned in close to her ear. Grace's table was set for six, with Clive on one side of her and a familiar-looking woman on the other. Beside her was a man, who, on closer inspection, Dax recognized as Clifton Webb. The room was teeming with movie stars.

"My friend wanted to compliment the man who carved the sign on the stage. I told her not to make assumptions." Grace placed a hand on the small of Dax's back and turned her attention to her tablemate. "Greta, meet Dax. She's the creator of that spectacular carving."

Dax's breath hitched. Grace's tablemate was Greta Garbo. The makeup around her eyes made them appear as smoky as they did on the big screen.

Greta extended her hand, which she accepted, eying Dax as if she were the entrée for tonight's meal. "It's a pleasure to meet you, Dax. You are an artist. If Grace can spare you a few days, I'd like to hire you to do something similar in a summer home I'm building in Monterey."

Dax's head swirled at the world she'd entered. She feared her life might go into a tailspin if she ventured in too deep. "Thank you, Miss Garbo, but I have my hands full with the Beacon Club."

"Perhaps I can change your mind." Greta continued her inspection of Dax.

"Down, girl," Grace said. "Dax is Rose's lover."

"Soulmate, actually," Dax added with a strong sense of pride. "If you'll excuse me, I have to check on her."

Dax stepped away and paused at the stage. The state-of-the-art microphone sat in the center. At the side, May's piano had been tuned by an expert from San Francisco, and Dax had sanded and stained it to match the wood on the bar. Vases of a dozen roses, each sitting on stools, lined the back of the stage, creating a brilliant, fragrant row of red. Grace and Dax had each sent one, and several guests had also brought some. The flowers from Dax were just the appetizer, though. She squeezed the box in her pocket again, confirming the main course hadn't fallen out. It had cost three months of profits from selling Logan's whiskey, but it was worth every penny.

One server walked past, and Dax called out, "Barbara." The woman stopped and retraced her steps to Dax. "Can you see where Kyle is? He might be on another break. Tell him to bring down another rack of glasses for Jason right away. And can you send out a thermos of coffee, some mugs, and some biscuits to the guards topside in the back?"

"Yes, ma'am."

Dax cringed for the second time tonight. She didn't want the staff to consider her unapproachable, so she would start with Barbara and make sure she understood everyone was on an equal footing. "Ma'am was for my mother. We're all a team here. Please call me Dax."

"Yes, Dax." Barbara scurried off, clearly not fully appreciating Dax's gesture. After a few more nights working here, though, Barbara should see that Dax had her interests in mind as much as hers.

Dax entered the back area through the swinging door. The supplies and equipment were arranged and stacked neatly on shelves to present a positive image to the guests traveling from the upstairs restaurant. Only a box of paper napkins was out of place, but Dax nudged it straight.

As she stood outside Rose's dressing room door, Dax's heart fluttered. This was Rose's big night—her grand return to the stage. She had put on a good front for four months, working side by side with May in the Foster House kitchen and said she enjoyed it, but Dax knew better. Rose was meant to be on the stage. That made tonight much more significant.

She knocked.

Moments later, Lester opened the door. The one flaw in the remodeling had been the lack of space for two dressing rooms, something Dax had addressed by adding a temporary plywood partition inside with curtains hung from a rod for privacy.

Rose was sitting at the vanity Dax had carried down from her bedroom. It fit nicely in the corner. The extra light the electrician added had turned the space into a perfect area for her to do her makeup and hair before each show.

"Hi, Lester. Would you mind giving Rose and me a minute alone?"

"Sure thing, Dax. I'll get Rose's hot tea and honey from the bar."

"Perfect. Thanks."

Once Lester closed the door behind him, Dax stood behind Rose, staring at her image in the mirror. Rose had added a dozen curls to her hair on the front and sides and gathered the long strands in the back into a broad black velvet ribbon. It perfectly matched her black sequined gown.

"You look stunning." Dax fixed her eyes on the patch of skin above the gown's scooped neckline. Only last night, after Logan had passed out drunk in his room, she had kissed every inch of it, careful not to leave a mark.

Rose blushed with a faint grin. "Are you wearing them tonight?"

"I am." Dax returned her grin.

"Let me see."

Dax unbuttoned her outer coat and carefully hung it over the last hat hook on the wall. She turned around slowly, displaying the suspenders Rose had given her last night after they'd made love.

"Oh my." Rose stepped out of her chair and moved closer. She hooked both hands beneath the strips of black silk at the shoulder and ran them down slowly, brushing against each breast. Dax shuddered as an ache built, ending at the tip of each breast.

"I might mess up your perfect hair and makeup if you don't stop."

Rose inched back. "Later tonight then?"

"That's a promise. But first, I have a surprise for you." Dax returned to her coat, fumbled in a pocket, and pulled out the small cardboard jewelry box. She wished it had come in a more decorative container, but it had only arrived this morning, and Edith was out of velvet boxes. Anticipating Rose's reaction, she felt her heart thump harder when she handed it to her.

Rose removed the lid, exposing a sterling silver ring. The setting was carved into the shape of a rosebud with a small diamond in its center. Rose gasped, her eyes dancing with excitement. "How did you get this? Edith said she couldn't get it for weeks."

"I had Edith put a rush on it. I couldn't let you take the stage tonight without it." Dax removed the ring from the box and took Rose's right hand. "I know the left hand is the traditional side for wedding rings, but I offer this ring as a pledge of my love. A promise that I'll always protect you and will never leave your side." Dax slid the silver onto Rose's ring finger.

Tears filled Rose's eyes. Her lips trembled. "This is beautiful, Dax. I'll never leave your side either."

Dax ran her thumbs below Rose's eyes to clean the newly formed black streaks. "I've messed up your makeup."

"Then I'll mess it up a little more." Rose pulled Dax in for a deep, passionate kiss. Lips molded perfectly together. Tongues caressed in a slow, sensual dance. Arms embraced. Hands sought every inch of their mate. Dax was sure they would be connected like this for life. They would grow old together, walking the beaches of Half Moon Bay by day and falling into each other's arms by night.

A knock on the door broke the moment. "I have your tea, Rose," the voice said through the door.

Rose pulled back. "One second, Lester." Rose ran a thumb across Dax's lips. "You have lipstick."

Dax clutched Rose's hand to stop her. "Don't. I want to taste you all night." She kissed Rose's hand before opening the door. "I'll let you get ready."

Customers ate and drank, servers scurried about, and Dax watched Rose's show from the end of the bar, sitting with Charlie, Jules, and May. Logan sat at the other end, his face buried in a glass of something. Rose had been on the stage for more than an hour with no sign of stopping. Song after song, Dax felt Rose's confidence grow. She was right about the ribbon microphone. Her voice had never sounded clearer nor more enchanting. The lighting topped off the performance, making her glow like an angel. From Dax's perspective, it seemed like she and Rose were the only two people in the room. And when Rose performed the song Lester had written for them, her last song of the evening, she never felt more connected, more in love.

The lights brightened, and the room erupted in applause, filling Dax's heart with pride. Everyone stood, cheering. Everyone but Logan, who downed another drink from his lonely perch.

"Rose was incredible tonight," May said.

"Amazing," Jules said.

"Marvelous," Charlie added.

"Perfect," Dax sighed.

Guests soon filtered out in pairs and groups if Jason deemed at least one in their clutch was sober enough to drive. The mumblings Dax overheard as each group left gave her the sense that the night had been a roaring success. When the last guest left and Logan disappeared upstairs, Dax's bunch from the bar joined Rose, Clive, and Grace at the front table after pulling up two extra chairs. Jason delivered champagne all around and took the open seat next to Clive. They kissed.

Dax kissed Rose on the cheek. "You were perfect tonight." She turned to Grace. "How did we do?"

"Spectacularly." Grace raised her glass. "Ladies and gentlemen, the Beacon Club is a rousing success. And soon, Frankie Wilkes will be nothing but a terrible memory."

CHAPTER TWENTY-TWO

Two months of managing the Beacon Club had nearly accustomed Dax to working nights. The first few weeks were brutal, though. Broken sleep had plagued her, leaving dark circles under her eyes. At first, it felt odd waking up after the sun. For years as a carpenter, she had risen before dawn to get chores done before work, and that habit continued at the Foster House. But a speakeasy was inherently nocturnal, coming to life when most of the town was in bed. It gave Dax no choice but to adjust.

Monday nights, or early Tuesday mornings, were the worst, especially tonight when the fog stubbornly hung in the air. One would think June would bring warmer nights, but the California central coast was an odd beast. Summers there were often colder than the winters. However, having Charlie's company made waiting at the dock behind the Foster House for the weekly smuggled liquor load much more palatable.

"They're late." Charlie sipped a cup of May's coffee to counter the bone chill that had enveloped them every delivery night like an old friend.

"Captain Burch left word he was delayed a few hours in Ensenada picking up tequila but hoped to make it up with extra steam," Dax said.

"At least both of our shops are closed tomorrow," Charlie said.

Dax had tried to convince Charlie early on that she needn't work at the club to earn her share of the profits—that her bravery the night Riley King died had earned it ten times over—but she was stubborn. "You shouldn't have to deal with two Logans," Charlie had said.

"You're nothing like that freeloader," Dax had replied, "but I understand feeling the need to work for your pay." That night, they'd agreed Charlie's responsibilities would include tonight's task and managing the club transportation issues, including parking. Last month, to Dax's surprise, Charlie came to the Foster House on a Tuesday morning with paint, a roller, and two long two-by-four boards. By the end of the day, she had two dozen ample parking spaces painted with perfectly straight white lines.

There was no need for small talk while they waited. Neither liked it, and both appreciated comfortable silence in the near darkness. Dax had doused the dock lamps and left on only one dim light at the club entrance at the back of the Foster House. That would provide enough illumination to discern the markings on the crates and barrels and determine which items belonged to which outfit. Soon the hum of motorboats could be heard and the drone grew louder with each passing second. The smugglers were coming.

Suddenly, an armada of six small boats poked through the fog, bobbing up and down against the marina waves. The pilots were well trained and easily coasted their crafts into the dock slips. One man from each boat jumped out and secured the lines to the dock cleats. Two other men remained in each boat and created an assembly line to unload the barrels and crates to the dock men. In less than fifteen minutes, they dumped a warehouse full of illegal liquor onto the Foster House dock and were racing back out to sea.

Four pickups waiting in the dark parking lot came to life and caravanned to the top of the gangway. Eight men jumped out and began a long assembly line, repositioning the booty on the asphalt. Dax paid the leader two sawbucks for their help when they were done. Twenty dollars was an excellent investment. It saved her from hiring another man and a ton of time for her and Charlie. The men loaded half into their trucks and disappeared into the night. That left only the Seaside Club. The rest belonged to the Beacon Club.

Dax ensured that each item stacked for The Beacon Club had a red 'X' on the side, including the single barrel as payment for the use of the Foster House dock, and the ones reserved for the Seaside had a white circle. As they waited for Seaside's driver to retrieve their delivery, she and Charlie began the tedious task of safely hauling the red "X" items to the basement. There she discovered Logan at the bar, drinking up a good portion of the profits. She had given Jason strict orders to measure each bottle behind the bar at closing and note any differences the next day. Grace would deduct the same amount from Logan's weekly cut. Thankfully tonight, he was staying to himself and merely grunted each time Dax and Charlie came down.

On their third trip back up, headlights appeared around the corner of the building. Dax hadn't heard a warning shot from the guard street side, so she didn't retreat and lock up. However, she remained alert. The vehicle took shape, resembling the pickup for the Seaside Hotel. Dax's tense shoulder muscles instantly relaxed. She wondered which underpaid employee would show up this week. Since Grace had stolen Jason to work at the Beacon Club, Frankie Wilkes had sent a parade of different men each week to take the Seaside's haul to the hotel.

Whoever was driving, they'd angled in awkwardly at the top of the gangway and parked too close to allow for easy loading. Clearly, the driver was inexperienced at this. Dax snickered when Frankie stepped from the driver's side, mumbling several loud and clear curse words. Dax waited for someone to exit on the passenger side, but no one did. She snickered again. Wilkes was there alone to retrieve his own liquor. Either every man working at the Seaside was sick, or Frankie had run out of employees. His business had taken a nosedive since Rose's opening night.

He stomped to the Beacon Club collection and grabbed a barrel. Dax rushed toward him and placed a hand on the wooden container, keeping it in place. "That's ours." She gestured a thumb at the barrels along the railing. "Those are yours."

Wilkes eyed his paltry four containers before turning his gaze to Dax's mountainous stacks. Side by side, they looked like a rowboat next to a steam liner. "You Fosters need to be taken down a peg or two."

"Maybe you should sell to Grace before you lose everything." Dax could not help poking a stick at Wilkes. Besides firing Rose and leaving her homeless, he was responsible for the deaths of Logan's father and Riley's accomplice. He deserved everything she and Grace could throw at him.

"Not on your life. And not on your lame sister's or on stuttering Rose's. You certainly know how to pick them."

Dax's rage pounded in her ears. "No one makes fun of Rose." She threw a punch, hitting Wilkes directly on the left eye. He appeared dazed but for only a moment. Taller and more muscular than Dax, he let loose a crushing blow to Dax's head. The second sent her to the ground. A third landed on her jaw, sending the coppery taste of blood to her mouth.

Charlie growled and tackled Wilkes, driving him to the asphalt and likely embedding gravel into his cheek. While he rocked back and forth, groaning in pain, Charlie crawled fast to Dax and helped her to a sitting position.

"Are you okay?" Charlie said, her words rushed, before pulling Dax to her feet.

Wilkes came to his knees. "On second thought, I'll start with the fix-it freak." The light to his back wasn't enough to illuminate his face from that position, but Dax sensed his rage. He pushed a foot against the gravel, pawing it like a bull preparing to attack.

The moment he appeared ready to pounce, the muzzle of a pistol pressed against his temple. Logan's figure became more visible when he slurred, "One move, and you'll get a bullet in your skull."

Wilkes stood tall and inched his hands up, palms open, but the rage pouring from him failed to recede. Logan stepped back but kept his gun at the ready. Wilkes sneered, "I should have gotten rid of you Fosters when I had the chance. One is lame. One is a freak. And the other is a drunk like his old man."

Logan's posture stiffened. He cocked the hammer, adding more firmness to his earlier threat. "What did you say?"

"I said all of you need to end up at the bottom of the stairs with a broken neck like your drunk father."

Oh boy, Dax thought. She and May had intentionally kept the truth from Logan about his father's death, fearing this exact situation. Emotions would run high and lead to more death. While she and May were no fans of either man, neither wanted to set the stage for another killing.

Dax hurried toward Logan, ignoring her throbbing jaw and eye. She pushed his gun-wielding arm toward the sky. "There will be no killing tonight. We don't want a war." Dax turned her attention to Wilkes. "Just get your liquor and get out of here."

Wilkes turned his nose up at Dax before loading his minuscule load into the back of his truck. Boarding the driver's seat, he slammed the door shut. Before he drove away, he rolled down the window and yelled, "If any of you ever steps foot in any of my businesses again, you're dead."

A seething took root in Dax. Inhaling deeply only made the ache on her face worse. Logan's drunken brashness had pushed things across a line. "You've done it now, Logan. Before this turns into a war, I'll have to find a way to smooth things over with Frankie." She knew that was going to be much easier said than done.

CHAPTER TWENTY-THREE

Frankie Wilkes parked his company pickup in the delivery area behind the Seaside Hotel. The scrapes on his face still stung, and so did his bruised ego. Minutes ago, he had been bested by two women and a drunk—not his finest hour. On the verge of bankruptcy and disgrace, he was baffled by his current circumstances. Not one of his childhood dreams had anticipated this dismal outcome.

At ten, he had had fantasies of robbing trains like Butch Cassidy or Jesse James—only he would get away with his riches and live a long, happy life off the spoils. At twenty, he'd shed the silliness of youth and set his sights on making the family name one to respect. His father was a con artist, shilling arrowheads he'd forged as authentic relics from Little Big Horn. His grandfather wasn't any better, carpetbagging his way across the South until he'd worn out his welcome and was forced to move west.

At thirty, Frankie had bought his first hotel near San Francisco with his brother, and they were well on their way to meeting his youthful goal. By forty, his brother bought him out so he could follow his dream. He took that money and found a silent investor to buy up half of the businesses in Half Moon Bay. The Wilkes name had finally become synonymous with success.

Now, at forty-five, he was on the brink of losing it all. Of course, he could say it was because Rose Hamilton had pushed him past his limits, sending Grace Parsons on a rampage to destroy him. But he knew the truth. He could have appeased Grace if he hadn't made the worst mistake of his life—bringing in his nephew to handle old man Foster.

Running a speakeasy during Prohibition came with inherent risks. Risks he was willing to take because of the money it brought in. That operation, his only profitable business, had funded his other ventures in town. It had become crucial in completing his dream of making Half Moon Bay the West Coast's answer to Atlantic City.

The only thing that had stood in his way was old man Foster. His was the only marina business Frankie didn't own. Why did the old geezer have to be so stubborn? He'd declined his first, second, and third offers, despite Frankie besting each previous one by a thousand dollars. The idiot had held on to his pride. He had built that business from the ground up and was determined to die in it. Riley was stupid enough to make that happen. Frankie's nephew was an excellent foreman of the family cattle ranch in Fresno that Frankie's sister had married into but had no head for more subtle business. Scaring the old man had turned into murder, and when that freak Dax started asking questions, Riley's buddy, the only witness, had to go. Frankie's fundamental mistake was not asking his brother to clip that thorn. It was a mistake he refused to repeat.

He dragged tonight's whiskey delivery into the club's basement storage room, one barrel at a time. He hadn't done this since the week before the club first opened five years ago. Even then, he had a team of men with him to make sure the load was properly picked up, transported, and stored without attracting the attention of law enforcement not on his payroll.

Until last month, Frankie had had a full staff at his businesses—then the Beacon Club had peeled off three-quarters of his customers. He could survive losing the locals and the off-season tourist, but Grace had stripped away her deep-pocket friends from Hollywood, Sacramento, and San Francisco. That had forced him to let half of his employees go. He shook his head. He went into business with Grace Parsons because of her money and connections to attract a wealthy clientele. Now, she was leveraging those very things against him. And he was sure she was about to break him, thereby wiping out his life's work.

Carefully tapping a barrel, he filled a dozen bottles and corked and stowed them beneath the bar. All but one. That one would serve as his crying towel until the sun came up in a few hours. Not only had Grace stolen his customers, but she'd also lured away two of his most valuable employees—Jason and Lester. In one day, he had found himself with a singer but no one to play the piano for her and lots of booze but no one to serve it. He'd spent the night behind the bar himself, and when his singer showed up, she quit, returning to San Francisco the next day to look for work.

The hardware store junior clerk he'd convinced to tend the bar was dumb as an ox, almost impossible to teach. A filled shot glass and a filled tumbler didn't equal one another. Frankie suspected he'd lost several hundred dollars in sales in overfilled glasses before correcting the matter. And despite finding a halfway decent replacement singer, he still hadn't found a piano player to accompany her. He was relying on instrumental recordings for her shows, but singing to a recording wasn't the same, as evidenced by the sparsely filled seats.

Frankie filled his glass for a third time and downed its contents, the sting in his throat reminding him that his life was burning around him. Minutes later, the main door to the club opened, letting in more light from the basement corridor. He'd locked the door when he'd brought in the last barrel, so someone must have used a key.

Frankie shifted his stare toward the door, discovering a shadowy figure in the doorway. He knew only one man who could fill an entrance like that—the brother he'd called last night. A call he'd dreaded because making it meant he'd failed. Another man, one Frankie didn't know, also entered, but he remained near the door.

"Join me for a drink, little brother." Frankie reached across the bar top to retrieve a second tumbler. He sloshed in about three fingers worth, an amount his idiot bartender would have rung up as a single.

Roy straddled the barstool to Frankie's left, towering over Frankie by a half foot, even sitting, making Frankie's nickname for his younger brother ironic. Both shared equally in looks and business sense, but Roy had gotten all the height. If he ever considered running for political office, he would be a shoo-in.

Roy grabbed him by the chin and inspected the side of his face. The one that felt as if he'd been dragged across the highway on it. "What the hell happened?" He released his grip.

"The Fosters happened."

"You should have called me sooner, Frankie." He slowly sipped his drink. Roy never rushed his liquor or overindulged. Unlike Frankie, he drank to savor the flavor, not drown his bad choices.

"I thought I could weather the storm until tourist season started next month, but none of the expected hotel reservations have come through. It appears Grace has poisoned the well."

"I warned you that going into business with a woman was a horrible idea. They let emotion get in the way."

"And, boy, can they hold a grudge." Frankie raised his glass to add emphasis.

"Hell hath no fury like a woman scorned." Roy twirled his glass before sipping again. "You should have learned that lesson from Mother. Why don't you let her buy you out? You can come back to the city and come to work for me. It would be like old times."

"And that, little brother, is where you're wrong." The muscles in Frankie's jaw tensed. He would not be relegated to the role of employee and certainly would not bend over and take it in the ass from Grace Parsons. He needed to outsmart that woman and offer something more than a nightclub on the central coast. "Can you loan me five thousand? I need it to rebuild and rebrand. I need to open Half Moon Bay to more than Hollywood. I want to convert the club into a gambling hall. That would attract a whole new crowd."

"It would take more than five thousand to make that happen. The number of government officials, politicians, and sheriffs we'd have to pay off regularly would be astronomical."

"Then I'm out of options." Frankie knew what had to be done, but he no longer had the means to do it himself. "I'll need your special help."

"That, big brother, I can give. But if we do this, we do it my way, no questions asked. Can you agree to that?"

"I don't have a choice." Frankie shook his head in defeat.

"I need to hear it, brother. There will be no going back once I start down this road."

Frankie stared his brother directly in the eye. "Yes, I agree."

Roy snapped his fingers, summoning the man near the door. He was not as big as Roy but was much scarier. His eyes were cold, as if death were his only friend. "I can't get my hands dirty, but you and Sam will. He'll show you what needs to be done tonight."

Frankie filled his glass again and swallowed it in one large gulp. He and his brother were about to spill much more blood over whiskey. If Frankie knew Roy, he would strike hard. And if the Fosters and Grace Parsons didn't get his message, he would burn and kill everyone in his path. The whiskey war was about to begin.

CHAPTER TWENTY-FOUR

Rose tossed and turned for a while, having no luck in falling asleep. A song from her performance last Saturday had bothered her. Something about the arrangement didn't feel right. She planned to talk to Lester about it when they rehearsed on Thursday, but first, she had to work out what would improve it.

She craned her neck to read the clock on her nightstand. It was three o'clock. May should wake in an hour to begin the breakfast prep. And since it was liquor delivery night, Dax had likely gotten to sleep just an hour ago and should not wake for at least another six.

Rose threw on a robe and slippers and cracked the door open. Thankfully the light in Logan's living room office was dark. She stepped into the hallway and discovered his door was shut, suggesting he was asleep like the rest of the household. Rose was about to tiptoe past Dax's room, but the pull between them was too strong. She stopped at the door and twisted the knob. If luck was with her, Dax would be awake, and she would drag her downstairs to her dressing room and they would make love until the Foster House came to life again. But when the door creaked open, Dax appeared sound asleep. She left the door open to avoid waking her with another loud creak and went downstairs. A rendezvous would have to wait.

Rose sneaked downstairs and past May's bedroom. While she didn't miss sweating away in the kitchen, she missed being with May all day. They'd made a perfect team, as if they were extensions of one another. And judging from her interaction with May that evening, Rose got the impression she and the new cook, Sheila, had yet to develop a similar symbiotic relationship.

Rose flipped on the light at the basement stairs and quietly descended. She needed only a single light to illuminate her way to the stage, so she turned on the one in the storage area and propped open the swinging door leading to the main room with a chair. The near darkness and solitude provided an ideal setting to rehearse in. It allowed her to stretch her comfort zone and make mistakes.

Ascending the two steps Dax had built, Rose took center stage. She took a moment to reflect on the last two months. Performing in front of a crowd at the Beacon Club was transforming. That first night on stage had been electrifying and revealed she'd missed it more than she realized. She loved singing—and she was darn good at it. The club and sound system were top-notch, and having Lester play for her again was a dream come true. The only thing that could make the entire experience more perfect would be to be able to perform on more than Friday and Saturday nights.

Without a hotel in town for Grace's friends to stay overnight, their visits only extended to the weekends. It made no sense for her to perform to only the locals and the stray traveler on other nights. Once tourist season started or Grace bought the Seaside, though, she would be back to singing four nights a week. Until then, she and Lester regularly took advantage of the extra time during the day to work on more songs and prepare four distinct sets to keep her performances fresh. And when she could not sleep, like tonight, she would head down after hours to work out some nuance for a particular song.

The state-of-the-art microphone Grace had gifted her was still center stage and was turned off, ready for her to practice. She cupped it with both hands and visualized Lester playing the blues song she'd had trouble with during her last performance. She wanted to reduce the tempo and change when she came in on the second verse. Counting the beats, she sang at a slower pace, and instantly it felt more natural. When she finished the first verse, she counted four beats in her head before starting the second. *Much better*, she thought.

"That was nice." The deep male voice came from the direction of the bar.

Rose jumped at the unexpected intrusion, her heart nearly thumping out of her chest. A figure appeared from the shadows engulfing the tables. It grew larger until a stubbled face came into view. "Logan. You scared me."

Unsteady on his feet, he wobbled up to the stage, nearly stumbling when he reached the top stair. "Well, we can't have that. My little canary can't sing when she's frightened."

A whiskey-scented cloud preceded Logan by five feet, forcing Rose back several steps. Since he first called her doll, she got the same vibe from him as from the handsy patrons at the Seaside Club who'd had too much to drink. They were all out for a kiss or a grope, with their eye set on taking Rose home for the night. Most nights, with Dax in the next room and May downstairs, she had little fear of Logan taking his intoxicated hounding beyond talk. But he'd become increasingly pushy, and with him a mere five feet away, Rose felt cornered.

"Go to bed, Logan."

"Only if you'll come with me." His words had a ring of foul intent, just like his breath. The hair on the back of her neck tingled at the notion that if he was close enough to smell, he was close enough to be a threat. He had blocked the stairs, and the only other way off the stage was to jump three feet off the front. Her robe and slippers would not make that easy.

"You're drunk." Rose curled her lip.

"So what if I am?" He moved closer, and Rose matched him step for step backward until her bottom hit May's piano. "I've had my eye on you, Rose. You're much too pretty to spend time with that freak upstairs. She'll turn you into a freak too. I'm here to make sure that doesn't happen."

He gripped Rose's upper arms and leaned in for a kiss. Rose remembered the tips Lester had given her on handling unruly club guests and kneed him in the groin. She missed the edge of his inner leg, so she stomped the top of his foot on the way down. Unlike the heels she would wear for performances, though, her slippers could not deliver a crushing blow. Logan groaned but not as much as Rose had hoped.

His eyes turned fiery. "You are a feisty one." He tightened his hold, sending fear coursing through her. At twice her size, Logan had superior strength, and her feeble attempt to get the best of him had only fueled his anger. He pushed his lips over hers in a nauseating, forceful kiss.

Rose pushed against him and thrashed until she forced their lips apart. "Help, Dax! Help!" She prayed her voice could penetrate the layers of walls and floors between her and anyone else. May and Dax were solid sleepers, but maybe the man on guard in the parking lot could hear her shouts.

Logan pressed a hand over Rose's mouth, muffling her screams, and forced her to the stage floor, pinning her down; she could not break free and could barely breathe. She felt a hand slip between her legs. It was rough and forceful, his jagged fingernails pricking the skin between her thighs. Flailing her head, Rose could not loosen the hand covering her mouth. She was helpless against his sheer size.

There was a loud crack. Logan flinched, his hand fell from her mouth, and he rolled off her.

Rose got her bearings, and her fear of being raped turned on a dime. Her protector had arrived.

Dax was standing over Logan, beating him repeatedly with a splintered chair leg in a relentless rage. She had never seen her this possessed. Dax wound up without pausing, connecting blow after blow, mere seconds apart.

"Dax! Stop!" Rose yelled, but the beating continued. If she didn't stop her, Dax would beat him to death. She climbed to her knees and closed in on her, intending to grab her arm, but when Dax pulled back for another rapid blow, the end of the chair leg nicked her on the forehead. Rose moaned in pain and tumbled to her bottom.

Dax froze in midstrike. She turned with a sickly expression on her face. "Rose!" She dropped her weapon and went to Rose's side, helping her to a sitting position. "Are you okay?"

Rose's vision momentarily blurred but cleared quickly. She brought a hand to the stinging spot over her right eye. "I'm fine. Just dazed."

"My God. I hurt you." Dax brushed back her hair on that side and winced. "You're going to have a lump. I'm so sorry."

Rose glanced at Logan. His still, limp body gave birth to a fresh fear. The sheriff would arrest Dax for murder if he was dead. He had been in Frankie Wilkes's pocket for years and could twist the facts to look like revenge, not her defending Rose from a rapist. No one would believe them. Dax would face decades in prison for protecting Rose against a worthless, vile man.

Logan moaned. He was alive but hurt. He grimaced and covered his midsection with his forearms. Rose suspected a broken rib or two. *Good*, she thought. He deserved each blow.

Now that the danger had passed for Dax, Rose's hands trembled as the events of the last few minutes soaked in. She had been moments away from being raped. Never had she felt more trapped. She was at the mercy of a horrible excuse of a man and could do nothing to stop him. Thank goodness Dax arrived when she did. If she'd come a minute later, Rose was sure Logan would have had his way with her.

Rose's lips quivered. Too much violence accompanied the illegal whiskey business and many of the men in her life. From Frankie to Riley to Logan, they were all bad men. If not for Jason, Lester, and Clive, she would believe every man was evil. Even her father, who had abandoned her in Half Moon Bay. Thank goodness Dax was there at every turn to protect her.

Logan moved more and appeared less groggy when he shifted to his knees and feet. He held an arm close to his ribs. "Get the hell out of my house, both of you."

Ever the protector, Dax positioned herself between Rose and that horrid man, appearing ready to fight to the death after picking up the chair leg again. "Why do we have to leave? You're the one who raped Rose."

"Because it's my damn house." Logan pointed toward the stairs, wincing in pain. "Now, get before I call the sheriff on you."

Dax helped Rose to her feet and slung an arm over her shoulder to steady her legs, which were still weak from the brush with danger. "Come on, Rose. Let's get a few of your things and get you somewhere safe."

After dropping her weapon, Dax guided her through the storage area, past her dressing room, and to the base of the stairs. The first step required considerable effort for her to climb, but with Dax holding her tight, she found her strength gradually returning with each step. Midway up, the door to the kitchen opened, and May appeared at the top landing.

"What's going on? I thought I heard yelling. Is everyone all right?" Concern cut through May's questioning. She hadn't bothered to put on a robe over her knee-length nightgown, making her leg brace visible below its trailing edge.

Rose's thoughts went to May and how she would react to the news of what Logan had done to her. Their marriage had been in name only for months, and May had clearly given up on him. She'd stayed married out of necessity and for the future of the Foster House, overlooking Logan's selfishness and drunken behavior. But tonight, he'd proved himself a scoundrel of the lowest caliber. No woman, especially May, should have to put up with a man like that.

"I have to get Rose somewhere safe." Dax guided Rose to the top step. Unfortunately, safe meant anywhere but here, the place Rose had called home for four months.

"Safe?" May retreated several feet into the kitchen. Rose and Dax followed.

"I need to get her away from Logan. He forced himself on her."

May gasped and flew a hand to her chest. Color left her face, leaving a pale, frozen expression that broke Rose's heart.

Rose gripped her by the arms and shook her head with the vigor of a relieving truth. Her throat thickened around her words. "He didn't. Dax stopped him."

Moisture pooled in May's eyes before she pulled Rose into a tight embrace. "I'm so sorry, Rose. When he knocked the other night, I should have let him in my bed."

The floodgates finally opened, letting an ocean of tears pour from Rose. May should not have to endure sex with a husband she detested, doing so in the hope that it would keep him from going after Rose. That was no way to live for either of them. Both would live in constant fear. At least the terrible circumstance was now out in the open, and Logan could not deny his part.

When they pulled back, Rose turned to find Dax. She was standing several feet away, dressed only in her nightclothes, her head held low and arms akimbo. Anger and frustration had clearly consumed her. Rose suspected she was blaming herself for what had transpired downstairs.

"We can't continue like this, May." Dax raised her head. The tightness in her stance had given way to a look of exhaustion. "Logan kicked Rose and me out. So now we have no place to live. The restaurant can run itself, but who will run the club? And sing? Grace will have a fit when she finds out what he's done."

"As the owner, he has the law on his side. Is there anywhere you can go until I can work things out with him?" May asked.

"We'll go to Charlie's. She has only one bed, but we can sleep on the floor."

After gathering a few of their things into suitcases, Dax loaded the truck and returned to the kitchen's back door, where May stood in quiet concern. Her uneasiness was infectious. Dax had to split her worry between Rose and May, but her priority was getting Rose out of the Foster House, where Logan posed a threat. She grabbed her newsboy cap from the wall hook.

"Take this for safekeeping." May handed Dax the tin box they'd hidden in the baseboard of May's room. It contained the money left over from selling the whiskey barrels from Riley

King's load and May's share of the profits from the Beacon Club. "Logan is no longer the man I married, and I don't trust him. Put it somewhere so he'll never find it."

"I know exactly the spot." Dax accepted the box as if it were a sacred scroll, handling it with care and reverence. The money in that box contained May's entire life savings and would shape her future. "Remember where we first hid the whiskey?" May nodded her head in concurrence. "I'll put it there. Why don't you come with us, May? I beat up Logan pretty bad, and he'll be as angry as hell. I can build you something to sleep on."

"Someone needs to talk sense into that man when he comes upstairs. I'll make him see he's jeopardizing everything."

Dax was torn. She didn't trust Logan one bit, but if anyone could calm him down, it was May. "All right but be careful around him. I'll come back to check on you in a few hours."

Dax kissed May on the cheek and closed the door behind her. She feared the worst was yet to come tonight. First, Logan pulled a gun on Frankie Wilkes, and later he nearly raped Rose. He was a man on the edge, and, if Dax's suspicions were correct, so was Wilkes. She feared for Rose, May, and herself, but she could not show it when May and Rose were counting on her strength.

After helping Rose into the passenger seat, Dax jumped in behind the wheel, sensing her helplessness. They were in an impossible situation, and Rose's blank expression suggested she thought the same. She cupped Rose's hand before starting the engine. "It will be okay, Rose. I'll protect you."

After coasting the truck to the back lot of Charlie's garage, Dax grabbed their suitcases, led Rose to the side door, and knocked loudly. A continuous, muffled, deep bark came from inside. Dax trusted Brutus would wake Charlie, so she forewent a second knock. Soon the door opened, and Brutus quieted.

"Hey, boy." Dax bent down to give the dog a vigorous scratch. His body wagged his excitement at the extra attention.

"Dax. Rose. It's not even four. Is something wrong?" Charlie was dressed in jeans and a man's undershirt like the one Dax slept in and held an arm tight to her chest in the chilly air. Her bare feet must have been cold on the concrete floor as well.

Dax stood tall. "I'd say so. Can we come in?" When Charlie opened the door farther, Dax entered first and Rose followed. She placed the suitcases on the floor, which Brutus gave a good sniff.

"What happened?" Charlie asked.

Dax rested a hand on the small of Rose's back to comfort her. "Logan forced himself on Rose tonight."

Charlie pinched her brow and took in a deep breath. "Did he—"

Dax shook her head. "No. I beat him to a pulp before he could. Then he kicked us out. Can we stay on your floor for a few days until we figure things out?"

"Absolutely. I have a ton of blankets we can stack together as a makeshift bed." She picked up one suitcase by the handle and headed toward the stairs. "Let's get settled so you can sleep for a few hours."

"We really appreciate your help," Dax said.

Brutus led the way and jumped on Charlie's bed. He pawed at the already rumpled covers, bunching them up further, before plopping down in the center of the newly formed pile.

Charlie retrieved a stack of blankets from beneath the bed. "Sorry, guys, I have only one extra pillow."

"Thank you. We'll make do." Rose rubbed Charlie's arm. She accepted the items with what Dax would characterize as a forced smile. Her drooping body suggested that tonight's events had drained every ounce of energy from her.

"I'll give you two some privacy and set out some towels in the bathroom downstairs. Take your time." Charlie slapped her thigh once. "Come on, boy. These two need a moment." Brutus stubbornly kept his head glued to the mattress until Charlie issued a stern "Come." He forced himself up and jumped down with all the get-up-and-go of a sloth. Before she disappeared downstairs with him, Charlie said, "Crack the door open when you're ready for company."

"Will do." Dax moved some of Charlie's clothes from the floor and repositioned a small chair to clear an area for a temporary bed.

Rose moved slowly, meticulously laying out each blanket, one atop another. She took extra time to align the corners perfectly and smooth them as if doing so would make sleeping there more palatable. Dax understood Rose's underlying purpose; she did the same thing with her carpentry. Whenever things around her went haywire, she would pour herself into her work and focus on every little detail. The same was happening to Rose, which meant she was restoring order in her life.

Dax waited patiently for Rose to finish and change into the nightclothes she'd packed, not the ones she'd been wearing when Logan attacked her. Finally, she crawled between the blankets, settled onto her left side, and lay her head on the far edge of the pillow. "Lay with me." Rose's voice sounded as drained as she appeared.

Dax remained in her street clothes, slipped under the top blanket, and faced Rose. She touched the bump on Rose's forehead. It had gotten bigger and redder since leaving the Foster House. "Does it hurt?"

"I've been hurt worse." Rose's indirect response meant that it did.

"Remember the first time we sneaked into Neptune Beach in Alameda from the bay, and you slipped on the rocks?"

"How could I forget?" Rose said. "I had a knot on my forehead for weeks. But it was so worth it because that was the first time I saw you in your underclothes."

"I loved the little cotton rose accent sewn to the lowest part of your camisole collar. I couldn't take my eyes off it all day." Dax stroked the lump on Rose's brow again. "This bump looks as bad as the one you had that day." She kissed it. "I'm so sorry I hurt you."

"It was an accident. You were protecting me. I'm glad you showed up when you did." Rose had yet to say how far Logan had taken things before Dax broke a chair over his back. And, Dax had been patient, but she needed to know whether she should go back and finish the beating she'd started.

"Can you tell me what happened?" Dax softened her voice as much as she could.

Rose's eyes turned sad. "I couldn't sleep, so I thought I'd work on a new song Lester and I added last week. I checked on you first, but you were asleep."

"I wish I would have heard you." After the altercation with Wilkes and Logan, Dax was so tired that she'd gone straight to bed. Maybe if she'd gotten a few hours of sleep before the smuggler came, the way Charlie had, she would have woken when Rose had peeked inside her room and been there earlier.

"I didn't know he was there until I f-f-finished the song. He came o-o-onto the stage, smelling like w-w-whiskey."

Rose's stutter had returned. That meant she was even more upset than Dax had initially suspected. "He can't hurt you, Rose. I won't let him."

Rose nodded in a short rapid burst. "He grabbed and kissed me. I tried to get away and screamed, but he pushed me to the floor and covered my mouth. Then he…he…" Rose's voice trailed off.

"You'd said he didn't rape you, but did he touch you?" Rose gave another quick nod, breaking Dax's heart. She thanked her lucky stars that Rose had left her bedroom door open. When she'd heard a faint scream, instinctively she knew Rose was in trouble and where to find her—the place she felt most at home. She had flown down the stairs faster than ever. She hated to think what might have happened if the door hadn't been open. She would not have heard Rose's screams, Logan would have had his way with her, and Rose would have been broken for years.

"I'm so glad I heard you." Dax caressed Rose's beautiful brown hair, kicking herself for not following her instinct. She had known Logan was agitated following the confrontation with Wilkes but had done nothing to protect Rose from him. "I wish I could have been there sooner."

"But you got there." Rose ran a finger down Dax's cheek, love flowing from her touch. "You've been my protector since we were kids. I knew you'd save me." She knitted her brow, focusing on Dax's tender left eye. "You're bruised. What happened?"

"It's nothing. We had a run-in with Frankie tonight at the dock."

"Grace's plan must be working." Rose winced, tracing Dax's eye.

"It is. Now get some sleep. I need to check on May in a bit." Dax wrapped an arm around Rose and pulled her close until their bodies molded together. Rose trembled. Ragged breathing marked the coming of tears. Dax held her tighter, strengthening the dam she erected inside her. Her heart was wounded at having failed Rose. But this night was far from over, and she had to remain strong to get through it.

Rose's crying stopped within minutes, and her head became heavy on Dax's chest. Dax hated leaving her, but she didn't trust Logan in his state. He might take out his anger on May. Once she was sure Rose was in a deep sleep, she slid her arm out, eased Rose's head to the pillow, and covered her with the blanket.

Dax put on her jacket and hat, grabbed the tin of money, and descended the stairs to the main garage floor. Charlie had bundled up in her coat and fallen asleep in a chair. Brutus was sleeping at her feet but raised his head when Dax's foot landed on the concrete floor. His body wiggled enough to wake Charlie.

"Sorry to wake you, Charlie, but I'm going to check on May. Logan was pretty mad when I left him in the club."

Charlie bounced to her feet. "Do you want me to come with you?"

Dax placed a hand on Charlie's shoulder. "I need to know that Rose is safe. Can you stay with her?"

"Of course. I'll keep my eye on her."

"Thank you, Charlie. I don't know what I'd do without you." Dax gestured at her with the tin box. "This is our life's savings, including May's. Is it okay to stash it here for the time being?"

"Of course. It will be safe with me."

After hiding the box under the stairs behind the tire rack, Dax exited the garage, anger building with every step to her pickup. She twisted her hands around the steering wheel, every muscle tensed. Before this night was over, Logan would pay for what he had done.

CHAPTER TWENTY-FIVE

Charlie woke to an annoying growl from Brutus and a dark room. Noises bothered him most nights, and he alerted whenever the wind creaked the downstairs windows or sliding garage door. She had tried to break him of the habit years ago, but the more she chastised him, the more skittish he became. Finally, she had given up, and broken sleep had become the norm.

Concerned he would wake Rose on the floor, she nudged Brutus with her foot from beneath the blankets. "Hush, boy." Another growl earned him a second shove, and a third made him jump down. He walked around. Instead of curling up on his blanket in the corner, he went to the foot of the closed door. His growl grew louder and turned into a bark.

"What is it, boy?" Charlie came to a sitting position, her senses up. Brutus only barked when he felt threatened or smelled a person or an animal he wasn't familiar with.

Rose woke with a start, rising at the waist. "What is it? What's wrong?"

The sound of glass breaking downstairs sent Brutus back to the bed, cowering by Charlie's pillow. He was an excellent alert dog but was worthless when the situation required courage.

Charlie's stomach tightened hard as a rock. She would think hooligans were at it again if it were any other night. But she suspected foul play after the run-in she and Dax had with Wilkes and what Logan did to Rose. Unfortunately, the phone was in her office, so she would have to sneak downstairs to call for help.

"I'll check it out." She jumped from the bed and slipped on pants, shoes, and a shirt before rummaging through her rickety dresser. "If you hear a ruckus, hide in the closet. Use this if you have to." She handed Rose her father's five-inch buck knife, a weapon she could not bring herself to use. She'd already killed once and had sworn to herself to never do it again.

"You're scaring me." Rose trembled.

"After the night we've all had, I'm a little scared myself." Charlie grabbed the baseball bat leaning upright against the wall in the corner near the door. Not being willing to use a deadly weapon didn't mean she would not defend herself. "Lock the door after me."

Charlie twisted the knob and eased the door inward. The only illumination below came from the office desk lamp that signaled customers peeking through the glass on the side door that someone was in the building. She stepped onto the top landing and scanned the dark floor below. Nothing seemed out of the ordinary, so she tiptoed downward. When she was halfway down, a shadowy figure dressed in an overcoat and newsboy cap appeared at the bottom of the stairs. She halted, gripped her Louisville Slugger tighter, and drew it back.

"The garage is closed. I open at eight."

"I'm not here to get my car fixed." The voice sounded vaguely familiar. The man stepped upward. "I'm here for you." Four steps from Charlie, he stopped. His face took shape.

"I don't want any trouble, Frankie."

"The only reason you're still alive is that you didn't hold a gun to my head." Frankie rubbed his cut-up cheek and took another stride upward. "But I owe you for this."

Charlie moved backward, and again, with Frankie matching her step for step.

"I'm going to teach you a lesson in manners. Then I want you to send a message to Grace Parsons to stop this feud, or I'll burn down the damn town."

There were only three steps remaining. She needed a distraction, something to catch him by surprise before he got off the first punch. She lowered the bat, holding it by one hand halfway up the shaft, and yelled, "Get 'em, boy!"

Brutus barked uncontrollably and scratched wildly at the door. When Frankie paused, shifting his stare to the source of the racket, Charlie stabbed the bat in his gut with as much force as she could muster. Frankie teetered backward, his hands whirling fruitlessly in the air like a windup toy. He grabbed Charlie by the hand, and they both tumbled down the steps, bouncing off the wall, the railing, and the wall again. Each roll was a novel experience in pain—back, shoulder, leg, knee, head. Hitting the concrete floor, Charlie had no sense of up or down. It was a miracle that nothing felt broken. If she hadn't landed on top of Frankie, she was sure she would be in plaster casts for months.

After several consecutive thuds and bangs, Brutus barked and clawed at the door more frantically. Charlie had told Rose to hide if she heard a ruckus, but she'd spent years working in a kitchen and knew how to use a knife. She could not sit huddled in a dark closet without learning what had happened to her friend.

Rose held the knife in her right hand with a reverse grip like a well-trained soldier. She whipped the door open with her left. Brutus rushed out and thumped down the stairs at lightning speed. In seconds, he was at the bottom landing, barking at a lumpy pile. Rose wasn't far behind in her nightgown. Halfway down, the mystery of the lump became clear to her. Charlie was lying atop Frankie Wilkes following an apparent horrid fall down the stairs.

Brutus stopped barking when Charlie groaned and rolled to the concrete floor, then commenced the wildest lick fest from dog to owner she'd seen. Rose rushed to her. "My God, Charlie. Did you break anything?"

Charlie brought a hand to her head delicately. "I don't think so, but everything hurts."

Rose was relieved. She placed the knife on the floor and helped Charlie to her feet, steadying her when she briefly wobbled. After guiding her to a metal chair in front of her office a few steps away, she inspected her injuries. Other than a lump on the head, she looked unhurt, but the room was too dark to confirm her findings.

"Where's the light switch for in here?"

"Base of the stairs."

Rose scurried over and flipped on the lights. Several bulbs strung from the ceiling came to life. So did Frankie Wilkes. He moaned and rolled on the floor, cradling his left arm with his right hand. Propping himself up to his butt, he focused on something on the floor. The knife! It was within Frankie's reach. She dashed toward it, snatched it in one swift move, and switched to a forward grip, ready to defend herself.

"You best get out of here before I dice you into today's entrée." Rose got a good look at Frankie. He looked nothing like the dapper man who walked into Ida's Café five years ago full of promise and optimism, hiring her on a whim. That man was gone, replaced by a worn-out, bitter person surrounded by a cloud of evil.

"I think my damn arm is broken." He grimaced.

"It serves you right, coming here to beat up a woman. If you can walk, I suggest you leave before I run this buck knife through you."

Frankie crawled to the stairs and used the nearby wall as a prop to get himself to his feet. He spun around. Rose expected a fight, and she was prepared to give it to him. She crouched, flipped the knife to her left hand, and returned it to her right. She was ready to counter any move he might make, but he appeared groggy and exhausted.

"You've won this time." Fire returned to Frankie's eyes. "But you haven't heard the last of me." He limped out the side door and disappeared into the darkness, leaving a chill in the air. Experience with him had taught Rose one thing: he would not stop until he was back on top, no matter what it took.

Rose closed the door behind him, noting its broken window and the breaking sunlight that was painting the coastal mountains in deep orange and purple. She returned to Charlie. "I knew Frankie had a run-in with Dax, but why is he so angry with you?"

"I got in a good lick. Then Logan showed up and pulled a gun on him."

"Logan and Frankie are cut from the same cloth." Rose was tired of powerful men and their greed. She tried to shake the bitter taste from her mouth. "Everything that happened tonight was for whiskey and money."

"I won't disagree with you." Charlie pushed herself from the chair but instantly faltered. Rose supported her by the elbow. "Whoa. There are two of you."

"You probably have a concussion or maybe a cracked skull." Rose helped her back to the chair. "We need to get you to the doctor."

Charlie shook her head gently left and right. "I'm not a fan of Doc Hughes. Let's get Jules."

"If we call the boarding house this early, we'll get Jules in trouble. The only one who can call without Mrs. Prescott throwing a fit is Doc Hughes. But I know where she hides a key. I can sneak in and wake Jules."

This posed a dilemma. She needed to get to the far side of town, two miles away. It would take too much time to walk there. Charlie was in no shape to drive, though, and Rose had never driven a car in her life. That left her with only one option that didn't involve scaring the daylights out of her and Charlie. "I'll be right back."

Rose went into Charlie's office and lifted the phone in one hand and the receiver in the other, clicking the hook several times. Following a polite operator greeting, Rose said, "Good morning, Holly. This is Rose. Can you connect me to the Foster House?"

"I can try, Rose, but they have their hands full over there. The sheriff and Doc Hughes were called there for a shooting."

"A shooting?" Rose stopped breathing. She didn't make out what else Holly had said beyond the word Dax. This awful night had turned into her worst nightmare. The love of her life could be hurt, dying, or dead while she was on the other side of town dealing with Frankie Wilkes's bruised ego.

She dropped the phone on the desk without hanging up and darted to Charlie. "We have to go. There's been a shooting at the Foster House. It could be bad. Doc Hughes was called."

"Who was shot?" Charlie asked.

"I don't know. Where are your keys?"

"In my top desk drawer." Charlie inspected Rose up and down. "But I think we're underdressed."

Rose had forgotten about her nightgown. "I'll be right back."

Once they were appropriately dressed, Rose fed Brutus and locked him inside the garage, then helped Charlie to the truck's passenger seat. She jumped into the driver's seat and gripped the wheel. "What do I do?"

"Have you driven before?"

"Never."

"I'll drive." Charlie reached for the door handle.

"You're seeing double. Tell me what to do, dammit." Rose didn't have the patience to argue. She inserted the key.

"I'd rather walk than take a chance you wrecking my truck. You can help me steer. Now let me in the driver's seat."

Rose let out a loud, nasally breath. "Fine." She jumped out and dashed past the front of the truck while Charlie slid over into the driver's seat. Once seated again, she gave Charlie a dry smile.

"Make sure we don't hit anything." Charlie started the engine, engaged the gear, and put the truck in motion, keeping a tight grip on the wheel. Under any other circumstance, Rose would be scared witless to let someone with double vision drive her across town, but time was of the essence. She tucked her fear aside and issued instructions, telling her to steer a little left or right and when to slow and stop for the three traffic signs on their route. Meanwhile, worst-case scenarios played in her head, each ending in a gut-wrenching fate—Dax lying dead on the floor.

When they turned onto the main highway, the Foster House was a block away. The sun had risen enough for her to see that Doc Hughes's vehicle was parked near the entrance. The county sheriff wasn't there yet, though. Half Moon Bay didn't have its own police force; it was just patrolled every few days by deputies venturing over the coastal mountains from the east.

"Slow, slow, slow, and stop," Rose said, guiding Charlie to park the truck.

"We make a good—"

Before Charlie could finish her sentence, Rose yanked the truck door open and dashed to the front door. She skidded to a halt, coming face-to-face with her worst nightmare. Her heart stopped beating at the possibility of never being whole again. A lifeless body lay at her feet, covered with woolen blankets from head to toe. Actually, a shroud looked big enough to cover two people. Was Logan under there too? She could not gasp, could not even breathe. Paralyzed, she could not reach out to confirm her greatest fear. Tears formed and fell.

Doc Hughes emerged from deep inside the main dining room, carrying his physician's bag. His expression was unreadable.

Rose dug deep, trying desperately to not fall apart. "Doc?"

"It's a shame what happened here tonight. Jules said you're a friend of May's, living upstairs." Hughes paused at Rose's numb, shock-filled nod. Charlie caught up and buoyed her with an arm to the small of her back. "May was nearly catatonic, so I gave her a sedative to help her sleep for a few hours. Jules will watch over her, but you should be there when she wakes."

Rose's mind caught up with what Hughes had said. May was alive, leaving only one other person Logan could have shot. Her legs went weak.

"Who—?" Charlie paused her question when the doctor's attention drifted to new street-side activity.

"If you'll excuse me, the sheriff is here." Doc Hughes sidestepped the body as if it were nothing but a nasty puddle full of muck that might dirty his beautiful new wingtips. He didn't seem to care that only hours ago the body was full of love and the brightest part of Rose's life.

Rose had always thought that when a person lost a spouse they loved more than life itself, the one left behind would tremble so much they'd crumble into a thousand pieces. But she was frozen and could only do what she was told, letting tears lead the way.

"Just breathe," Charlie said. Rose did, but the air was stale from the ugly cloud of death. "Let's get you inside." She nudged Rose over the threshold. Her legs moved, but she didn't feel like she controlled them. Somehow the powerful force that was crushing her soul out of existence was moving her forward.

Tears clouded her vision, making it seem like she was seeing the room through the concave bottom of a soda bottle. Every object shimmered in Rose's river of grief. Two questions rocked her. How was she supposed to live without the other half of her heart? And, how was May supposed to survive without her sister, the person who had made living with a disability possible?

Wobbling a bit, Charlie guided her toward the kitchen and the door that had swung open a hundred times a day while she helped May as her second cook. And each time it did, she had glanced in its direction, hoping Dax would walk through to caress her with a smile.

That would never happen again. The door into heaven would separate them until Rose took her final breath.

Charlie pushed the door open with one hand, encouraging Rose to enter first, but she hesitated. Seeing Jules hovering over May in her bed would make the unfathomable real.

"It's all right, Rose. Jules and May would want to see you."

Rose willed herself to keep moving. If she didn't, she feared she would never move again. She took one step and another to the threshold, her legs as heavy as anvils. What she saw in the kitchen nearly made her faint. Her heart beat so fast that she had to clutch Charlie's arm to keep from tumbling to the floor.

Then…

A firm hand lifted Rose into her arms. "Are you okay?"

Rose flung her arms over Dax's shoulders and hugged her so tightly she might have broken a rib. Surprisingly, relief made her tremble, not grief. "I thought you were dead."

"No, it was Logan." Dax pried Rose's hold loose. "May said she heard a gunshot and found him on the ground."

Rose's heart still thumped her reprieve. "If neither of you shot him, who did?"

"We're not sure, but my guess is Frankie Wilkes."

"If Logan was shot in the last twenty minutes, it couldn't have been him," Charlie said. "He broke into my garage to give me a beatdown for last night and send Grace a message to stop the feud."

She staggered briefly, but Dax caught her. "Whoa. Did he hurt you?"

"We tumbled down the stairs. I cracked my head, and he broke his arm," Charlie said. "Before he left, he sent a warning for Grace to stop this feud or he'll burn the town down."

"It will never get that far." Dax patted Charlie's hand before shouting over her shoulder, "Jules, Charlie hit her head."

Jules charged from May's room to Charlie's side. Her eyebrows drew together. A well-trained nurse with a year of medical school, she could turn off emotion and focus on the needs of her patient, no matter how gruesome they were. That applied to everyone but Charlie. Jules agonized about her if she even got a splinter. "What happened, baby?"

"She rolled down the stairs," Rose said. "Luckily, Frankie Wilkes broke her fall."

"Lord, woman. You could have broken your neck." Jules sat Charlie on a stool and examined her head meticulously with her hands. "I don't think you cracked your skull. Follow my finger." She pointed an index finger straight up and moved it left and right and up and down. "But I bet your vision is a little fuzzy. Am I right?"

"I was seeing double a bit ago, but it's getting better," Charlie said.

"Your pupils are dilated, so I think you have a concussion again. If you're not careful, you could end up with brain damage. So it's bed rest for a day with me waking you up every hour for the next twelve hours."

"Then you two need to stay here," Dax said. "I'll fix up a room for you two with some clean sheets."

"That can wait," Rose said, splitting her attention between Dax and Jules. "You two need to tell us what happened here tonight."

Dax rubbed the back of her neck. "It was like this…"

CHAPTER TWENTY-SIX

An hour earlier

As Dax approached the Foster House, torn between her anguish about what had happened to Rose and her fears about what might be happening to her sister, the street was empty save for the figure of someone walking the sidewalk toward the Seaside Hotel, a block away. Likely one of the few employees Wilkes had left, Dax decided, and reporting for the early shift. The night guard wasn't standing watch at the restaurant, but she wasn't alarmed. Thomas sometimes went inside to use the bathroom or get a cup of coffee to warm his bones, leaving his post for a few minutes.

She made the left turn shy of the building, drove down the access road to the back, and parked in her designated spot next to Logan's car. She thought the "Reserved" sign was unnecessary but sometimes found it handy. However, the reason for it made her snicker. When Logan had returned from an errand late one Friday night, he discovered every parking spot was taken in front of his own house. So the next day, he posted a sign reserving a slot for the Foster House owner. Charlie later put up a second one for Dax.

Unlocking the back door, she walked inside. The overhead kitchen lights were still on there, and the room was silent. Two steps farther in, a chill shot up her spine. One of May's stools was lying on the floor. Then the rancid smell of vomit hit her nose. Both were unnerving. The foul puddle on the floor likely belonged to Logan, which meant he'd come upstairs. The stool could have been Logan's doing, too, toppled either by him tripping into it or, alarmingly, pushing May from it.

The quiet made the back of her neck tingle. She envisioned Logan coming upstairs drunk, fuming mad, and lashing out at the first thing in his path—May. But where was she? Dax considered calling out, but she was afraid of what it might mean if May didn't respond.

May's bedroom door was cracked open but not enough to see inside. Dax slowly inched it open, her heart thumping wildly at the thought of what she might find. As the door slid open, light from the kitchen spilled into the room, inch for inch. First, the upright dresser. Then the foot of the bed. Dax gulped. An inch more would reveal whether May was lying dead in her bed. The hinges squeaked as she continued to push.

The bed was empty.

The tension in Dax's shoulders instantly released to a breathy sigh. She pressed on toward the dining room, pressing her hand against the swinging door. The hinges whined as it opened. Slivers of light from the kitchen poured into the next room, casting a bright rectangle across the floor. Dax scanned the room. Everything looked in place, but the front door appeared to be wide open.

"May?" Dax called out, holding her breath for a response.

Several beats later, a woman's voice replied, "By the door."

Dax sprinted toward the front, weaving her way through the tables in the near darkness. She stopped as a horrible scene came into view near the entrance. May was sitting in a chair next to the open door, holding a pistol in her lap. Logan was lying across the threshold, motionless on his side, with a dark pool of thick liquid near his belly.

"May, what did you do?" Dax stood frozen, processing what she was seeing. So much had spun out of control tonight, all of it surrounding Logan.

"I heard a gunshot and found him like this."

"Where's Thomas? Did he do anything to help?"

"I don't know where he is."

Dax dashed through the door, sidestepping Logan. Looking up and down the street, she discovered a man lying on the sidewalk ten feet down to her right. The sheer size of him told her it had to be Thomas. She hurried to him but didn't see any signs of bleeding. She placed a hand in front of his nose and, feeling a weak exhale, shook him by his coat lapels. "Thomas, wake up."

She confirmed he was still breathing, but it was clear Thomas wasn't coming to any time soon and that she needed to get help fast. Her mind racing, she darted back to the door and placed a hand over Logan's nose. He was breathing. Barely.

"He's alive."

"I know." May's flat, unemotional response confused Dax. Where was her urgency?

"Did you already call for the doctor or an ambulance?"

"No, and I don't plan to."

"He'll die." Dax had no problem beating Logan for what he'd done but letting him die? Was that the right thing to do?

"After what he's turned into and what he did to Rose, I'm not lifting one finger to help him. But I won't stop you if you want to call a doctor to save his life."

Dax hurried to the phone and lifted the receiver, but her protective instinct overpowered her instinct to render aid. Logan had been the source of much of their misery. First, he'd abandoned Dax and May for months to fend for themselves, only to return when he had no other choice. His presence had turned Dax and Rose's idyllic life upside down. He'd stolen the whiskey barrel Dax was saving for a rainy day, his greed later causing a man's death in a traffic accident. Finally, his depravity had nearly resulted in Rose being violated in the worst possible way.

It all added up. Logan didn't deserve their help. Letting a man die wasn't the same as causing his death. Was it? Dax wasn't sure if the law would consider her and May killers, but if May was willing to take that chance, she was too.

Dax returned the phone to the counter and turned toward May. "Are you sure you want to do this?"

May locked eyes with Dax for the first time since she arrived. The conviction in them appeared strong as steel. "I've been sure of only two things in my life. Your devotion and this. Logan needs to die."

"Before I agree to this, I need you to tell me what happened."

"I was waiting at the center chopping block for my waste of a husband…"

* * *

May folded her arms over her chest like a schoolmarm, ready to scold an unruly student, when the basement door opened. A lecture was the last thing she wanted to give, but she needed to put Logan in his place.

When he stepped toward the door leading to the main dining room, May kicked a stool into his immediate path, causing him to trip. He tumbled to the linoleum floor, landing on his side, hitting his jaw. He rolled over and vomited up a putrid puddle of bile and whiskey.

"I'm ashamed that I once loved you enough to marry you. I considered divorcing you when I thought you were a lazy, drunken deadbeat, but I loved the life Dax and I had built at the Foster House. After what you did to Rose tonight, though, I'm done with you."

Logan picked himself up from the floor, wiped the corner of his mouth, and laughed. "Good riddance. I'll let Grace buy me out, and then I'm out of here."

May laughed. He had no idea who he'd gone into business with. "Grace Parsons won't let this stand, especially since she and Rose are special friends."

Logan rolled his eyes. "Of course, they are. Everyone involved with the Beacon Club is depraved. They're all freaks. I'm glad I kicked them out."

"Then I'm leaving too. I'll pack my things in the morning and find somewhere to stay until Grace Parsons deals with you."

"What do you mean deals with me?"

"A woman who can put together the swankiest speakeasy on the West Coast in a matter of months, arrange for more illegal liquor than this city has ever seen, and pay off every government official between here and Sacramento has power. Power like that means she's dangerous if you cross her. And you have."

"I'm dangerous too." Logan teetered, pulling out a pistol he'd stowed in his waistband. May flinched, unsure what he would do with it in his drunken state. But she relaxed when he waved it around, alternating the muzzle direction between the floor and ceiling. "If she comes after me, I'll put a bullet in her."

"Put that thing down before it goes off." May tapped a finger on the chopping block, identifying where she expected him to place it. "You might shoot yourself or me." He returned his pistol to his waistband, but May put up her hand in a stopping motion. "Oh no, you don't. You're too drunk to handle a gun. You can get it when you're sober."

Who was he kidding? The gun was his father's, not his. If memory served May correctly, Logan had shot it exactly once years ago, in target practice, shortly after their wedding. He'd missed the soda bottle on the dock railing but had put a bullet-sized hole in his father's only fishing boat. His father never let him handle it again. Logan could not hit what he was aiming at sober, much less in his current state.

"Fine." He slammed it on the chopping block. "I'll deal with her later."

* * *

"Logan went out to the dining room," May said, "and a few minutes later I heard a shot. You came a few minutes later."

"All right. I'll check on Thomas again. If he's okay, I won't call for the doc. At least it's Tuesday, and the restaurant is closed. The sun will be up in a bit, and the town will start waking up. We'll wait for Logan to pass to call the sheriff."

Dax thought of Rose, but she was safe with Charlie. Her primary worry at the moment was her sister. She gestured her chin toward May's lap. "Is that Logan's gun?"

May nodded slowly. "He threatened to use it against Grace if she came after him for what he did to Rose."

"Let me have it. I'll hide it before the sheriff comes." Dax stuffed the pistol in her coat pocket. "Keep an eye on him. I'll be right back."

Dax returned to the street. Thomas had moved and was sitting propped against the Foster House storefront with a palm pressed against his head. He appeared dazed but otherwise unhurt. "Are you okay, Thomas? What happened?"

"I'll be all right. Someone hit me over the back of the head. Is May okay?" Thomas's lack of concern for Logan's well-being was very telling. No one liked him.

"She's fine. Can you get up and walk?" She could not lift him if he could not right himself.

"I think so." Thomas pushed himself up gingerly, with Dax at the ready to steady him. Before she guided him inside, she considered what to tell him about what was waiting for them in the doorway.

"Thomas, I need to tell you something, but before I do, I need to ask that you keep it to yourself. Can you do that?"

"I'll do anything you need. You and May have been very good to me."

"Thank you, Thomas. Logan was shot in the belly and is bleeding out. I'm assuming by whoever hit you over the head. We have yet to call the doctor and the police. Do you understand what I'm saying?"

"I wouldn't lift a finger to help that pill either."

"May said the same thing." When Thomas teetered, Dax pulled him upright. "So you're okay with this?"

"It couldn't have happened to a better guy."

"Let's get you inside." Dax guided Thomas to the Foster House front door and past Logan's dying body. She pulled out a chair at the nearest table for Thomas to sit in. "I'll get you some water and a wet towel for that bump on your noggin."

Dax went to the kitchen to retrieve the promised items. While wetting the towel, she thought about what to do with Logan's gun. She wanted to believe May's story that she found Logan shot. It made sense, what with Thomas being knocked out, but her gut told her May might have pulled the trigger herself. Coming up with a story and sticking to it was imperative, but Dax wasn't about to take any chances. She ran out the kitchen door and down the newly built gangway to the end of the dock. Standing at the railing, she threw the gun into the water, hoping Half Moon Bay would forever keep May's secret.

Dax returned to the kitchen and brought Thomas the water and wet towel. "Thank you," he said. "I think you better check on Logan. He hasn't gurgled since you left."

"Thanks, Thomas." Dax patted him on the shoulder before standing at Logan's side, careful not to disturb the pooled blood. She held her hand over his nostrils but felt no sign of breathing. She pressed a hand on his chest. He was lifeless. One part of their nightmare had ended. The only one left to deal with was Frankie Wilkes.

"He's dead," Dax announced. "When the police arrive, we all tell the truth but leave out the part about waiting. Are we in agreement?" At May's and Thomas's firm nods, she went to the counter and lifted the candlestick phone. She clicked the handle three times and waited for the operator to respond.

"How may I direct your call?"

"Holly, this is Dax. There's been a shooting at the Foster House. We'll need Doc Hughes and the sheriff." When Dax returned the earpiece to its holder, headlights appeared on the street. They slowed before crossing in front of the Foster House. Fearing whoever did this had come back for more, she suddenly regretted tossing out Logan's gun.

CHAPTER TWENTY-SEVEN

Rose knelt at the threshold next to the blanket-covered mound. The congealed dark-red puddle soaked her knees but failed to faze her. Minutes ago, that blood had flowed through Dax's veins, vibrantly blushing her cheeks, warming her smile, and filling the heart that had belonged to Rose for a decade. But that heart was now still. It would never again pulse to the rhythm of love that had given Rose and Dax purpose.

Rose dragged back the blanket, exposing the lifeless body on the cold ground. Dax appeared to be sleeping, not dead as the doctor had proclaimed. He'd shown her the blood and the gun and had said there was nothing he could do. So Rose had said nothing. She didn't tell him that the bullet that had gone through Dax had also hit her. That it was killing her too. She would rather join the stillness than exist with emptiness.

She didn't cry or tremble. The pain of grief would be short-lived. She would soon join her other half. But first, a kiss. "It's all right. I'll soon be with you." Rose ran a fingertip across Dax's lips. They were cold and unresponsive, the polar opposite of what they had been during their goodbye kiss an hour ago.

Rose leaned in, pressing their lips together for the last time in this world. It would not be long now. Blood had drained from her more slowly than was merciful, but she was nearing empty. She lay beside Dax, placing her head on the stilled chest. It didn't rise and fall to the rhythmic intake and expression of air. She pulled a lifeless arm around her midsection, holding it down with her last ounce of energy. But the once strong and comforting arm failed to convey the reassuring message that Dax would always protect her. How could it? Dax had died keeping that promise.

She was almost there. Rose closed her eyes and took one last breath into the darkness.

Gentle shaking brought back the light. Rose took a gasping breath, feeling as if she'd just surfaced from a watery grave. She opened her eyes to the bright room, the weight of dreamed grief still holding her down.

"Are you okay? You were wheezing." Dax tightened an arm around her.

"I had a bad dream." The nightmare's fog had lifted, but the sense of dread hadn't. They were in bed. Entwining their legs and pulling Dax into a firm embrace, Rose felt warmth and the reassuring pulse of life touching every inch of her. The lifeblood pumping through Dax was as strong as the day they first kissed and gave one another their hearts.

Dax pulled back. "What about?"

"It was horrible." Rose shivered. The grief from her dream still chilled her to the bone.

"Was it about Logan?" The pain in Dax's eyes said she still blamed herself for not getting there sooner.

"No. It was about you. I dreamed you'd been shot protecting me and died at the front door. I was shot too and lay down next to you to die in your arms."

"I'll always protect you," Dax whispered, pressing their bodies together again.

"I know you will." Having their bodies molded together was all Rose needed to know it was true.

Dax rocked her hips in a slow, predictable pattern, sparking the first hint of desire. Rose matched her movement, fanning the spark into a flame. Lips collided, but unlike in her dream, Dax's were infused with heat. Pushing nightclothes out of the way, they drove a hand to each other's center. Unlike when Logan had violated her, this touch was wanted and invited. It meant Dax was alive, and that horrible man was dead. And soon the contact sent Rose tumbling into ecstasy, with Dax following her soon after.

Moments later, as Rose was lying quietly in Dax's arms again, Jules and Charlie's muffled voices in the next bedroom broke the silence. She could not make out most of what they were saying, but Charlie was clearly upset. Perhaps she'd had enough of Jules waking her every hour to check her pupils and pain and simply wanted to sleep.

"Since they're up, we should check on May again," Dax said. "Then we all need to talk about when to reopen and what to do about Frankie Wilkes."

Rose and Dax dressed and let Jules and Charlie know they were up and heading downstairs. Once on the main floor, Rose stopped and stared at the front door. The pool of blood was gone, but knowing it had been there reassured her that Logan would never hurt her or torture Dax and May again with his selfish greed.

Dax wrapped her arms around Rose from behind, resting her chin on a shoulder. "I'm so sorry you thought I was dead."

Rose took strength from Dax's embrace. "I'd never felt more empty."

"May felt the opposite. She was relieved when Logan died."

"Then why did Doc Hughes give her a sedative?" Rose asked.

"The doc assumed she was a grieving widow, but she was upset over what he did to you. We didn't want him asking questions about his death, so we didn't correct him. He stuck a needle in her arm, and the next thing I know, she was out."

"At least May got some sleep." Rose recognized the familiar scent quickly filling the dining room. "I smell bacon. She must be up."

Stepping into the kitchen, Rose walked straight to May at the stove. She spun her around and pulled her into a tight hug.

May's nightmare was finally over, and she had Dax and Rose to look after her. "This will be a new beginning," Rose said before releasing her hold.

"It was long overdue." May's expression grew long. "I'm sorry it wasn't soon enough for you. I feel responsible because I brought him into our lives."

"You have nothing to be sorry for. If you hadn't married Logan, you would have never come to Half Moon Bay, and I would have never reunited with Dax. So I have you to thank for bringing her back to me."

"Let's make a pact." May glanced between Rose and Dax. "Once we bury that man, we never speak of him again."

"Deal," Rose and Dax said simultaneously.

The door to the dining room swung open, and Jules and Charlie stepped through. "Good morning, May. How are you feeling?" Jules asked.

"Like I'm ready to start my new life," May said. "How about you, Charlie? How's your noggin? Jules told me what happened when she checked on me earler. I'm glad you're all right."

"Much better," Charlie said. "But I need to head back to take care of Brutus."

"I bet you two are hungry. If Rose gives me a hand, we can have breakfast ready lickety-split."

"Happy to help," Rose said. Then, as if they'd rewound the clock and Logan had never been there, she and May worked seamlessly to prepare and plate the food. *Just like old times*, she thought.

They gathered at the center table in the main dining room and ate. A few words passed about how they slept before Dax dove into the weighty topic lingering in the room. "We need to talk about last night. I think we're all in agreement that Frankie Wilkes shot Logan or had him shot. The question is: What do we do about it?"

Clearly upset, Charlie lowered and shook her head. "We're in way over our heads." Jules lovingly rubbed her back.

"Last night proved that one guard isn't enough at night when the club is closed," Dax said. "We'll need two."

"I want security around the clock," May said. "My customers need to be safe during the day too."

"Agreed." Dax was sure Grace would provide an army if that was what was needed to keep Rose safe.

"You're fooling yourselves if you think a few men will deter Frankie Wilkes," Charlie said. "You didn't see the fire in his eyes last night. He's at the end of his rope. Shooting Logan proves it. Plus, someone must have been with him. There was no way he could have operated the brake lever in his car with a busted left arm. We're going to need many more to stop him."

"Then we better get the ball rolling." Dax went to the cash register, pulled a folded piece of paper from her front pants pocket, and picked up the phone and mouthpiece. "Holly, I need to make a long-distance call to Hollywood." The call connected.

Following Dax's recounting of the night's events, Grace said, "Thank you for the call, Dax. I suspected something was awry when Captain Burch called me early this morning. He said that Frankie had suggested we'd become a bad risk. That we weren't doing our part to keep the Prohibition agents happy and the barrels his crew were unloading at the marina were likely to get confiscated."

"He's grasping at straws," Dax said.

"I realize that now. Tell Thomas and Jared they're both on duty until we arrive with reinforcements and that I'll compensate them well for their loyalty." Grace bit back her seething anger. She'd decided nothing short of bankruptcy would sufficiently punish Wilkes. If Rose had been the one to answer the door at the Foster House last night, she would be dead.

"When will that be?" Dax asked.

"I can have six men up there by midnight, though I don't recommend opening the restaurant until I arrive. I need to bring in a specialist, which might take longer to round up." Grace considered the logistics of protecting both the Foster House and Charlie in her garage. She would need many more men if she had to split her resources. "And one more thing. How amenable would Charlie be to staying with you until this is over? I don't think I can adequately secure both locations."

"I'm sure I can convince her to stay."

"Dax..." Grace paused, searching for the right words to take responsibility for the untenable situation she'd put everyone in. "Everyone's safety is my highest priority. I'll make sure Frankie Wilkes won't get close to any of you again. If he tries, he'll die doing so."

"You need to protect Rose at all costs." Dax's plea confirmed one thing. They both loved Rose more than life itself.

"And I will. You have my oath on it."

Grace disconnected the call, mad at herself and at Frankie. Both had been equally arrogant, but she was more determined. Frankie was protecting his legacy of money and power, but Grace was protecting the love of her life—the most powerful motivation in history. She would bring to bear every weapon on Earth to safeguard her sweet Rose.

Clive finished his ministrations at the corner bar and walked across the drawing room, carrying two martini glasses. He handed one to Grace, which she gladly accepted. She needed to numb her wrath before it spun out of control. The last time she failed to keep it in check, she'd dug the hole now engulfing her. She downed the cocktail in four consecutive gulps.

"What has Frankie done now, my sweet?" Clive asked.

"It wasn't enough for him to make trouble between Captain Burch and us. He killed Logan Foster. That works to my advantage in the big scheme of things, but he also attacked Charlene Dawson—with Rose right upstairs! He told her to tell me to end this feud, or he'll burn down the entire town. That means Jason is at risk."

"He's declared war." Clive's eyes turned steely black seconds before the martini glass in his hand cracked into pieces. "It's time that slacker got a taste of what he missed out on during the real war."

"Dax said he has help." Grace inspected Clive's hand, though she expected to find not a single drop of blood. His hands were too calloused from his gardening hobby to be cut by fine shards. Spending hours of solitude with his flowers had, thankfully, provided him moments of peace. "It's time to enlist Hank."

"You'll have to ask. He'll only do it for you."

"We have no choice." Grace squeezed her husband's strong, steady hand. "Will you come with me?"

"Of course, my sweet."

After arranging for six well-armed men to drive all afternoon and evening to Half Moon Bay, Grace led the way to the sunroom. Years ago, she'd converted it into a studio for Clive's cousin. His recovery from the horrors of war rested on having a daily creative outlet, especially following the death of his wife. Hank O'Keefe had experienced enough sadness and depravity for ten lifetimes. And Grace was about to ask him to face more. She knew this might destroy his progress, but she was out of options and time.

No one, she knew, would ever suspect that the gentle-looking man sitting at the easel was capable of unspeakable violence, but that was what made him lethal. Not tall or broad-shouldered, Hank was creating a colorful abstract landscape of blues, greens, and yellows from his memory of the last trip he took to the ocean with his late wife. This one was beautiful, but his first attempts at painting years ago had been rudimentary. But after his sister stayed for a month and taught him proper technique, his creations had taken on a vibrancy worthy of a showing at the Met.

"Georgia would be proud," Grace said. "Your brushstrokes are impeccable."

Hank cocked his head, inspecting his painting more intently. "I still can't capture depth like she can."

"You're just as gifted. Your sister has been painting for twenty-five years. Give it time. You'll catch up." She rested a hand on Hank's shoulder. "Do you have a moment to talk? I have something to ask of you."

She phrased her words carefully. Six years ago, she'd paid off the Los Angeles District Attorney to lose a particular police report, one detailing how Hank choked the life out of the drunkard who had mowed down his wife in the middle of the street. Grace moved him into the mansion that day. When he asked how he could repay her, she said, "One day I will ask something of you. I hope you will find the strength to carry it through when I do."

"I pledge my life that I will do as you ask," he'd said.

Hank put down his paintbrush and slowly turned to face her. "I've been waiting for this day. Now I can finally repay your kindness."

"You might not think me kind after I give you your task."

"I gather you need special skills beyond my scribblings on canvas."

"I do. The people Clive and I love are in danger."

"Then all the more reason to keep my promise." Hank wiped his hands with a clean towel as if they were already dirty from Grace's coming request. A look of determination filled his eyes. "Tell me what needs doing."

CHAPTER TWENTY-EIGHT

Grace sensed their car slowing. The timing seemed right, so she opened her eyes to the darkened cabin and pushed herself upright from her sleeping position on the back bench. They'd taken their rarely used Cadillac Town Sedan instead of her preferred Roadster because Frankie Wilkes would not recognize it. This was the first time she'd ridden in the back seat, and to her surprise, it was a comfortable ride. She'd used her overnight carpetbag as a pillow and Clive's overcoat as a blanket to sleep most of the seven hours from Hollywood to Half Moon Bay. Hank, having tossed his bags into the trunk attached to the sedan's back, his rifle case was the only item she had to maneuver around. It contained everything he needed to keep his promise.

Approaching the first set of buildings in the marina area, Clive slowed again to turn onto the access road to the back of the Foster House. Hank waved him off. "Drive past the hotel. I want to scout."

Clive acknowledged the request with a nod and continued down the street. "The Foster House is the only high ground we'll have access to, but it's on the same side of the street as the hotel." He gestured toward a row of shops on the east side of the road across from the Foster House. The storefronts faced west. "The glare at sunset on those windows is brutal."

"That would be perfect if I have to do this during the daytime," Hank said.

"Every business on this stretch belongs to Wilkes," Grace said. "Soon, though, they will be mine." Her claim wasn't bravado but confidence in Hank's abilities to end this war. But before he could take his shot, she needed to set the stage. "We should get going. I have a meeting tonight, and we have to be in San Mateo before sunrise."

"Of course, my sweet." Clive flipped the car around. One guard waved them forward when they reached the access road to the back. Another trained his shotgun on them until he clearly recognized Clive. A third man stood watch at the other end of the building—an obvious chokepoint between the business next door and the dock. "I'll double-check the posts and make sure the men are positioned correctly."

"Thank you, dear." Grace trusted Clive and Hank to set up security. As former Army snipers, they were well trained to spot weakness in every type of defensive line. Unless the guards were overwhelmed by sheer numbers, the Foster House would be impenetrable.

Once they parked, Dax let them in. Everyone except the men standing guard assembled in the main dining room with coffee and dessert prepared by May. Grace first approached May with two open arms. "It's safe to assume your loss is welcomed, but I'm sorry for what you went through."

"We're all better off now that he's gone," May said, "but I'm worried about more violence."

"Which is why I'm here. I intend to put an end to this within a few days. In the meantime, I've brought enough men to keep everyone safe." Grace glanced at Rose standing next to Dax, letting her stare linger long past social graces. It teetered on longing, she feared.

May shifted her stare in that direction. "We need to keep both of them safe."

"That goes without question," Grace swore. "We should get down to business. I'm expecting visitors soon."

"Of course. Everyone," May said loud enough to command the room's attention, "Grace has something to say."

Rose, Dax, May, Charlie, Jules, Clive, Hank, the four off-duty security guards, and the town's most adorable bulldog formed a semicircle around Grace. She began. "Our feud with Frankie Wilkes has reached a flash point. We can no longer wait for his business to dry up, so I intend to force a speedy resolution."

"What do you mean, 'speedy resolution'?" The pronounced edge in Charlie's tone suggested she would not be agreeable to the details of Grace's plan if it included violence.

"The less you know, the better. I can say that Frankie Wilkes will never bother you again when this is done."

"I want nothing to do with whatever you have planned, Grace. There's already been too much killing." Charlie didn't have to explain. The guilt she still wore on her sleeve for her part in Riley King's death was evident to those who had been there.

"Then I suggest you and Jules stay upstairs and wait this out."

"We can't do that. We'll stay here when we're not working, but I have a garage to run, and Jules has a job."

"I can't force you to stay, but all I'm asking for is two days. Three at the most. Until I conclude this ugly business, I've brought in extra security." She gestured to her left. "This is Hank O'Keefe. He's well trained in security matters and will be in charge until Clive and I return."

"You're leaving us?" Rose clutched Dax's arm. The worry cutting through her voice was a sucker punch to Grace's gut on two levels. First, leaving meant exposing Rose to greater risk, but she had to lay the groundwork to protect Hank. Second, a part of Grace wished she was the one Rose clung to when fear gripped her. Grace wanted only happiness for Rose, though, and Dax could do that for her.

"It can't be helped. I have an important meeting that will make all of this possible. Also, if we hope to continue our business relationship with Captain Burch, I must meet with him Thursday night in San Francisco. He'll only be ashore for two hours." Grace's explanation did little to curb Rose's anxious expression. "We shouldn't be more than two days."

Dax turned to Rose, locking gazes with her. "Do you trust me?"

"Of course I do." Rose had a quizzical look.

"I won't leave your side. You'll be safe with me." Dax earned Rose's instant relief, convincing Grace that letting go of Rose was the right thing. She had never affected her that deeply. She swallowed the last bit of hope she'd had that Rose might change her mind and focused on their immediate dangers. "I think it best that only Hank knows of the plan. That way none of you can be implicated if anything goes wrong."

"With all due respect," May said, "this is our house. We have a right to know."

"I agree." Dax turned to her sister. "But I want to keep you and Rose out of this. So I'm going to ask you the same question, May. Do you trust me?"

"With my life."

"It's settled. I'll look after our interests." Dax turned her attention to Grace. "You keep me in the loop on everything." It was not a question.

Grace replied with a silent nod.

While Clive and Hank surveyed the building exterior and met with the on-duty guards, everyone else retired to their rooms. All but Dax, who kept Grace silent company in the dining room. Soon there was a knock on the back door. Dax rose and let in the two Prohibition agents assigned to the Half Moon Bay area, the same ones who had been in Frankie Wilkes's pocket for years. The ones whose loyalty followed the money.

Paxton did not look happy. "Couldn't this wait until a decent hour?"

"I wish it could." Grace gestured to a table and chairs in the center of the room, where a pot of hot coffee was waiting for them. "Please have a seat. I assume you heard what happened here last night."

"We heard from the sheriff that the slug bought it, and there were no witnesses."

"That is true, but we know Frankie Wilkes was behind it. He crossed a line and needs to pay the price. That is why I called you here tonight. I want him shut down."

"This is your war. Our part is to look the other way for whoever pays," Paxton said, shaking his head.

Grace slid an envelope across the table and asked him to read the letter inside. The letter of introduction, given to her months ago, had been meant as a last resort to get Grace out of trouble with the law, not entice them to do her bidding. But she was desperate and hoped the name below the signature would alone be enough to get her what she needed.

"Do you know the man who wrote this letter?"

"I wouldn't be a very good agent if I didn't know the name of the United States Attorney General."

Grace slid a second envelope across the table, this one with five thousand dollars. The money represented two years of salary for each agent. "I want you to raid the Seaside Club and detain Frankie Wilkes. You'll get the other half when it's done."

Paxton inspected the contents. "When do you want it done?"

"As soon as possible."

"It will take a few days to get the right number of agents here from the San Francisco field office, but I think we can do it on Friday."

"That's satisfactory, but I also need you to confiscate his vehicles and make sure he doesn't stay in the hotel for the night. I want him walking home. Do not release him until the streets are empty. Then get word to us here a half hour before you do."

"What for?" he asked.

"I'm paying you to do, not ask questions."

"Toss in another thousand, and you have a deal."

Grace detested graft, not from a moral perspective but from a practical one. Once a government official tasted how much their services were worth to the right people, they always wanted more. In her experience, these agents were particularly greedy, and she needed to make clear to them the power dynamic in this situation. "The name on that letter should tell you that my offer is sufficient. Otherwise, you might find yourselves working in Oklahoma next month." Grace handed him a folded piece of paper. "Call me at this number when resources are in place."

Paxton slipped the envelope into his inside suit breast pocket. "Expect my call on Friday."

Dax escorted the agents out and led Clive and Hank inside. "So what's the other half of the plan, Grace?" she asked, glancing at Hank with his rifle case slung over his shoulder. "How is Hank going to shoot Frankie?"

"You're very smart, Dax." Grace was never easily impressed, but Dax had astounded her from their first meeting. She was bold, telegraphing her intention to fight for Rose, and smart, not letting the relationship Grace and Rose once had shared to become a stumbling block. Jealousy would have bred doubt and mistrust. "Clive was the Army's number-two sniper in the Great War. Hank was number one with the most kills ever recorded. He can put a bullet in a man's eye from a hundred yards."

Dax eyed Hank up and down. Her appreciation was palpable.

"Wilkes is a smart man," Hank said. "The hotel is well guarded, and he likely won't leave it until he has to. So, a close-quarters kill is out of the question. Fortunately, the upper window here gives me the high ground. The Prohibition agents will flush him out and steer him to the street. That's when I'll take my shot."

"Once he's dead," Grace said, "I can file the agreement I signed with him in the probate court. My lawyer tells me it's ironclad. Ownership of his properties in Half Moon Bay will be transferred to me."

"Is that it?" Dax asked.

"No. Clive and I are driving to San Mateo tonight. I have a similar envelope to persuade the sheriff there to look the other way and write up Wilkes's murder as unsolved when it happens. After that, I'm off to smooth things over with Captain Burch."

Dax let out a deep, weighty sigh. "All right. I want this to be over."

"With a little luck and Hank's sure hand, it will be."

CHAPTER TWENTY-NINE

Dax shifted her back to ease a crick in her neck. She'd been sitting silently at the head of the bed, watching Rose sleep as the morning sun broke into the room. She'd missed spending this part of the day with her. On the nights when she'd stayed overnight, before Logan reappeared, Dax often woke before her and would sit or lay awake, studying the nuances of her body. She'd learned Rose was a side sleeper who often tossed and turned during the night.

Rose had rested a hand atop the pillow and cradled her head in its palm. The position painted her with the aura of innocence, almost childlike, bringing Dax back to when they first met. Dax had turned twelve, and Rose was still eleven. The playground at school was awash with kids running around during lunch recess, but the most beautiful thing Dax had ever seen stood alone in the playground corner, leaning against the fence. It took five days of standing near her, receiving the cutest smile for saying hello, before Rose replied with a hello of her own. The next day Dax socked a bully in the face for ridiculing Rose's stutter—and became Rose's sworn protector.

Frankie Wilkes was the latest bully in a long line of them, but he was the most dangerous. Neither the playground bullies nor Riley King had been armed with guns. Frankie had already proven he was ready to use one. Dax's skin prickled as she considered how much further he was willing to go. Would the team Grace had assembled be enough to repel a man who had nothing left to lose? No matter the case, Dax was prepared to lay down her life to protect the woman peacefully sleeping beside her.

Dax brushed Rose's hair back, exposing more of the face that had imprinted itself into her memory since that first hello. Rose had suffered too much pain and misery for someone her age. "I won't let anyone hurt you again," she whispered.

The floorboards outside Dax's room creaked, likely from the footsteps of someone staying upstairs. Charlie and Jules had taken Rose's room. The four off-duty guards were sleeping on cots in Logan's old room. Hank had insisted on taking the couch to be closer to his perch.

Having a house filled with armed men was both unnerving and comforting. Their presence was a glaring reminder of the threat Frankie posed, but it was also proof that Grace would do whatever it took to end this feud in their favor.

Unable to get back to sleep, Dax crawled out of bed, careful to not wake Rose. She dressed in her well-worn carpenter clothes of knickers, a man's flannel button-down shirt, and boots. The outfit was a far cry from the one she wore while managing the Beacon Club, but it was the one she was most comfortable in. Grace had insisted Dax and the men wear black suits with bow ties in the club and that the women wear black dresses decorated with gold fringe. Rose was the exception. She chose whatever struck her fancy when she performed. Dax's favorite was the red dress that highlighted her curves instead of hiding them.

She looked back at those curves peeking out from the covers before stepping into the hallway and closing the door quietly behind her. Diffused light from the east windows cast a yellow-golden glow in the living room. Hank was sitting on the couch, oiling and wiping down the components of a long rifle with a scope attached to the sights. He handled each part as if it were the world's finest crystal.

Dax sat in the chair across from the couch. She had a healthy respect for guns but didn't fear them. Other than Logan's firearm, she had never touched one. But considering the war that had now ensnared her, she needed to become more acquainted with them and the man who could teach her.

"Did the Army teach you to shoot?"

Hank continued cleaning his weapon without shifting his stare from it. "My pop taught me to shoot. The Army taught me to kill." The candid distinction conjured images of a sniper's work, staring through a telescopic scope, waiting for the right conditions to pull the trigger.

"How do you do it?"

"Do what?"

"Muster the courage to shoot someone."

"I don't think of them as human. They're a predator who would kill me if given a chance, so I think of it as sport. A challenge to hit a target in the bullseye." Hank stopped performing his task and studied Dax for a few beats with a penetrating stare as if he were sizing her up for a kill. "You and Rose are like Grace, aren't you?" His soft tone made Dax think his question was more curiosity than accusation. She answered with a slow nod. "It explains why she's so protective of you."

"How do you know Grace?"

"I'm Clive's cousin." Hank's eyes turned distant. "Grace took me in six years ago when I was at my lowest."

"Which explains why you're so protective of her." Dax sensed a painful story behind Grace's generosity, deepening Dax's respect for her.

"I owe her my life," Hank said.

"And now you're prepared to take a life for her."

"Wilkes is a predator who intends to kill Grace and the people she loves. I won't give him a chance. Once I get him in my crosshairs, he'll never be a threat again."

"Not that I don't trust your ability to get the job done," Dax said, "but could you teach me how to handle a gun? As much as you want to protect Grace, I want to protect Rose."

"Do you have a gun?" Hank asked.

"No, we don't." At least not any longer. Dax had been premature, perhaps, in tossing Logan's pistol into the marina at the first opportunity when she'd thought May's story about Logan's death might not stick.

Hank pushed himself from the couch and retrieved a suitcase from the corner of the room. He placed it on the coffee table and opened the lid, exposing a collection of at least a dozen handguns of various sizes and calibers. "Considering your business, we should train everyone in the house."

"Train us on what?" a voice said from the other end of the room. Dax turned her head in that direction. Charlie was dressed in her work clothes, ready for a day in her garage. Brutus lumbered by her side, step for step.

"Hank wants to teach us how to handle a gun," Dax said. Charlie's stiff body posture telegraphed her aversion to violence. "But I know you have to work today."

"So does Jules," Charlie said. "I don't want her anywhere near a gun, Dax."

Dax placed a hand on her friend's shoulder. "I won't mention it to Rose and May until you two leave."

"Thank you."

Moments later, the rest of the floor came to life. Rose and Jules took turns in the shower, and the off-duty guards filed downstairs to start the next twelve-hour shift securing the perimeter of the Foster House.

After Charlie, Jules, and Brutus retreated to the main floor, Rose stepped out of their room. Her jaw-dropping outfit brought Dax to a dead stop. Women's slacks, Dax's white button-down shirt, and the suspenders Rose had gifted her were the world's sexiest combination on her.

Dax remained silent while she came closer, enjoying the sway of her hips in those pants. Finally, she wrapped an arm around Rose's waist, pressing their bodies together. "Wow."

Rose pulled back and glanced in Hank's direction. He was studying the street from his seat at the window. "We shouldn't."

"Hank lives with Grace and Clive, so he knows the score."

"Still," Rose said.

"Grace is doing all this to create a safe place for us. Right now, right here, this room is a safe place." Dax pulled her closer again. "You look amazing in those suspenders."

Rose draped her arms over Dax's shoulders, lowering her voice. "Now you know what I go through every time you wear them." She pressed their lips together in a brief yet fiery kiss. When they pulled apart, a glance confirmed Hank still had his attention glued to the street below.

"Hank." Dax waited for him to turn his head in her direction. "Breakfast should be ready."

"I'll be down when everyone is done. I'm not good company." Hank's reticence strengthened Dax's earlier theory. He was a lost man, and Grace was helping him find his way again.

"Suit yourself," she said.

After both guard shifts ate and the day shift assumed their posts, the night shift took over the bed and cots. Charlie and Jules left for work, leaving May, Dax, and Rose in the kitchen for cleanup.

"It's strange being closed on a Thursday," May said, cleaning the grill.

Before Dax or Rose could respond, Hank entered the kitchen through the swinging door, carrying the suitcase of guns. He placed it on the floor next to the door.

"If all goes right, ma'am," Hank said, "you'll be open on Saturday."

"I hope so." May gestured the scraper toward the counter with the warming lamps. "I saved you a plate, Hank. And it's May, not ma'am."

"Thank you, May." Hank grabbed his plate and headed toward the door.

"Please stay," Dax said. "I've talked to Rose and May, and after breakfast, the three of us would like to learn how to use a gun." Considering Logan's attack, she had expected Rose to be receptive to the idea. However, May's eagerness had been a surprise. Logan's shooting must have frightened her more than Dax suspected.

"I brought my inventory." Hank cast his chin toward his suitcase.

"Later." May pointed her tool at the center chopping block and an empty stool. "Eat first."

"Yes, ma'am." When May gave Hank the side-eye, he corrected himself. "Yes, May."

While Dax dried the last of the dishes, Rose stored the containers of ingredients in the pantry and on the spice shelf. May finished her task in two more passes, hung up her scraper, and brought Hank a glass of orange juice and coffee. She joined him, sitting at the stool to his right, propping her injured leg on the produce crate positioned there for that purpose.

"If you don't mind me asking"—Hank pointed his fork toward May's leg—"what happened?"

"A careless driver ran a traffic sign." May patted her leg. "It's been, what? Five years, Dax?"

Still ashamed about her role in the accident that crippled May, Dax turned her back to her sister. "Yes, five." Logically, she knew the other driver was at fault. However, she could not help but think May would be whole if she had been more attentive that day. Rose came to her side and stroked her back between the shoulder blades. Dax instantly drew strength from the tacit support. "Thank you," she whispered.

Hank finished his meal, wiped his mouth with a paper napkin, and laid it on the plate. "Let me see your arms and hands, ladies."

"What for?" May asked.

"To pick the right weapon for you. The size of your hands and strength of your arms will be the determining factors."

Dax was first. He inspected her biceps and palms before asking her to squeeze his hands. "My, you're strong."

"I'm a carpenter."

"That explains the strong grip. The Army-modified Colt M1911 for you. A single .45 can take out a bear, and I'm betting you can handle the recoil." He moved on to Rose.

"I'm a singer, so don't expect much," she said.

Hank harrumphed. His expression was unreadable. "You're stronger than you think, but you have little hands. A Detective Special for you. It's half the weight, two inches shorter, and has much less recoil than the Colt."

Hank finally made his way to May. Inspecting her hand, he asked, "You're the widow?"

"Technically, yes, but I haven't considered myself married for some time. My husband turned into a dreadful man after the accident."

Hank let a half-cocked smile form before asking, "Was he driving?"

"No, but he'd made it abundantly clear that he didn't sign up for a crippled wife. He kept me around to cook and clean."

He flipped her hands over to inspect the palms. "It's a shame. A woman like you shouldn't have callouses." He held onto her hands longer than the others, eliciting something Dax had rarely seen—a blush on May. "I think you could handle the Colt Police Positive. It has a longer barrel than the Detective Special but is light, so it could easily holster to that brace of yours."

"Does it pack a punch?" May withdrew her hands slowly. Clearly, the extra attention wasn't unwanted.

"It will make a man think twice about messing with you." Hank glanced around the kitchen once before returning his full attention to May. "The dock is a good place for target practice. Do you have any empty tin cans we can use to shoot at?"

"This is a restaurant. Of course, we have tin cans." A shy grin grew on May's lips, one Dax hadn't seen since her sister was a teenager and soft on a boy.

"I'll need a dozen," he said.

"I'll get them," Dax said. When she returned minutes later with a burlap sack full of rattling cans, Hank retrieved his suitcase full of guns.

"Give me a few minutes to set up." He headed outside.

When the door closed behind him, Rose snapped her head toward May and drilled her with her eyes as if an interrogation was about to begin. Dax did the same.

"You clearly have the hots for each other," Rose said. May waved her off as if the suggestion was absurd.

"Then what was all the grinning about?" Dax asked. "I haven't seen you blush like that since Allen Fisher brought you daisies when you were sixteen." Redness returned to May's cheeks. "Just like that."

"Will you two stop?" May spun on her stool and started for the door. "We better not waste Mr. O'Keefe's time."

"So now it's Mr. O'Keefe." Rose snickered and followed.

"Well, May Foster…" Dax walked steps behind. "I do believe you have a crush."

May retrieved a light coat from the hook near the door and put it on. "That's silly."

Rose put her coat on before resting a hand on May's back. "I think it's wonderful. That square jaw of his makes him a handsome fella."

"I don't have the time to show interest in a man, especially one that might not accept you and Dax."

"But he does," Dax said. "He knows about us like he knows about Grace and Clive. He's been living with them for years." May harrumphed on her way outside. Maybe, just maybe, Dax hoped, May might leave the door open to finally finding happiness.

The ladies descended the dock ramp where Hank had set up a half-dozen tin cans evenly spaced atop the railing facing into the marina. They lined up near his suitcase and waited for him to join them.

"All right, ladies, we begin by learning the four golden gun safety rules." Hank looked each of them in the eye before starting. "One. Treat all guns as if they are loaded. Two. Never point a gun at anything you aren't willing to destroy. Three. Keep your finger off the trigger until your target is in sight and you're ready to shoot. And four. Be sure of your target—and what is behind it." Hank's stare went distant when he recited the fourth, making Dax suspect there was a sad story about violating that rule.

For the next hour, he demonstrated to them the mechanics of each gun and how to hold, aim, and fire it properly. Surprisingly, Rose was an excellent shot. Dax was too, but she was hard on herself for missing the can the first time. She could not afford to miss her target a single time if Rose was ever in immediate danger.

May needed extra guidance on aiming, so Dax and Rose waited farther up the dock for them to finish. They watched Hank come up behind May and wrap his arms and hands around hers, helping her line her sights up on the target.

"I'm beginning to suspect May missed her target on purpose," Dax said.

"You're just now figuring that out?" Rose giggled. "I've seen her toss a balled-up towel and make the laundry basket from the other end of the room. Trust me, she has no trouble with her aim."

"Good for her." A warm feeling took root in Dax and grew. Not since before the accident had she seen May relaxed around a man. Even if Hank left after their ugly business was finished, it was good seeing May happy for a day.

Dax and Rose didn't rush them. Instead, they waited in silence as May received the attention she deserved. Soon, May and Hank rejoined them. Her eyes sparkled with joy.

"It took you long enough to hit your target." Dax forced back a smile.

"May's a great shot." Hank winked at May. "As are you two."

Dax removed the magazine from her weapon and turned the muzzle toward herself, exercising proper gun safety before offering it to Hank. "Thanks for the lesson. Can you recommend a place for us to buy guns for ourselves?"

Hank waved Dax off. "Those are yours to keep. I can always get more. I have a shoulder holster you might like, Dax. But Rose, you should keep yours in a handbag. And May, I know a man who can fashion a holster to attach to your leg brace. Until then, your handbag will have to do."

"Thank you, Hank." Dax reloaded her weapon and stuffed it into her coat pocket. "We appreciate your help today. I feel safer already." She turned to May. "Edith should have an order ready for us this morning. I'll pick it up and come right back."

"I'll come with you," Hank said. "I'm already concerned that Charlie refused to have a guard at the garage. I don't want to worry about you too."

"I'll come too," May said. "I need Edith to place a special order for a new coffee machine. Ruth said ours is on its last legs." Though Dax could have placed the order herself, she agreed without hesitation. May's motivation was transparent, and Dax could not deny her the opportunity.

"Sure thing, May." Dax walked Rose back inside and kissed her on the cheek before whispering in her ear, "She's definitely interested."

"So is Hank," Rose whispered back.

While Hank returned his case of guns upstairs, May studied the small purse hanging on the wall hook near the door. She handed Rose her gun. "Can you put this under my pillow? I'll have to find a handbag big enough to hold that thing."

Hank returned with a leather shoulder holster and an extra loaded magazine for Dax's pistol. "This should fit you perfectly."

"I'll figure it out when we get back. Let's head out." Dax placed the items on the chopping block and snatched her truck keys from the peg. She led the way outside. Hank opened the passenger door for May, offered his arm to help her up, and slid in beside her. Once Dax jumped in, the tight fit required their bodies to touch from shoulder to thigh. May's upturned face suggested she appreciated Hank's special attention and was enjoying the contact. Dax grinned, started the engine and coasted the truck toward the front where Thomas was standing guard.

"Hold on, Dax," Hank said. "Roll down your window." She cranked as fast as possible until the window retreated inside the driver's door. He called Thomas over. "We're heading to the department store. It shouldn't take more than thirty minutes. No one but Charlie, Jules, Grace, and Clive are to get past you."

"Gotcha, boss." Thomas wagged two fingers in a salute.

Dax pulled onto the main road. It was busier than it had been in recent weeks, a sure sign that tourist season was around the corner. She thought about what might happen if the feud between Wilkes and Grace continued into the summer months. Without decent entertainment at the Seaside and with the amenities at the Beacon Club unknown to many, tourists might stay away. Fewer tourists would mean less income for local merchants like Edith. For everyone's sake, Hank had better make his one shot count.

Parking in front of Edith's, Dax stuffed the truck keys into her coat pocket next to the Colt .45 Hank had given her. Hank offered his hand to May, helping her step down onto the street and generating another smile Dax enjoyed seeing.

The moment Dax stepped inside, she cringed. The biggest thorn in Rose's side since her first day in Half Moon Bay was at the register. Hopefully, her cousin Ida would buy her things from Edith and be on her way without making a scene.

Dax veered to the area near the front door where Edith kept the orders for the locals, separated by labeled boxes. May stepped to the register while Hank remained near the door, the perfect vantage point from which to vet anyone coming inside.

"I'll be right with you, May," Edith said before directing her attention toward the front of the store. "Everything should be there but the paper bags, Dax. I can get them in a minute." Dax's scan of the box labeled "Foster House" confirmed the missing bags.

"No problem. I'll do it." Dax started toward the back, where Edith kept the paper products.

"I can't believe you're out and about a day after your husband was shot and killed by a thief." Ida's tone was unmistakably judgmental.

Dax stopped in midstride, waiting for May's counterpunch. At least the theory they provided the sheriff about Logan's shooting had made the rounds in town. Keeping the ongoing feud under wraps was key to providing cover for when Hank took his shot at Wilkes. If the conditions were right, it could be written off as another robbery gone wrong.

"Some of us have a stronger constitution than others," May said, raising her chin at the busybody.

"Well, I never." Ida stiffened her posture.

"Do you really want to go there again, Ida?" May placed both hands on her hips, telegraphing her lack of patience. "Maybe if you did once in a while, you might not have a stick up your back end all day."

Dax let out a loud guffaw, sending Ida out the door in a cloud of dust.

"Dang, May," Edith howled. "No one has ever put that woman in her place, not even her husband."

"Someone had to." May shrugged, prompting Dax to grin with pride. When they were little, May had socked one of the older girls who teased Dax about having short hair. From that day, Dax knew that slapping down a bully was the right thing to do.

"I'll get the bags before Ida comes back for a second round with the bone crusher here." She made her way to the back wall and eyed the shelves until she located the paper bags May liked to use for customer leftovers. She was reaching up to grab two boxes when someone shoved her against the display shelf. She hit metal, a sharp pain radiating from her ribs. She turned toward her attacker.

"You Fosters don't learn lessons very well, it seems." A large man threw a punch into her gut. Dax doubled over, gasping for air. A second punch landed on her left flank, a direct shot to the kidney. Pain came in waves and sent her to her knees on the hard floor. Dax fought the urge to throw up but lost the battle. Breakfast ended up on the linoleum.

There was a crunch.

A grunt.

A thud. A second. A third.

Dax looked up, discovering Hank straddling the man on the floor, pistol-whipping him into a bloody pulp. He stopped just short of killing him.

"Can you walk, Dax? We need to get out of here." Hank steadied her to a more upright stance. Pain shot through her on both sides. Nothing felt broken, but her midsection hurt like hell.

"Yeah, I can walk. Where's May?" Dax felt her coat pocket to make sure her gun was still there.

"She's safe with Edith."

Hank guided Dax to the front of the store. May rushed toward her. "My God, Dax. What happened?"

"A man from the Seaside. I recognized him from one of my walks last night." Hank turned his attention to Edith. "I'm sorry for the trouble, ma'am. The man back there might need medical attention."

"What in tarnation?" Edith said.

"I think he was beating on Dax because she dresses differently." Hank continued to steer Dax toward the exit. "She'll be fine, but I need to get her home."

"Let me get your order." Edith grabbed the box of goods and followed them out to the truck. She placed their items in the back bed. "You should take her to see Doc Hughes."

"Thank you, ma'am, but I've got this. I have medical training." Hank turned to May. "Can you get yourself into the truck and help me get Dax in?"

"Yes." May pulled herself onto the front bench and reached out for Dax when Hank maneuvered her into the truck cabin. Each shove and pull sent waves of pain cresting through her like waves against the cliffs in a storm.

"Keys are in my right"—Dax paused for another wave of pain—"coat pocket."

Hank fished in her pocket, retrieved the keys and Dax's gun, and hopped into the driver's seat. "We need to get you back."

"No." Dax's first worry was for her friend. "We need to check on Charlie."

"Dammit, Dax. I need to keep you two safe." Hank's tone turned sharp.

"Charlie."

Hank let out a breathy sigh. "Fine, where is she?"

"Her garage," May said. "I'll show you."

Hank drove through town and pulled around the back of Charlie's garage. He handed Dax her gun. "Stay here."

Dax sat straight and clicked off the safety on her pistol though she wasn't sure if she was strong enough at the moment to pull the trigger. She kept an eye on the truck's perimeter, occasionally glancing in the rearview mirror. Minutes later, Hank exited the garage through the back door with Charlie and Brutus behind him. Thank goodness she was safe.

Hank opened the driver's door, and Charlie peered inside. "Geez, Dax. Frankie's man did a number on you."

Dax winced through another wave. "Which is why you should come back to the Foster House. You'll be safe there."

"All right, Dax. I got Mr. Getty's car running, left the keys under the seat, and left him a note on the windshield. I also grabbed the tin box you asked me to hold on to. I figured it would be safer at the Foster House now."

Dax managed a nod.

"Do you want us to pick up Jules too?" Hank asked.

"She's not associated with the club, so she'll be fine." Charlie lifted Brutus into the truck bed and jumped in after him.

Hank returned to the driver's seat and started the engine. Concern cut through his voice, "Things are getting hot. We stay in the house until this is over."

"And when will that be?" May asked.

"If the Prohis do their jobs"—Hank twisted the steering wheel—"before dawn." That meant the Prohibition Agents would raid the Seaside Club and force Frankie Wilkes into Hank's trap. One shot could bring this war to an end. Or so Dax hoped.

She glanced over her shoulder, pain punctuating her turn. Charlie had her back against the side of the truck bed and was focused on petting Brutus, no wiser to what was about to transpire. Considering her loathing of violence, her ignorance was a blessing.

CHAPTER THIRTY

Frankie stood at the end of the bar, his arm in a sling, surveying the sudden surge in customers. It had been months since the Seaside Club had had a crowd large enough to need more than the two waitresses left serving food and drinks. The room was three-quarters full—a sign that his brother Roy was on the right track with his plan to bring Grace Parsons to her knees. The Beacon Club was closed tonight, and if the Fosters had a lick of sense, it would stay closed. But on the off chance they were thickheaded, he had Roy's fixer to make sure Grace and those sisters ended up like Logan Foster.

The bartender, unaccustomed to the brisk pace, appeared frazzled. If Jason were there, he would have a grin a mile wide and handle every customer without dropping a single ice cube. But that was when Frankie had a complete staff with a club manager who kept the bar stocked with liquor, mixers, and glasses throughout the night without a single complaint. At least the two maids Frankie dragged in for the night were helping enough to keep the regular waitresses from walking out.

He checked the clock on the wall behind the bar. The new canary he hired to replace the one who replaced Rose Hamilton should have taken the stage five minutes ago for her last show of the evening. Unfortunately, within a week of hiring her, Frankie realized he didn't know how good he had it with Rose. Rose had missed very few shows, was on time, and performed impeccably. She made the audience fall in love with her, which had customers coming back for more entertainment, food, and drinks. But her replacement's replacement was also no Rose Hamilton. She canceled more nights than she sang, citing that singing to an empty house was an insult. When she sang, though, she frequently started late, was drunk, and her song choices bored the clientele.

His practical side said he'd made a mistake in firing Rose, but his pride would never let him admit it and reverse course. He'd made his choice. Rose and Dax were more than thick as thieves. They *were* thieves, and he would rather lose everything than crawl on his hands and knees to ask her back. This feud would end on his terms, not theirs.

Ten minutes later, Rose's second replacement stepped through the swinging door to the left of the stage and staggered up the stairs. The coffee cup in her hand was a sure sign she was about to deliver a less than stellar performance. She stepped up to the microphone, placed her cup, likely filled with booze, on the nearby stool, and said, "Hit it."

Without a musician to play the piano and announce her performance, the bartender turned on the microphone next to the Victrola record player Frankie had brought from his home and started the instrumental record. Surprisingly, the singer was sober enough to remember the words to the first song, but that didn't last past the fourth when she continued to gulp her drink between selections. Replacing her would be Frankie's first act once he made enough money to pay the bills.

"Hey, boss," the hapless bartender called out after the lackluster performance. "I'm out of glasses."

"Did you send one of the girls to the kitchen to bring out more?"

"I forgot."

"You'd forget your head if it wasn't attached." Frankie buried his face in the palm of his only working arm. Firing this idiot would be his second act. "I'll go."

After directing the busboy to restock the bar, Frankie took a moment to marvel at the organized chaos in the kitchen. His restaurant was the only part of the hotel that didn't suffer from Grace's vendetta. Though bookings from the Hollywood crowd, their primary source of revenue during off-peak season, had come to a grinding halt, the locals had maintained their dining routine. Tonight's increased business resurfaced his vision of adding a fine dining restaurant to the main floor. He could see the most delicate crystal glassware, bone china plates, and sterling silver flatware adorning the tables. The room would be filled with wealthy philanthropists and financiers from all corners of the Bay Area and…

Loud voices in the club were followed by the sound of breaking glass and a building commotion. *Great*, Frankie thought, rolling his eyes. The last thing he needed was a brawl on the busiest day his club had seen in months. He steeled himself for an unruly scene before marching down the corridor. When he pushed through to the main dining area, he got the shock of his life.

"What the hell?"

"Hands up." A man in a suit spun around, pointing a long-barreled handgun at Frankie's face. "Prohibition agent." He patted Frankie down and confiscated his pistol.

"This has to be a misunderstanding. Who's in charge?" Frankie clenched his jaw, struggling to tamp down the anger boiling in his belly. He thought he'd greased the right palms to stay out of this mess, but apparently, more grease was needed.

"They are." The unknown Prohi pointed toward two men behind the bar, who, as if on cue, began wielding baseball bats aimed at the Seaside's stock of whiskey, champagne, and other liquor. They also took out the glassware there with targeted swings, each strike adding hundreds of dollars to the tally of mounting debt.

Frankie glared at the two he'd hosted at the Seaside Club a hundred times over the last three years. They'd drunk his booze, eaten his food, and taken his money without thinking twice about the illegality of doing so. Their presence tonight confirmed his long-held suspicion: their loyalty was extended only to whoever was the highest bidder.

"Against the wall with the others." The Prohi gestured toward the wall where other agents had lined up the bartender and the servers against one wall and patrons along another. Several women customers were trembling, hiding their faces in their hands or in their male partner's arms.

Clearly, this was Grace Parson's handiwork, but it was anemic, thought Frankie, compared to the death blow Sam, his brother's "fixer," had administered the other night with a single pull of the trigger. By tomorrow, with the help of Roy, he would have the state officials paid off, the charges dropped, and the club restocked. He and Sam would take the war to the next level after that.

When Agent Paxton and his partner, Harris, finished making their point by smashing the last whiskey container behind the bar there, they turned toward where the guests had been herded. They walked up and down the line as if memorizing the faces of the patrons. If the purpose was to intimidate, it clearly worked on most customers.

Harris slapped the bat he carried into his other hand several times. "The Seaside Club is shut hereby down, and the hotel is off-limits until further notice." He pointed the bat toward Frankie. "As long as this man runs the place," he said, "we will arrest you if we see you here again. Now go home." Guests filed out quickly but in an orderly fashion, most leaving unpaid bills. Sam, Roy's muscle, quietly exited with them.

Harris turned then to face Frankie's staff. "Is there any more alcohol on the premises?" The women remained silent, but the hardware store clerk-turned-bartender shook like a little baby, reinforcing Frankie's opinion that hiring him was a giant mistake.

"Furnace room. There's a hidden compartment behind the clothes washers." The coward volunteered the location of the club's stash without having to withstand even a single threat of violence. Frankie eyed him, trying to decide whether the bottom of the marina or Devil's Slide should be his fate.

Paxton directed two agents to locate and destroy whatever liquor they found before turning back to the Seaside staff. "You can leave, but I suggest you find other jobs. Frankie Wilkes won't last long in this town."

"He owes us a week's pay," a maid said, "and we have bills to pay."

Paxton opened the till at the bar and handed each employee forty dollars. "This should cover it and then some. Go home."

Once the employees left, the two traitors dismissed the other agents, leaving Frankie with his tormentors as his only company. He glared at them. They had burned a bridge tonight. If Roy's fixer neutralized Grace and the Fosters as promised, they would be next on the list, he swore, envisioning them agonizing for several harrowing seconds over their impending death and then plunging into a watery grave at the bottom of Devil's Slide.

"What now, fellas?" Frankie asked. "A bullet to the back of the head?"

"We wait," Paxton said before directing Frankie to sit at a table. Waiting suggested these guys expected someone else to make an appearance. And, with his protection gone with the wind, Frankie had no other choice.

Harris grabbed three soda bottles from behind the bar, popped off the caps, and joined Frankie. He distributed the bottles and propped his feet atop the table. "You really screwed the pooch on this one, Frankie."

"What is she paying you?"

"More than you ever did. But it's not about the money. Grace has the Attorney General in her pocket."

"Webb? I'm not worried about him. He supports whoever provides the biggest envelope of cash."

"Not Webb. The new guy, Mitchell. In DC. Which means you're out of luck."

Frankie sensed the walls closing in on him. The Attorney General of the United States would be impossible to grease, though several had tried. He wondered what Grace Parsons had on him. She traded in information surrounding the rich, famous, and influential, which had made her a formidable ally. Now, though, she was his enemy, one, evidently, with a much farther reach than he had imagined. He would never again be able to operate a speakeasy in this country. Would have to find another way to make his fortune back.

After a time, Harris went outside. He returned twenty minutes later, offering only a nod. He extended a hand to Frankie. "Give me the keys to your car and the hotel truck."

"Why?"

"That's the price of getting out of here."

"Fine." Cooperating was clearly his only way out. Frankie could address Grace and her misguided campaign after a good night's sleep in one of his hotel's many vacant rooms, so he handed over the keys.

"All right, let's go," Paxton said. After retrieving his coat and hat, he and Harris led Frankie to the main floor lobby. Not a single employee or guest was in sight, suggesting the agents had cleared everyone from the hotel. "Go home, Frankie."

"Someone has to watch the hotel. I'll stay here if you don't mind."

"I do mind. Start walking."

An unnerving feeling seeped into Frankie's bones as he pulled his newsboy cap low on his head and the agent threw the coat over his shoulders. It was two in the morning, and the streets were empty. He was going to have to make it a mile to his house with no weapon and an arm in a sling, and Sam was nowhere in sight. He walked through the main doors onto the sidewalk, fearing the worst.

CHAPTER THIRTY-ONE

Two hours earlier

Barking woke Charlie with a start. She sat up in bed. "What is it, boy?" Brutus barked again, standing on his makeshift bed of bunched blankets on the floor of Rose's room.

"Jules had a call. Doc Hughes needs her at the clinic," a security guard said from the other side of the door.

"Wonderful," she whispered. A middle-of-the-night call when things were heating up between Frankie and Grace wasn't good. "Thanks. I'll get her up." Charlie placed a hand on the back of the very, very sound sleeper beside her, giving her a gentle shake. "Jules, wake up." The lack of movement prompted a second round. "Jules, wake up."

"What?" Jules mumbled.

"Doc Hughes called. You need to head into the clinic."

Jules sighed and pushed herself out of bed. "I need to ask for a raise if this keeps happening."

"I'm coming with you." Charlie got up and slipped trousers over her sleep shorts. "After everything that's happened, I don't want you walking the streets alone at night."

After turning on the overhead light, Jules pulled off her nightgown, revealing the body that had been the source of many sleepless nights for Charlie. Those generous curves, small breasts, and tanned skin were what she craved every night. But this town was full of narrow-minded people. Since she lived at the boarding house, Jules could not have overnight guests; she stayed at Charlie's only once a week when her job allowed. Spending two consecutive nights with her at the Foster House, like this, was the ultimate treat, even if the second one was cut short.

Charlie had gotten one arm into the sleeve of her shirt but stopped, focusing on Jules's alluring lines. "You're so beautiful."

"I'm putting on weight. May's cooking is too good." Jules put on her underwear and brassiere, bringing the best part of the show to an end.

"I love curves on you. They mean you're happy and eating when you want, not when you can."

Jules slipped her nurse's uniform on and backed up closer to Charlie, gesturing for her to zip her up. "You're the best girlfriend in the world." After Charlie completed her task, Jules turned around and gave her a luscious, pulse-pumping kiss.

"If you don't stop, I guarantee you'll be late."

"Then we better go. Doc Hughes gets grumpy when he's called in the middle of the night. So late might get me fired."

After she finished dressing, Charlie opened the door for Jules and Brutus. Dax was waiting for them in the living room. "Are you going to drive her?" Dax asked.

"Yeah. Can I use your truck?"

"Of course." She wrinkled her brow. "I'm worried for you two. Let me wake a guard to go with you."

"We'll be fine, Dax. Besides, I'm bringing Brutus. He's a great alert dog."

Dax relented but warned, "If anyone follows you, come straight back."

Minutes later, Charlie pulled up to the side door of the clinic. "I'll wait for you out here."

"Don't be silly. I don't know how long I'll be," Jules said.

"It doesn't matter. I'm waiting."

"At least come inside. I'll get a pot of coffee going, so help yourself whenever you want. You two can stay in an exam room and use the blankets there to get some sleep."

"Deal."

After delivering a cup of hot coffee to Charlie, Jules exited the exam room to tend to her patient. Charlie pushed two chairs close together, facing each other, as a makeshift bed, stretched her legs across them, and covered her lower body with a blanket. Brutus curled up in a corner atop a scrunched-up blanket on the floor.

"Get some sleep, boy. We might be here a while."

Eventually Brutus laid his head down, and Charlie finished her coffee. Despite the caffeine, her lids grew heavy, and she finally closed her eyes. The next thing she saw was Jules nudging her awake.

"We're all done here," Jules said.

Charlie shook off the haze of sleep. "What time is it?"

"A little after one."

"That didn't take long."

"Sprained ankle."

Charlie rolled her eyes. "Couldn't that wait until morning?"

"It was a tourist. The wife slipped on the stairs coming out of the Seaside Club, so they came here." Jules pushed Charlie's legs off the second chair and sat on it. "You'll like this. Her husband said they were staying at the Seaside overnight, and Prohibition agents raided the place. They kicked everyone out, including guests."

"So, that's Grace's plan? Shut down the hotel? The town won't survive without it."

"Don't be so negative." Jules playfully slapped Charlie's leg. "I'm sure she has a plan for that too."

"I don't trust her, Jules. She brought in men with guns."

"Frankie Wilkes brought in the guns first. He killed Logan, had Dax beaten up, tried to get to you, and is probably responsible for old Mr. Foster's death. I'm happy Grace has brought in firepower."

"Well, I'm not.   There's already been enough killing."
Charlie folded her blanket and returned it to the cabinet. "Let's
go back to the Foster House so you can get some sleep. What
time do you have to be back?"

"Not until noon. Half-days are the benefit of nights when
I'm called in."

Charlie drove slowly down Main Street. They were the
only ones on the road. The sky was cloudless, and the moon
was unobstructed, providing ample illumination. She stopped at
the traffic signal, preparing to make the turn onto the highway
where the Foster House was.

Her headlights swung at an angle, highlighting the front
of the building less than a block away. The light cone lit the
bottom of a second-story living room window and caught her
eye. That window was never open. Charlie raised her gaze. A
long, thin metal cylinder was sticking past the window frame. It
had to be the barrel of a long rifle. A rifle that likely belonged
to Hank.

As she turned the corner, she saw that the rifle was pointed
at a shop across from the Foster House. She swung her gaze
to follow the rifle's aim. A hunched-over figure dressed in an
overcoat and newsboy cap was lumbering along the sidewalk.
She glanced back at the Foster House. The barrel was trailing
the person.

She had just seconds to decide what to do. If she did nothing,
Hank would let a bullet fly and kill whoever it was a hundred
feet in front of her. Even if it were Frankie, could she live with
the fact that she let him die? But what if that person wasn't him
and had nothing to do with the feud? The person was dressed
like her and Dax. What if it *was* Dax? She could not tell from
this distance with the hat pulled down so low. She could not
take that chance, could not live knowing she let someone die
when it was in her power to prevent it.

She honked the truck's horn and kept her hand pressed on
it. Brutus howled. The walker ducked. She heard the distinct
sound of a bullet ricocheting. The person scampered along the
sidewalk. There was a second ricochet. A third. The final blast

shattered a storefront plate glass window. Charlie lifted her hand from the horn when the person came even with the truck. It wasn't Dax, but someone who looked her straight in the eye with an expression of pure evil. The next second, he scurried around the corner.

"That was Frankie," Jules shouted. Her head swiveled, following his direction of travel.

"I know." Charlie twisted the steering wheel with both hands. She didn't regret her choice, but she knew what this meant for her and Dax's friendship. It might end it.

She turned the truck to the mouth of the access road at the side of the Foster House. A guard waved her through, and she parked in the back. Before getting out, she gave herself a silent pep talk, trying to stay positive. Maybe this would not kill their friendship. Maybe the sniper shot was improvised and not part of the grand plan. And maybe Grace had something else up her sleeve to send Frankie packing and keep the town afloat. That was a lot of maybes, but Charlie had nothing else on which to hang her hopes.

She let herself in the back door, using the key Dax had attached to the truck key chain. The kitchen was dark, just as it was when they left. She and Jules tiptoed past May's room, out of the kitchen, and up the stairs to the residence floor. The living room was dark, so Charlie turned down the hallway to the bedrooms. The floorboards creaked when she reached the door to their room. A door swung half-open at the end of the hallway, spilling light onto the floorboards and the wall.

"In here." Dax's voice didn't have its usual warmth. Charlie stepped inside with Jules right behind. Brutus remained in the hallway. "Close the door." Dax's voice and expression sent chills through her.

Inside the room, silent, stood Dax, Rose, and Hank. At the click of the latch, Dax laid into her. "What the hell, Charlie? That was our one chance to take out Frankie and end this war. You let him get away. Now he'll fortify and have time to retaliate with force."

Rose placed a hand on the small of Dax's back. The touch seemed calming, relaxing Dax's tense muscles and turning down the heat in her fiery eyes. "I'm sorry I got mad, but I take nothing back. What were you thinking?"

"I thought that person on the street might have been you. He had a newsboy cap on."

"So you thought you were saving Dax," Rose said.

Charlie could leave her explanation at that and preserve her friendship, but holding back the truth was not healthy for any relationship. She had too many lies in her life. She hid her sexuality from the public. She hid her role in Riley King's death and the theft of the missing whiskey. She hid the truth about her role in the speakeasy business. Her entire life was a lie to everyone but Jules, Dax, Rose, and May. Much as she needed that island of honesty, blurring those lines with them would make every relationship she had a sham. She had to tell the truth.

"Yes and no. Even if I was sure it was Frankie, I couldn't stand by and let him get shot. I couldn't cause another man's death."

Dax's chest heaved at Charlie's confession. Her hands formed into fists, and in a flash, she charged, grabbing Charlie by the lapels and pinning her against the wall. "Dammit, Charlie. Your cowardice may have killed all of us."

"Is that what you think of me? That I'm some lily-liver?" Dax's accusation stabbed her in the heart. She'd pushed Riley King over a cliff to save Dax's life and nearly broke her neck twice after being forced down the stairs. Wasn't that enough to prove she wasn't a coward?

Dax tightened her grip on her jacket lapels. "I think you're not willing to do what it takes to keep us safe."

Charlie threw off Dax's hold and pushed her backward a step. If Dax could not see the difference between cowardice and an unwillingness to take a life unless forced to save another, her friend wasn't the person she thought she was. "Then we have nothing else to say." She turned to Jules. "Let's get our things. We're leaving."

Dax firmed her fists again, but Rose pulled her back. "Don't. Let them go. Let's get some sleep, and we can all talk this out tomorrow."

"I won't have anything to do with someone who thinks me a coward, Rose." Charlie took Jules by the hand, gathered their items from Rose's room across the hall, and they left. As they started the long walk to her garage in the dark night, the reality of the night's events sank in. Hank's sniper bullet had missed Frankie but hit an unintended target. It had damaged Charlie and Dax's friendship. Likely forever.

CHAPTER THIRTY-TWO

The twenty-minute walk to the garage chilled Charlie to the bone, but she was more concerned for her shivering girlfriend and dog. Brutus's thin coat and pink belly and Jules's light jacket and dress exposed them more to the chilly night ocean air. If she had to do it again, she would have jogged home to get her truck for her loved ones, but her anger had clouded her thinking.

She placed her key into the lock and pushed the side door open. The boarded-up windowpane was a reminder of the danger besieging them. Perhaps cutting her ties with Dax was for the best.

Once Jules and Brutus stepped inside, Charlie flipped on the main floor overhead light. "Let's get you warm."

Jules led the way upstairs, followed by Brutus. By the time Charlie entered her room after filling the dog's water bowl downstairs, Brutus was already nuzzled under the blankets on the bed. After placing her bag on the floor, Jules sat on the edge of the bed, shivering and blowing into her cupped hands. Charlie tossed an extra blanket over her lap and rubbed her arms.

"I'm sorry I made you walk." Charlie sat on the bed next to her. "I wasn't thinking."

Jules caressed Charlie's cheek, running a fingertip to her lips. "It's okay. Let's get some sleep." She pressed their lips together in a brief, tender kiss.

"I love you, Jules. Thank you for standing by me."

Jules pursed her lips. "Rose and Dax are my friends, but you are the love of my life. I will always stand by you."

Dax's harsh words still stung. She tried to convince herself that it was because no one had ever called her a coward. Or that it hurt only because her best friend had said it. But down deep, Charlie knew the accusation carried some truth. She knew what Frankie Wilkes was capable of and wanted nothing to do with it, though for Jules's sake, not hers. Frankie had proven he would come after anyone who crossed him, and she could not risk Jules becoming collateral damage by crossing him again. Maybe that made her a coward in Dax's eyes, but she would rather risk their friendship than her woman's life.

Charlie leaned her head against Jules's shoulder, accepting a comforting arm. She uncorked the emotion she'd successfully bottled up for days and let the first tear fall. She could not remember the last time she cried. She thought it might have been when her parents died. But she had had no one then to soothe the pain.

Jules lifted her chin with a hand and gazed deeply into her eyes. "I love you with all my heart."

Charlie could not imagine a life without this woman. She gently guided Jules flat against the mattress, shooing Brutus away with a hefty shove. Capturing her lips in a passionate kiss, she pressed their bodies together and rocked her hips until Jules hooked her legs around them.

Brutus growled. The next second he dashed to the door and barked nonstop. A crash and the sound of breaking glass came from the bottom floor, bringing Charlie to full alert. She bounded from the bed, readying the baseball bat by the door as a weapon. "Stay here," she said over her shoulder to Jules before inching the door open. She stepped onto the landing.

Orange tendrils of flames were consuming the tire rack below her, lapping at the stairs. A shot rang out. Charlie slammed the door shut but not before dark smoke seeped into the room.

"Was that a shot? Is that smoke?" Jules's voice contained the unmistakable shrill of terror, matching the fear beating wildly in Charlie's chest.

"Yes." Charlie glanced at Brutus, who had gone quiet. He was lying on his blanket on the floor, completely still with his legs straight as boards. He'd fallen into another of his scared stiff stupors and would be of no help. The garage was ablaze, and they would be trapped if she didn't act quickly. She needed to fight fire with fire. "Tear a six-inch strip off my sheets." She dashed to her dresser, where she kept some home remedy items. She rummaged through the drawer and retrieved the glass bottle of rubbing alcohol and her Ronson lighter.

Jules ripped a corner off the bedsheets in three hard pulls. "How are you going to use it?"

"I'm going to give Frankie a taste of his own medicine, which might flush him outside."

Charlie unscrewed the top of the bottle of rubbing alcohol and stuffed the torn section of the sheet into the bottle opening, leaving half of it sticking out. She opened the door, coughing as choking smoke and heat poured into the room. She waited for another gunshot, lit the makeshift fuse on fire, and threw it where she thought Frankie had taken up position. "Take this, Frankie!"

A bright flash. A scream. The side door flew open, and two figures scrambled outside. The flames had grown stronger, nearly reaching the stairs. Black smoke from the burning tires engulfed the garage in a toxic cloud.

"We have to get out of here." Charlie glanced at her dog, who was still motionless. "I'll carry Brutus."

Jules stepped out to the top landing, but flames had reached it. "It's too late. We're trapped."

"We have no choice." She and Jules coughed. Charlie draped the wool blanket over Jules and pushed her toward the door. "Wool burns slowly. Go now or die."

"Come with me." Jules's eyes shimmered with fear.

"I can't leave without Brutus." Another cough. "Hold your breath. Now go!"

Jules darted out the door and disappeared down the stairs. The absence of screams was a good sign.

Charlie bent over Brutus, sliding her arms under his stiff body. He was fifty pounds of dead weight, but a rush of adrenaline pushed her into action. She cradled him with both arms like a groom carrying his bride and stepped onto the landing. A black cloud filled the entire garage, and flames lit the stair railing like a string of Christmas lights, dancing like serpents.

The heat had become unbearable, leaving her skin feeling like it might melt from her bones. The air was unbreathable and had her gasping. Her awkward grip on Brutus made her wobble on the first step downward, but she leaned right into the flames. Her wool coat protected her arm, but Brutus let out a gut-wrenching continuous yelp. She overcorrected on her second step and hit the wall to her left but regained her balance quickly. The next few steps were a blur. Finally she reached the concrete floor. A scan of the room confirmed the flames had reached every corner, leaving few areas untouched. Thankfully, one was the path to the open side door. Holding her breath, she dashed toward it, hoping Jules was waiting on the other side.

Once outside, Charlie gulped the frigid night air. Brutus's yelp turned into a whimper. Charlie inspected him. His ears were pinned against his head, and a back paw looked red and blistered. She struggled to remain strong, fighting back a flood of sobs. She looked right before locating Jules to the left near her truck. Thank goodness. She appeared unhurt. "Brutus is hurt."

Jules threw off her blanket and examined the dog's leg. She winced. "It looks like a second-degree burn. We need to get him to the clinic, but I don't have my key."

"I'll get us in." The clinic was only blocks away, but Charlie wasn't sure she could carry him that distance. She loaded Brutus onto Jules's lap inside the truck and sped through Half Moon Bay's empty streets. She ignored the two traffic signs and came to a gentle stop at the clinic's front entrance. Picking up a fist-sized rock in the nearby flower bed, she broke the windowpane in the front door and opened it. She lifted Brutus from Jules's lap and followed her inside.

Jules hurried down the hallway to the first treatment room, turning on the lights along the way. "Put him on the table and hold him down." She gathered supplies and approached the table. Brutus squirmed and kicked, making it impossible for Jules to treat him. "The only way I can do this is to give him a sedative. Are you okay with that?"

Charlie nodded. She trusted Jules with her life and now with Brutus's.

Jules prepared a syringe, drawing a small amount of liquid from a small bottle with a printed label.

"What is that?" Charlie asked.

"Barbital. I figure he's about fifty pounds, so I'm giving him a quarter of the adult dose. It should calm him enough to let me treat him. Hold him tight." Jules held down the dog's injured leg and administered the shot high on the thigh muscle. He yelped.

Within five minutes, the sedative took effect, and Brutus fell asleep. Over the next thirty minutes, Jules meticulously cleaned and bandaged his burn. "It's important to keep the wound clean and dry for the next few days to avoid infection. The bad news is that we'll have to keep an eye on him to keep him from licking it. The good news is that he'll be his old self in a few days, and the burn should heal in a week or two."

"Will he be in much pain?"

"For the first day, yes, but I can keep him sedated to get him past the worst. The burn was pretty bad near his knee. Unfortunately, the scar tissue might leave him with a limp."

Charlie petted the little guy's head, taking in how peaceful he looked. A wave of guilt crested inside her. She had saved Frankie's life tonight, and he repaid her by burning down her home and business, trying to kill her and Jules, and injuring her loyal companion. And he probably wasn't done exacting his revenge. If anyone deserved to die, Frankie Wilkes did. But it would not be by Charlie's hand.

"We should warn Dax," Charlie said. "Where's the phone?"

"At the reception desk." Jules rubbed Brutus's side. "I'll stay with him."

Charlie reached the front and lifted the phone, clicking it several times to raise the operator. She asked Holly to connect her to the Foster House. The phone rang and rang and rang, but no one answered, confirming Charlie's fears. Frankie Wilkes wasn't done. She had to warn Dax.

CHAPTER THIRTY-THREE

When Charlie and Jules walked out, Dax's temples throbbed so hard she thought her head might burst. What Charlie did tonight was unforgivable, but she hadn't deserved to be called a coward. That was a step too far, and she regretted taking it the minute the words passed her lips. Her friend deserved better, but first, Dax had to calm down and focus on the immediate threat. Once they got through the night, she was confident she would figure out a way to let go of the anger and apologize properly to her friend.

She placed her hands on her hips and turned her attention to Hank. "What do we do now?"

"Plan B."

"What is that?"

"I hunt him down and put a bullet in his head." Hank exited the bedroom, and Dax and Rose followed. He pounded on Logan's old door. "Everyone up." Seconds later, the four off-duty men filed out of the room, receiving instructions from Hank to augment the on-duty guards and to remain on high alert. They hurried down the stairs in a stampede. Hank turned his attention to Dax. "Get your guns. The eight guards will protect you while I hunt down Wilkes. Once I leave, lock the door after me and don't open it for any reason until you hear my voice."

The urgency in Hank's commands lent credence to Dax's growing fear. Frankie was already a loose cannon, but now that he'd evaded Hank's sniper bullet, he would not stop until they were all dead. She sensed Frankie would not chance an attack in bright daylight, for all the world to see, but sunrise still was an hour or two away. Until then, they were in mortal danger.

She watched Hank sift through his suitcase of weapons and select a sawed-off shotgun and three handguns, stowing the pistols in his boot and two shoulder holsters, one under each arm. He slipped on a dark coat and hat and disappeared down the stairs. He wasn't going off to war but to kill. That realization tugged at Dax's conscience, but not in the way it would have affected Charlie's. She was willing to pay the price of guilt to keep Rose and May safe.

She turned to Rose. "Let's get May up. We need to stick together until this is over." She went to her bedroom, retrieved her Colt .45, and stuffed it into the waistband of her pants. Dressed again in slacks and Dax's shirt, Rose did the same with her smaller pistol.

Dax slowly pushed open the door to May's room. When light from the kitchen reached May's head in the bed, her eyes snapped open. "It looks like I'm not the only one who can't sleep with all the activity tonight."

"You might want to get dressed, May," Dax said, turning on the overhead light in her room. "Things with Hank didn't go as planned."

May flipped the covers back, popped up from her pillow, and swung her feet over the edge of the mattress. "I'll be right out."

While Rose brewed coffee, Dax assembled sugar, cream, mugs, and spoons. May changed into her day dress and leg brace, entered the kitchen minutes later. She sat on a stool at the center chopping block. When Rose poured coffee all around, May said, "Tell me what happened."

Dax stalled, stirring in cream and sugar to her coffee as she tried to find words that would not scare May or leave her thinking that her sister was heartless. She and Grace had left May in the dark about Hank's role by design. But now that the situation had worsened, Dax carefully detailed the raid on the Seaside Club and how the Prohibition agents had funneled Wilkes into the street. "Hank had him in his sights, but Charlie stumbled upon the trap at the worst time, and Wilkes got away. Now Hank is out to get Wilkes before he gets to us."

"Where are Charlie and Jules? Shouldn't they be down here too?" May's eyebrows drew together.

"They left," Rose said.

"But why? Aren't they in danger too?"

"It's my fault." Dax regretted the earlier knee-jerk reaction that had driven her friend away. She would never forgive herself if something happened to Charlie and Jules. "I accused her of being a coward."

May drew her head back. "Why would you do that? She's anything but."

"My temper." Dax lowered her head, too ashamed to explain further.

"I don't understand."

Rose caressed Dax's back, but the comforting touch failed to lessen her regret. Rose said, "Charlie alerted Frankie before Hank could get off a shot. She said she couldn't cause the death of another man."

May pressed her lips tight. Her disappointment was palpable. "I understand your frustration, Dax, but Charlie is such a gentle soul. She didn't deserve your ire."

"I know." Dax looked her sister in the eye, accepting the rebuke. "I'll make it right."

The distinct sound of gunshots rang out from the front of the Foster House. No, the back. The front. Concurrent and consecutive volleys made Dax's pulse race and her stomach turn rock hard. She drew her gun.

Glass broke in the main dining room. The fight had come to their doorstep. Even if they had time, Dax could not get May upstairs or into the basement for shelter. Her only choice was to stay put.

The gunshots stopped, creating an eerie silence. Dax's mind settled on the possibility of only two outcomes. Either Frankie Wilkes's men were lying dead on the ground or Hank's were. Then the knob to the kitchen door rattled. If Hank's men had lost the battle, Wilkes's men would overrun the Foster House in seconds. Dax, Rose, and May were fully exposed and needed to take cover in a place that would not be explored first.

"Go to the pantry," Dax said firmly but quietly, urging Rose to help May to the storage room. Dax darted toward the short corridor leading to the back door and rolled a rack of dishes and glasses against five stacked tubs to block the entrance. She doused the lights and dashed to the long, narrow pantry, closing the door behind her. May and Rose were huddled in the back corner, Rose with her pistol at the ready.

Standing in the dark, her heart pounding harder than it ever had, Dax knew they were trapped. The Wild West shootout that ended moments ago made it abundantly clear they were also outgunned. "Where's your gun, May?"

"Under my pillow." Which was of no help.

They had thirteen rounds of ammunition between them. Seven in Dax's gun and six in Rose's. Unless Rose hit him in the head, only Dax's .45 was powerful enough to stop a man with a single shot.

Dax placed her gun on the shelf and quickly stacked the fifty-pound bags of flour and sugar in front of her, creating a two-and-a-half-foot high embankment. Retrieving her weapon, she told May and Rose to get down and stay behind her. May lay flat, but Rose knelt beside Dax, elbows resting on the flour bag and her gun pointed toward the door.

"I said get back." With no time for stubbornness, Dax's order came out extra sharp.

"I won't let you do this alone." Rose's voice was firm. She turned to face Dax. The small storage room was too dark to make out her expression, but Dax was certain confidence was in her eyes, fueled by the same blind faith she'd had when she and

Dax were dangling over the cliff at Devil's Slide. For the second time, they would face the prospect of death together.

"Then we die together."

Their connection needed no light to see it was stronger than steel. More formidable than a bullet. More resilient than time itself. If Dax's and Rose's bodies didn't survive tonight, their love would.

Bangs, crashes, and the sound of shattering glass followed. The stronger the sounds grew, the heavier Dax's breathing became. Their nemesis was inside their business and home, forging a path of destruction. Dax didn't voice it, but she didn't fear a possible hail of gunfire peppering the door. Instead, she took Frankie Wilkes at his word and feared he was about to keep his threat to burn the town down. The smoke seeping through the crack at the bottom of the door confirmed it. He was out to incinerate his enemies.

A gunshot sounded inside the kitchen.   Another. And another. And another.

Silence.

Another shot.

Dax held her breath.

Silence.

Silence.

The stillness gave no hint of what lay on the other side of the door. The smell of smoke remained but hadn't grown stronger. Hank's last words to her were to not open the door until she heard his voice. But what if he was dead? What if they were all dead? She could not wait for them to be burned alive.

Dax took in a shaky breath. "Wait here," she told Rose. She moved to push off her knee, but Rose clutched her coat sleeve.

"Kiss me," she begged. Her tone didn't contain pain or fear but desire. The same desire from when they shared their first kiss beneath the poplar trees a decade ago. But this time, with the possibility this kiss might be their last, the craving had a more powerful, irresistible pull.

Dax pressed their lips together, re-creating perfection. Every kiss with Rose was beautiful, warming her like a fire on a cold winter night. Each movement of her soft, moist lips was a gentle caress reaching deep into her bones. And this kiss contained the certainty that their love would survive no matter what happened next.

When the kiss ended, Dax traced Rose's cheek with a fingertip. "We'll always be together."

"Yes, we will."

Dax stood, stepped around the sacks of flour and sugar, pressed her left hand against the door, and released a breath of relief. The wood felt cool, suggesting fire wasn't waiting for her on the other side. A test of the metal knob confirmed it. She raised her gun to eye level, released the safety, and placed her index finger against the trigger. If Frankie or his men were out there, she would have to fire in a fraction of a second. Surprisingly, despite a pounding heart, she was steady but a far cry from calm. She placed her hand on the knob and twisted.

"Dax, are you in there? It's Hank."

Every muscle in Dax relaxed at the deep voice. She pulled the door open to the darkened kitchen. She made out Hank's familiar silhouette in the shadows. He had his sniper's rifle slung over his shoulder.

"We're here, Hank."

"Is anyone hurt?" he asked.

"No, we're all fine." Dax pivoted to look behind her. "Rose. May. It's Hank. We can come out." She returned inside and cleared a path for May to maneuver around. After helping both women out, she clung to Rose's hand, refusing to let it go.

Hank turned on the overhead lights, revealing a bloodbath on the floor. Frankie and two other men she'd never seen before lay dead, each in a growing pool of blood. The spatter on Hank's face was evidence that the fight had been at close quarters.

"Your men outside?" The answer was obvious, but Dax had to ask.

"All dead, and so are all of Wilkes's men."

May gasped. Two of those men had stood guard at the Beacon Club entrance and eaten May's food for months. Thankfully, neither left behind a family.

The smell of charred wood was more pungent in the kitchen, but Hank's lack of urgency suggested the blaze was out.

"Where was the fire?"

"In the dining room," Hank said. "Thankfully, I had some help to put it out. We limited the damage to one corner."

"Help? Who?" Dax asked.

Hank gestured his chin toward the dining room. "See for yourself."

The smell of smoke nearly choked Dax when she pushed through the swinging door. She flipped on the dining room lights, revealing the charred street-side corner. Sadness tugged at her heart. The burned window wall had housed the booth where she first saw Rose on opening day.

She stepped farther in and spotted someone hunched in a chair with their back to her. She picked up her pace, intent on thanking the person who had saved her restaurant and home. When she closed within a few feet, she said, "I can't thank you enough for—" She stopped in her tracks when she glimpsed the identity of her rescuer. "Charlie."

Charlie's slumped body and smudged and haggard face telegraphed her exhaustion. Her stare remained fixed on some spot on the damaged wall. "I couldn't save it."

"What do you mean?" Dax knelt in front of Charlie. She looked like she'd been broken. "You saved the Foster House. You're a hero."

"My garage." Charlie finally met Dax's gaze. "They burned it down."

Dax gasped. Her mind jumped to the worst probable outcome. "Jules and Brutus?"

"She's taking care of him at the clinic. I burned his leg getting him out."

Dax held back a gasp. "I'm so sorry, Charlie." She rested a hand on her knee, intending to comfort her, but Charlie brushed it off.

"I've lost everything, and Jules and Brutus nearly died because of this damn war."

"It's over. Frankie is dead."

Charlie's eyes turned from sad to cold in an instant. "You're naïve if you think our troubles are over because that man is dead. Frankie has a brother who is just as greedy. This is only the beginning."

"You're wrong. You'll see. We can rebuild your garage, and once Grace takes over the Seaside, this town will be rolling in money."

"You're a fool if you think that will ever happen." Charlie shook her head in resignation as clear as glass. "I'm done." She stood and lumbered out the door without another word.

Dax had won the whiskey war, but at what price? Winning had cost Charlie her life's work and Dax her best friend twice in one night.

Rose came from behind. "She'll come around. Give her time." She held Dax's hand, reminding her that they had each other despite the horrific events of tonight.

"I hope so, Rose. I hope so."

CHAPTER THIRTY-FOUR

One month later

"Don't...stop," Rose gasped between words, pressing her hands against the head between her legs. Her lover had perfected the slow tease, adding agony to her anticipation.

"Don't...stop," Rose repeated. Every coherent thought vanished, focusing on Dax's unrelenting touches and licks. Muscles tensed, starting at her toes and cascading up her leg like a rush of electricity. Her back arched, lifting her off the mattress as spasms rolled through, sparking thousands of nerve endings. Her body finally fell to the bed in a thump, leaving her trembling in pure satisfaction.

Dax crawled to the head of the bed, pulling the covers up with her. She cradled Rose in her strong, loving arms. Her breathing was as ragged as Rose's. "I got you." She held on while Rose's heart slowed and stopped reverberating in her chest like a drum.

Rose pressed her head against Dax's chest, waiting for its rise and fall to match her breathing rhythm. "Are you ready for tonight? We should have a packed house."

"I should ask you the same thing." Dax traced a fingertip up Rose's spine. "Grace said her Hollywood friends are all coming to hear you sing."

"I've been ready for weeks." Rose lifted her head to look Dax in the eye. "Have you checked on Charlie?"

Dax ended her attention to Rose's backbone. "She still won't talk to me." The pain in her voice broke Rose's heart. For weeks, Dax had said all she needed was a chance to give her best friend a genuine apology to mend their rift and convince Charlie to give up the notion that the war wasn't over, but nothing she said or did worked.

"She may not realize it now, but you two need each other," Rose said.

"I thought we did too, but I can't force what isn't there. She's turned me away eight times, Rose."

"Don't give up on her. She hasn't had it easy since Frankie burned her place down. Living at Edith's has meant swallowing her pride."

Dax rolled to her side, facing Rose, her head propped up by an upturned palm. "Is that what you had to do when you moved into the Foster House with May and me? Swallow your pride?"

"In a way." Rose matched Dax's posture. "I had a job and my own place. I wasn't getting rich, but I was making a living. It was reaffirming to know I was doing it all on my own. Yes, I moved in here when I had no other choice, but that wasn't why I moved. I came because you and May are family. We were Charlie's only family besides Jules, but since she wouldn't come here and couldn't go to the boarding house, she had to rely on the charity of acquaintances. And that is a hard pill to swallow."

Dax traced Rose's jawline with a feathery touch. "I'll keep trying."

"Thank you."

Soon Rose and Dax made it downstairs. What they were billing as Reopening Day had the main dining room abuzz with customers and staff. Despite the midmorning hour between the breakfast and lunch rushes, every table and booth was occupied, except one with a reserved sign. The town and tourists were hungry for the Foster House to return to its glory.

Rose caught the head waitress's attention and gestured toward the row of booths lining the window fronting the street. Ruth responded with a nod. "Our table is ready," Rose said, guiding Dax to the reserved booth, where a copy of the morning *Half Moon Bay Review* was waiting for them.

"Nice touch, Miss Hamilton." Dax sat in the rebuilt booth across from Rose.

"I want this to be *our* table and for us to have every meal here."

A wry smile grew on Dax's lips. "I had the same idea. Look at the bottom of the tabletop."

Rose lowered her upper body closer to the bench seat and shimmied to see Dax's surprise. The light coming through the window was enough to see Dax had carved a heart into the wood with "D+R" in the middle. The heart and letters weren't made haphazardly like a teenager's carvings with a pocketknife. Instead, they were pristinely etched and ornate—clearly the result of hours of painstaking care. The gesture was the perfect tribute to their love, despite it being hidden.

Rose returned to a seated position, her heart much fuller. "I love it."

While waiting for Ruth to come take their order, Dax flipped open the newspaper, displaying the headline that read "Foster House is Back. HMB Future Still Unclear." The townspeople of Half Moon Bay had been reeling since the night of the bloodbath, though most were relieved that Frankie Wilkes was gone after the sheriff—thanks to Grace's well-placed money—declared the entire ordeal Frankie's fault and promptly closed the case. But with the hotel closed and the aftertaste of bloody headlines fresh in the minds of tourists, many feared tourism would shrivel to nothing this summer. Today's reopening of the Foster House was sparking renewed optimism among the business owners, but Dax and Rose had their doubts. The probate court was taking too long to decide on the ownership of Frankie's properties.

Once Ruth delivered their food, they ate and chatted about the club's reopening. Jason had the bar covered, but Dax still had to check on the deliveries for the dinner service, and Rose had yet to settle on an outfit for her show.

"I was thinking the black dress since most guests will come formal," Rose said.

Dax shook her head slowly before a second wry grin formed. "Red. It will make you stand out. Plus, I want to see your curves tonight."

"You are a naughty one, Dax."

"Do I need to send her to her room?" a woman's voice said from several feet away. Rose glanced in its direction, finding Grace and Clive had arrived.

"It would only encourage her." Rose slid to the end of the bench closest to the window and patted a portion of the vinyl seat next to her, inviting Grace to sit. Dax did the same for Clive. "Join us."

Ruth promptly delivered two coffee mugs for Grace and Clive and filled them. "Would you like to order, Mr. and Mrs. Parsons?"

"We don't have time to eat. Just the coffee, thank you." Grace tore off a corner of Rose's toast and nibbled it.

Rose slid her plate over with the last triangle of toast. "It's all yours."

Grace smiled her appreciation.

"You're here early," Dax said. "Does that mean you have news about your court claim on Frankie's estate?"

"We can discuss that later when we're all together." Grace nibbled on more of the toast. "We arrived early to check on the construction. Would you care to come with us?"

Rose turned her attention to Dax with a questioning expression and received a heartening affirmative nod. "We'd love to."

Minutes later, Clive navigated their Cadillac Town Sedan through town with Rose and Dax in the back seat. When he turned off Main Street, a newly constructed building came into view. With its smoother features and much cleaner lines than its neighbors the modern structure definitely stood out on the block. Customers would indeed flock to it, expecting the latest conveniences and top-notch service.

Dax squeezed Rose's hand extra tight, tears pooling in her eyes. "I'm so happy for her."

"Charlie will be moved in and back in business by the end of next week," Grace said over her shoulder from the front seat. "The hydraulic lifts took longer than expected to install."

"The what?" Dax asked.

"You'll see," Grace said.

Clive pulled into the parking lot of Charlie's new garage. The sign blazoned across the front was big and bold and would brighten the street when lit at night. Two men were unloading crates from a large side panel truck. Clive hurried out of the car, unlocked the garage, and opened one of the bay doors. Surprisingly, it rose automatically without him having to use the pull chain.

The polished concrete floors and whitewashed walls made the space look more like a hospital than a garage. New metal racks and shelves filled with tires and other car parts lined a wall. In the center were two maintenance bays. Each had two thick, flat metal rods four feet apart on the floor, connected by another strip at their midpoint. They were situated where the cars would sit while Charlie worked on them.

"What are those?" Dax asked.

"I'll show you," Clive said. He pushed a button on the wall, and one set of the metal rods rose from the floor simultaneously, pushed up by a metal cylinder. "These are the hydraulic lifts. They're strong enough to hold up a car for Charlie to work underneath it while standing. They're supposed to revolutionize car maintenance."

"Absolutely amazing," Rose said. "Charlie will be thrilled."

"That's only part of it. The residence upstairs is four times as large as her old one. She'll have a bathroom, kitchen, living room, and two bedrooms," Grace said. Everyone moved to the side, making a path for the workers to haul in the crates. "And these are the tire spreader and mounting machines. Changing or fixing a tire should only take her minutes." She turned her attention to the older man. "Topper, did the special order make it on the truck?"

"Yes, ma'am. It's outside," Topper said. "We detoured to San Jose and picked it up this morning."

"Splendid." Grace smiled.

"Everything looks really nice, Grace." A thin, shadowy figure appeared at the open bay door and stepped forward. It was Charlie. She had her hands in her coat pockets and held her head low. Her reserved demeanor was on full display, but it was more than modesty. Her greeting lacked excitement and bordered on sadness.

Charlie approached the group but kept her distance from Dax on the other side of the semicircle. The six feet separating the once best friends might as well have been an ocean. They seemed that far apart. Rose crossed the divide, greeting Charlie with a warm hug.

"I've missed you," Rose said. "Did you get any of the pie I dropped off at Edith's the other day?"

"I did, thank you." Charlie had stopped coming to the Foster House for meals after Edith had taken her and Brutus in after the fire, taking most of her meals with Edith or Jules. The only times Rose had seen her since was during her visits to the department store. According to Edith, when Charlie wasn't upstairs in her daughter's old room, she insisted on earning her keep by stocking shelves and sweeping floors from opening to closing.

"It won't be long," Grace said. "You'll be back to work fixing cars and living in your home next week."

Charlie looked at Grace. "I don't know how I'll ever repay you."

"You don't. I'm repaying my debt to you." Sorrow filled Grace's voice. "If I hadn't pushed things with Frankie Wilkes, he wouldn't have taken out his anger on you. I hope you'll find it in your heart to forgive us one day and that we'll see you again at the Beacon Club."

Rose glanced at Dax. The sadness in her eyes showed her longing to reconcile with Charlie.

"I appreciate everything you've done to make things right," Charlie said, "but I've had my fill of killing." Tears formed in her eyes. Her lower lip trembled. Her gentle soul was clearly still deeply troubled and would require much more healing before she could be at peace again.

"And I respect your position. Though I hope time will prove your concern of future violence is unwarranted." Grace glanced at the workers who had brought in another crate. "Now, for the reason I'd asked you here today. I have a surprise."

Grace directed the men to place the crate against a wall and open the side, unveiling a five-foot-tall tool chest on caster wheels. They pulled it out.

"I know you'd said you'd salvaged enough tools to get you started, but I had the best mechanic in Los Angeles order every tool you might need to rebuild a car from the tires up. He assured me they're a mechanic's dream and should last a lifetime."

Charlie opened the drawers, one by one, inspecting the tools. Each was lashed down by straps or set into uniquely shaped insets cut into a foam insert. Charlie's eyes danced with unbridled joy. "My goodness, your friend wasn't kidding. These are incredible."

"I know none of these things make up for losing everything you'd built," Grace said, "but I hope they will provide you the new beginning you deserve."

"They certainly will help." Charlie walked to the tire equipment the workers had carried in and tested a few levers. "These will make changing tires a snap." She walked beneath the hydraulic lift, running a hand across the length of the metal supports. "This is life-changing. I'll be able to make repairs in half the time."

"Would you care to see the upstairs?" Grace asked. "It's not finished, but enough is done to give you an idea of how your new home will look."

"Sure." Charlie shrugged.

Dax opened her mouth as if to say something but closed it quickly. Her shoulders sagged in unmistakable disappointment.

"We'll stay down here," Rose said. After Grace, Clive, and Charlie went upstairs, and the workers closed the bay door and disappeared outside, she draped her arms around Dax's neck. "She didn't walk away, and that is a good sign. Give her time. She'll come around."

"I hope you're right. In the meantime, I have something in mind that might win her over."

"Oh? What's that?"

A smile popped on Dax's lips—the first sign of optimism. She tapped Rose on the nose with a fingertip. "More patience and kindness."

When they left, Rose had a positive vibe. The prospect of Dax and Charlie reconciling appeared attainable, the Beacon Club was reopening tonight, and Charlie's life would be back in order next week.

CHAPTER THIRTY-FIVE

The night of the fiery bloodbath had ended with Dax optimistic that the war was over and a new era for the Seaside Hotel and Club was on the horizon. But Charlie's warning about Frankie's brother and her pigheadedness over the last four weeks were giving her pause. Roy Wilkes had been fighting Grace in probate court with everything he had, vying for ownership of Frankie's properties. Perhaps Charlie was right and Roy planned to finish what his brother had started.

Dax checked the wall clock in the kitchen for the third time. The grocer had said he would deliver the Foster House's order by three for tonight's special reopening, and it was ten past the hour. She should not be this anxious, considering the grocer's sterling record before the fire. However, memories of their first opening eight months ago had crept into her head overnight. Riley King had sabotaged their grocery order, and she feared a quirk of fate might spawn a repeat.

She would give the grocer another five minutes but not a minute more. Until then, she would let May and Hank entertain her. Since that horrific night, Hank had stayed on as a one-man security force to give May "peace of mind," as he'd put it. However, Dax was convinced Hank had May on his mind. He'd given her more private shooting lessons and had asked for several cooking lessons. Surprisingly, May had become an excellent shot, and Hank had become a darn good cook. Dax was more surprised to learn how well he painted. His work rivaled anything found in museums.

Hank had hung around the kitchen since she and Rose returned from Charlie's garage, helping May and Sheila prep what they could for tonight's special event—individual salads, baked potatoes, steamed green beans, May's biscuits, and a selection of cakes and pies. Now, they were waiting on the final delivery of meats.

Like the first opening of the club, the guests had preselected their entrees from a limited list. This time, though, the Foster House and Beacon Club were serving one hundred and fifty guests instead of seventy-five. Every seat, upstairs and downstairs, would be filled for dinner. For Rose's performance, staff would remove the basement tables and line up chairs in straight rows divided by an aisle in the center. Rose wasn't kidding when she said they'd have a packed house tonight.

May worked at the prep counter, mixing the different salad dressing selections. She glanced over her shoulder. "Hank, would you mind grabbing the paprika?"

Dax snickered. The spices were closer to May than to Hank.

"Sure thing, May." He sprang into action from his stool at the center chopping block like a smitten teenager fawning over the class beauty. Instead of merely handing it to May, he stood close behind her, a little too close to be socially acceptable, especially for a grieving widow. But her beaming smile proved the only thing May was grieving was that she hadn't rid herself of Logan years ago.

The last four weeks had been a sugary display of wooing. Both had gone out of their way to get the other's attention. Smiles had turned into blushes, and passing comments had turned into laughs. But Hank had turned up the volume with subtle touches. He had started by always offering his hand to help her down from the truck and graduated to offering his arm when she walked into local stores.

Likewise, May's responses had advanced from a polite nod to letting her hand linger longer than necessary whenever it touched Hank's. But today, she took their flirting to a new level. "Thank you," she said, raking a fingertip down his hairy forearm before accepting the container of paprika. "It's so very nice of you."

"It's my pleasure, May," Hank replied.

Dax folded her arms across her chest, rolling her eyes. If this didn't stop, she would die from a sugar overdose. "Oh, for goodness' sake. I wish you two would get it over with and finally kiss."

Sheila snorted but continued racking the pies.

"Well, um. I need to finish the dressings." May snatched the spice jar and sprinkled a generous amount into the mixing bowl.

"Yes, well." Hank stepped back, his cheeks blushing beet red. "I should help with the tables in the club." He disappeared down the basement stairs in a flash.

May moved closer to Dax and slapped her playfully with a dishtowel. "You need to mind your own business."

"Every Foster House employee would say you've made it our business. We watch you two trot right up to the edge every day with smiles and sugary 'thank-yous.' Just kiss the man." May opened her mouth as if to object but closed it quickly. Dax kissed her cheek and encouraged her to sit at the center chopping block. "I know Hank has some issues from the war and the death of his wife, but from what I can tell, he's a good man."

"We've only known each other a month, though," May said.

"I'm just saying to kiss the man, not marry him. Let him take you to a movie in the city or to the beach for a picnic."

"Maybe." May struggled to force back a grin.

"Maybe is a good start." A honk at the back door meant their food delivery had finally arrived. Dax pushed herself from the stool, relieved the ghost of Riley King was only in her head. She gave her sister a wink. "It sounds like everything we need to make tonight memorable is here."

CHAPTER THIRTY-SIX

Guests came to the Foster House car by car, in pairs and in groups. Hank oversaw the parking, with only the early arrivals finding places in the back. The rest were directed to park at the Seaside Hotel, which had yet to reopen pending the lengthy court battle for ownership.

Both shifts of waitresses and bussers were brought in to serve dinner, and Jason had an assistant at the bar. The former hardware clerk might not have been reliable on his own at the Seaside Club, but under Jason's supervision, he followed directions remarkably well.

Every customer appeared satisfied with their meal. Those in the club were ushered upstairs to enjoy coffee or champagne while the staff removed the tables downstairs to prepare for Rose's grand return.

Dax knocked on Rose's dressing room door and opened it when she heard a muffled, "Come in." She considered stepping inside, but the vision sitting in front of the mirror deserved to be savored.

Rose ran a hot comb through her hair one last time to straighten a few uncooperative strands. "In or out," she said with a suggestive grin on her lips.

"You know the answer to that." Dax stepped inside and closed the door.

Rose stood from her chair and turned toward Dax. Her coral-red satin gown could stop traffic. Two sparkling rhinestone-studded shoulder straps led to a plunging low-cut bodice. The fabric was nipped in at the waist, accentuating her bust. The dress combined seduction and elegance perfectly. It skimmed her hips and flared out below the knee in a fishtail design.

"You are stunning," Dax said, kissing her on the neck, careful not to muss her makeup.

Rose took a step back, turned, and inspected herself in the mirror, pulling a section of fabric lower on the hips. "Are you sure it's not too tight?"

"You're asking the wrong person for that." Dax stepped behind Rose, wrapped her arms around her waist, and rested her chin atop a shoulder. "I think May and Hank might finally stop dancing around each other tonight."

"It's about time," Rose said. "They make a handsome couple."

"I gotta go make sure the VIPs have made it to their reserved seats. Do you need anything else before you go on?"

Rose pressed Dax's arms harder against her abdomen, giving them a warm caress. "I have everything I need right here."

"So do I."

Twenty minutes later, the guests had been seated and served more drinks. Dax took a position at the bar to keep an eye on the crowd, the stage, and May and Hank in the back row. One minute later, Lester sat in front of the piano and spoke into a microphone, "Ladies and gentlemen, the Foster House and Beacon Club are proud to present the finest vocalist to grace the stage. I give you Miss Rose Hamilton."

Accompanied by whistles and hoots, every set of hands in the room came together in deafening applause to welcome Rose to the stage. For the next hour and a half, while waitresses weaved in and out of the rows serving drinks, she performed, earning the crowd's roaring appreciation after each song.

In a rare moment, Rose spoke between songs, "Th-th-thank you for coming. I'd like to close t-t-tonight with a special song wr-wr-written by my dear friend Lester Nichols. This is for May and Hank." Rose performed the song he'd written about her and Dax as would-be lovers longing for the first kiss.

Dax shifted her stare to Hank and May in the back row. Hank slung an arm over May's shoulder and drew her face closer with his other hand. Several beats passed as they stared into each other's eyes. Dax could nearly feel her sister's pulse racing in anticipation. Hank pressed their lips together in a long, overdue first kiss. By the time they pulled apart, Rose had finished the song, the audience was standing in ovation, and Dax's heart was full.

Two hours later, the crowd had cleared, the club had been put together again, and the staff had gone home. All but Jason. He brought up two bottles of champagne and seven flutes from the downstairs bar. May and Grace repositioned chairs around three tables Hank and Clive had pushed together in the upstairs main dining room. Once everyone took their seats, Dax popped and poured the champagne, and Rose passed along the glasses for Grace's toast.

After Dax placed the emptied bottle on the floor beside her feet, Grace drew everyone's attention by clinking a spoon against a glass. "First, I'd like to thank everyone for making the reopening a success. It couldn't have been done without everyone in this room. Now, for the reason I gathered you here tonight. I'm happy to announce that the probate court ruled in my favor yesterday. I am now the sole owner of Wilkes's properties in Half Moon Bay, including the Seaside Hotel. It was a painful journey getting to this point, but I hope you will continue to walk it with me." Grace turned to May. "May Foster, I propose a partnership. I'd like to make the Foster House the Seaside's cornerstone restaurant. What do you think?"

A smile as wide as the bay formed on May's lips. "I think we have much to talk about."

Dax took stock of the people around the table. She started her journey in Half Moon Bay with her sister. Abandoned here to fend for themselves, she and May had survived. They were bound by blood, but their unbreakable devotion to one another was what had made it work. Dax would like to take credit for putting the smile on her face tonight, but that honor belonged to Hank, the man who had saved her, May, and Rose from certain death. After years of neglect from Logan, May deserved happiness.

Then there were Clive and Jason. Clive slung an arm over Jason's chair and whispered something into his ear, earning a laugh and a peck on the lips. They were the first men Dax had met who were like her and Rose. Seeing the love they shared made her realize she was part of a bigger community. It was heartening to see that some men were brave enough to follow their hearts, irrespective of society's expectations.

That made her think about Charlie and Jules, who weren't there tonight. They were part of her community, but they were also family. Though Charlie could not see it, Dax envisioned a day when all would be forgiven, and they would share a table like this one.

Dax shifted her attention. No sane person would blame Dax if she were jealous of Grace. Besides being rich, beautiful, and adored by millions of moviegoers, she had been Rose's first lover. Today Rose's every touch and kiss proved Grace wasn't a threat. But Dax was no fool. Anyone could see that Grace had started the war with Frankie Wilkes largely because she loved Rose. Dax was counting on that devotion. As long as Grace was breathing, she knew she would protect Rose if Dax could not.

Finally, Dax gazed at Rose—the other half of her heart. She could not imagine a life without her. Everything she had gone through during the nine years they spent apart, from May's accident to loving and losing Heather, had brought her back to the one person who completed her. And everything she and Rose had endured since, from Devil's Slide to a whiskey war that nearly cost them their lives, proved they were inseparable.

Grace stood and lifted her glass. "A toast." Everyone around the table raised theirs. "Here's to new beginnings."

The Speakeasy Series continues with Last Barrel

Sometimes winning comes at a high price.

Three years after *Whiskey War*, Dax and Rose live the high life at the Foster House, running the poshest speakeasy on the West Coast. Half Moon Bay is about to claim its place as the top tourist destination in northern California, with a remodeled Seaside Hotel and second club under Grace Parsons's ownership and Dax Xander's management. Repeal of Prohibition is on the horizon with the prospect of making their illegal liquor businesses legitimate. Dax's fractured friendship with Charlie Dawson is the only blowback from her battle with Frankie Wilkes for supremacy. If she could fix it, her life with Rose would be perfect.

Or so Dax thinks, until an election sweeps in Roy Wilkes as the new county sheriff. With the law behind him, he's hellbent on revenge for the death of his brother in the wake of the whiskey war and puts everyone involved in his crosshairs. On day one, he wreaks havoc in Half Moon Bay with arrests and beatings. Nothing is off the table. No one in Dax and Rose's circle is safe, and they must leverage every resource to protect the people they love. How far will Dax go? Will defeating Wilkes come at too high a price? Who will survive to open the last barrel?

More Titles from Bella Books

Hunter's Revenge – Gerri Hill
978-1-64247-447-3 | 276 pgs | paperback: $18.95 | eBook: $9.99
Tori Hunter is back! Don't miss this final chapter in the acclaimed
Tori Hunter series.

Integrity – E. J. Noyes
978-1-64247-465-7 | 28 pgs | paperback: $19.95 | eBook: $9.99
It was supposed to be an ordinary workday...

The Order – TJ O'Shea
978-1-64247-378-0 | 396 pgs | paperback: $19.95 | eBook: $9.99
For two women the battle between new love and old loyalty may prove
more dangerous than the war they're trying to survive.

Under the Stars with You – Jaime Clevenger
978-1-64247-439-8 | 302 pgs | paperback: $19.95 | eBook: $9.99
Sometimes believing in love is the first step. And sometimes it's all
about trusting the stars.

The Missing Piece – Kat Jackson
978-1-64247-445-9 | 250 pgs | paperback: $18.95 | eBook: $9.99
Renee's world collides with possibility and the past, setting off a tidal
wave of changes she could have never predicted.

An Acquired Taste – Cheri Ritz
978-1-64247-462-6 | 206 pgs | paperback: $17.95 | eBook: $9.99
Can Elle and Ashley stand the heat in the *Celebrity Cook Off* kitchen?

Printed in the USA
CPSIA information can be obtained
at www.ICGtesting.com
JSHW022236181123
52294JS00002B/3